Mr. Darcy's

Diary

AMANDA GRANGE

SOURCEBOOKS LANDMARK™
AN IMPRINT OF SOURCEBOOKS, INC.®
NAPERVILLE, ILLINOIS

Published by Sourcebooks Landmark, an imprint of Sourcebooks, Inc.
P.O. Box 4410, Naperville, Illinois   60567-4410
(630) 961-3900
FAX: (630) 961-2168
www.sourcebooks.com

Library of Congress Cataloging-in-Publication Data

Grange, Amanda.
  [Darcy's diary]
  Mr. Darcy's diary / Amanda Grange.
      p. cm.
  ISBN-13: 978-1-4022-0876-8
  ISBN-10: 1-4022-0876-6
  1. Darcy, Fitzwilliam (Fictitious character)--Fiction. 2. Bennet,
Elizabeth (Fictitious character)--Fiction. 3. Diary fiction. 4.
England--Fiction. 5. Domestic fiction. I. Title.

PR6107.R35D37 2007
823'.92--dc22

2006100788

Printed and bound in the United States of America
VP   10   9   8   7   6   5

Mr. Darcy's

July

Monday 1st July

Have I done the right thing in establishing Georgiana in London, I wonder? The summer is proving to be very hot, and when I visited her this morning, I found her lacking her usual energy. I think I will send her to the coast for a holiday.

Tuesday 2nd July

I have instructed Hargreaves to look for a suitable house in Margate, or perhaps in Ramsgate, for Georgiana. I wish I could go with her, but it is proving difficult to find a new steward to replace Wickham and I cannot spare the time.

Wickham! It is strange that one name can summon up such contradictory feelings. My father's steward was a man I admired and respected, but his son is a man I hold in contempt. I can hardly believe that George and I were friends when we were children, but George was different then.

I sometimes wonder how it is that a boy who had every advantage, who was blessed with good looks, easy manners and a good education, and who was the son of such a respectable man, could turn out so badly. When I think of the dissipation he has indulged in since his father's death...

I am glad I have not heard of him recently. Our business dealings last year were unpleasant. When he asked me for the presentation of the living my father had intended for him, he resented my refusal to give it to him, although he knew full well that he had relinquished all claims to it, and that his character made him entirely unsuited for the church.

Fortunately, a sum of money settled the matter. I feared he would approach me again when it ran out, but I have finally convinced him that he will get no more help from me. For the sake of the friendship we once had I have given him much, but I will not help him any more. The only man who can help George Wickham now is himself.

Saturday 6th July

Hargreaves has found a house for Georgiana in Ramsgate, and Georgiana's companion, Mrs Younge, has been to inspect it. She finds it suitable, and so I have taken it. Ramsgate is not too far away, and I will be able to join Georgiana whenever my business allows. I feel sure the sea air will revive her and she will soon be in good spirits again.

Tuesday 10th July

I had not realized how much I would miss my sister. I have grown used to calling on her every day. But she is in good hands, and I am persuaded she will enjoy herself. I dined with Bingley this evening. He is still in town, but he will be travelling north to see his family next week.

'I think, you know, Darcy, that I shall take a house for the winter,' he said after dinner.

'In town?'

'No. In the country. I have a mind to buy an estate. Caroline is always telling me I should have one, and I agree with her. I mean to rent a property first and, if I like it, I will buy it.'

'I think it is an excellent idea. It will stop you racketing all over the country,' I said.

'Exactly what I think. If I had a house half as fine as Pemberley I would not always be going from one place to another. I could invite company to stay with me, instead of travelling the length and breadth of the country to find it,' he returned.

'Where do you mean to look?' I asked him, as I finished my drink.

'Somewhere in the middle of the country. Not too far north, and not too far south. Caroline recommended Derbyshire, but why should I live in Derbyshire? If I want to visit that part of the country I can stay at Pemberley with you. I have told my agent to look for something in Hertfordshire, or thereabouts. I rely on you to inspect it with me when he finds me something.'

'If you go ahead with it, then I will be glad to.'

'You do not think I will?'

'I think you will change your mind as soon as you see a pretty face, whereupon you will decide to stay in London,' I said with a smile.

'You paint me very fickle,' he said with a laugh. 'I thought you were my friend!'

'And so I am.'

'And yet you think me capable of abandoning my

plan? Upon my honour, I will not be so easily dissuaded, and nothing will stop me from taking a house in the country. You will come and visit me?'

'Of course.'

'And you must bring Georgiana. How is she? I have not seen her for months. I must take Caroline and visit her.'

'She is not in London at present. I have sent her to Ramsgate for the summer.'

'Very wise. I cannot wait to remove from town myself.'

We parted after dinner. If it was still the Season, I would not hold out much hope of him fixing on a place, whatever he protests. But as London is empty of female company, then I think he may hold true to his course – unless a young lady in the north should happen to catch his fancy, whereupon he will stay at home until Christmas!

Friday 12th July

I had a letter from Georgiana this morning. It is lively and affectionate, and I am pleased I thought of sending her to the seaside. She has arrived safely in Ramsgate and writes of her pleasure at the house:

> *It is small compared to my London establish-*
> *ment, but it is very comfortable and it has a*
> *pretty view of the sea. Mrs Younge and I are*
> *going down to the beach this afternoon as I am*

eager to make a sketch of the coast. I will send
it to you when it is finished.
                    Your affectionate sister, Georgiana.

I folded her letter away and I was about to put it in
my desk with the others when I happened to notice the
handwriting on one of her earlier letters. I took it out so
that I could compare the two. She has made a great deal
of progress, both in her handwriting and in the style of
her letters, over the last few years. However, I confess that
I find her earlier letters charming, though the handwriting is poor and the spelling atrocious.

As I reread her earlier letter, I remembered how worried I had been that she would not be happy at the seminary, but I need not have been concerned. She liked her
teachers, and made a number of good friends there. I will
have to suggest that she invite one of them to stay with
her in London over the autumn. If I am to help Bingley
find his estate, then a friend will provide some company
for Georgiana whilst I am away.

Tuesday 16th July

I rode in the park with Colonel Fitzwilliam this morning. He told me that he had been to Rosings and seen
Lady Catherine, and that she had appointed a new
rector. For a moment I feared it might be George
Wickham, knowing that if he had heard of a wealthy
living at Rosings he might have tried to ingratiate
himself with my aunt.

'What is the rector's name?' I asked.

'Collins.'

I breathed again.

'A heavy young man with the most extraordinary manner,' went on Colonel Fitzwilliam. 'A mixture of servility and conceit. He bobs about praising everything and anything. He talks endlessly but says nothing. He has no opinions of his own, except an idea of his own importance, which is as ludicrous as it is unshakeable. My aunt likes him well enough, however. He performs his duties well and he is useful to her for making up a table at cards.'

'Is he married?'

'I believe it will not be long before he takes a wife.'

'He is betrothed, then?'

'No, but my aunt finds it tedious at Rosings with so few people to entertain her, and I believe she will soon tell him he must marry. A new bride will make a diversion for her, and then she will have someone to…help,' he said with a wry smile.

'She likes to be of service,' I remarked, returning his look.

'And she is so fortunately placed that other people have little choice but to thank her for her advice,' he added.

We have both had a great deal of advice from Lady Catherine. Most of it has been very good, but all the same I have often been relieved that Rosings is not in Derbyshire, but that it is far away in Kent.

'How is Georgiana?' he asked, as we left the park and began to ride back to my house.

'Very well. I have sent her to Ramsgate for the summer.'

'Good. It is too hot in town for her. It is too hot for anyone,' he said. 'I am going to Brighton next week. It is a pity I will not be able to see her, but next time I am in town I will make sure I visit her. Will you be joining her in Ramsgate?'

'Not yet. I have too much to do.'

'But you will be going to Pemberley?'

'Later in the year, yes.'

'I envy you Pemberley.'

'Then you should marry. It would enable you to buy a place of your own.'

'If I find a suitable heiress, I might consider it, but at the moment I am enjoying the bachelor life.'

With this we parted; he to go to his barracks, and I to return home.

Sunday 28th July

At last my business in town is done, and I am free to visit Georgiana. I mean to go first thing tomorrow, and surprise her.

Monday 29th July

I had no idea, when I set out for Ramsgate this morning, what lay in store for me. The weather was fair and everything promised an enjoyable day. I arrived at Georgiana's house and I was pleased to find it neat and well cared for. I was announced by the maid, the establishment being too small to allow of a full staff, and found Mrs Younge in the parlour. Springing up at my entrance, she looked at me in consternation.

'Mr Darcy. We did not expect you today.'

'I thought I would surprise my sister. Where is she?'

'She is…out…sketching.'

'On her own?' I asked.

'Oh, no, of course not, with her maid.'

'I did not hire you to sit at home whilst my sister goes out with a maid,' I said, displeased.

'I would ordinarily have accompanied her, of course, but I was forced to stay indoors this morning. I was…indisposed. I…ate some bad fish…I was most unwell. Miss Darcy was eager to continue her sketching, however, and the weather being fine I did not like to spoil her enjoyment. She asked if she might take her maid, and I saw no harm in it. Her maid is not a young girl, but a sensible woman who will see that she comes to no harm.'

I was mollified. Mrs Younge did indeed look ill, though at the time I did not know the true cause of her pallor.

'Which way did they go?' I asked. 'I will join her. I can sit with her whilst she sketches, and we can return together.'

She hesitated for a moment before saying: 'They intended to turn right along the shore, so that Miss

Darcy could finish a sketch she had already begun.'

'Very well, I will follow them and surprise her.'

I went out into the hall, but at that very same minute I saw Georgiana coming downstairs. I was startled. She was dressed for indoors and showed no signs of having been out sketching. I was about to ask Mrs Younge what she meant by such a fabrication when Mrs Younge herself spoke.

'Miss Darcy, I thought you had gone out already,' she said. 'Here is your brother come to see you.' Then she added: 'Remember, a little resolution is all that is needed, and you will achieve everything your heart desires.'

I thought her speech odd, but I took it to mean that if Georgiana applied herself she would be able to finish her sketch to her satisfaction. How wrong I was!

'Fitzwilliam,' said Georgiana, growing pale.

She stopped on the stair and did not come down. She looked suddenly very young, and very uncertain. I was alarmed, and thought she was unwell.

'What is it? Are you ill?' I asked. 'The fish – did you eat it, too?'

'Fish?' she asked, bewildered.

'The bad fish Mrs Younge ate. Did you have some as well?'

'Oh, no,' she said, twisting her hands.

'You are not well, however,' I said, noticing a sheen of perspiration on her forehead and seeing how white she had become.

I took her hand and led her into the parlour. Mrs

Younge was about to follow us when I said to her: 'Fetch the doctor.'

'I don't think -- ' she began, but I cut her off.

'My sister is unwell. Send for the doctor.'

My tone left her no choice and she departed. I shut the door.

Georgiana had walked over to the window, and was looking paler by the minute.

'Here,' I said, taking a chair over to her and helping her to sit down.

But she immediately sprang up again.

'No, I cannot,' she said unhappily. 'I cannot deceive you, no matter what he says.'

I was startled. 'No matter what he says?' I repeated, at a loss.

She nodded seriously. 'He says that if you know about it you will stop us,' she went on miserably.

'Who, Georgiana?'

'George,' she said, hanging her head.

'George?'

'Yes, George Wickham. Mrs Younge and I met him by chance on the seashore. He is holidaying here. We fell into conversation and he told me how much it grieved him that there has been some coolness between you lately. I, too, have been grieved by it. I liked it much better when you were friends. It does not seem right that there should be anything unsettled between you. I was relieved when he told me that it had just been a silly misunderstanding, and that it had all been cleared up, so that there was nothing now to prevent us being comfortable together. He reminded me of the time he sat me on my pony and led me round the yard, and of the time he brought me a pocket full of acorns,' she said with a smile. 'He said it was fortunate that we had met as it meant we could renew our friendship. I said I no longer liked acorns, so he laughed, and said that he would bring me diamonds instead.'

'Did he indeed?' I asked. 'And what did Mrs Younge say to this?'

'She said it was perfectly proper for me to entertain a family friend. I would not have done so otherwise,' said my sister.

'Entertain him?' I asked, feeling more and more alarmed.

'Yes. He has dined here on occasion, and joined us in the day if the weather was wet. He plays chess as well as he ever did, but I am improving and I have beaten him twice.'

There was some animation in her face as she said this, but she faltered again on seeing my expression.

'I have displeased you.'

'Not at all,' I said, striving for my composure. 'You have done nothing wrong.'

'I did not mean to fall in love with him, really I did not,' she said imploringly. 'I know I am very young, but he told me so many pleasing stories about the future that I came to look on our marriage as a settled thing.'

'Marriage?' I exclaimed in horror.

'He…he said he loved me, and he reminded me of when I had said I loved him.'

'When did you say so?' I demanded.

'When I fell off the gate in the courtyard and he picked me up.'

'But you were seven years old!'

'Of course, it was just a childish thing to say at the time, but the more I saw of him here, the more I became convinced I was in love with him in earnest. Only I did not like to think of deceiving you. I wanted everything to be open. I told him he must ask you for my hand in the ordinary way, but he said you would not let us marry until I was eighteen, and that it would be a waste of three precious years of our life together. He said we should elope, and then send you a letter from the Lake District afterwards.'

'And did you agree to this?' I asked, stricken.

Her voice dropped.

'I thought it sounded like an adventure. But now that I see you, and know how much it grieves you, it does not seem to be like an adventure at all.'

'It is not. It is trickery of the basest kind. He has made love to you in order to gain your fortune, and in order to hurt me! To persuade you to forget friends and family and run away with him to your utter ruin is monstrous!'

'No!' she exclaimed. 'It is not so. He loves me.'

I saw the fear in her eyes and I did not want to go on. For her to learn that the rogue had never loved her must hurt her. But I could not let her continue under such a misapprehension.

'I do not want to tell you this, Georgiana,' I said softly, 'but I must. He does not love you. He has used you.'

At this she broke down. I was helpless in the face of her tears. I did not know what to do, how to comfort her, and in that moment I missed my mother more than I have ever done. She would have known what to do. She would have known what to say. She would have known how to comfort her daughter, whose affections had been played upon. I could only stand helplessly by and wait for Georgiana's grief to spend itself.

When her tears began to subside, I handed her my handkerchief. She took it and blew her nose.

'I must speak to Mrs Younge and make sure she knows what has been going on behind her back,' I said. 'It has been negligent of her not to notice.'

Something in Georgiana's expression stopped me.

'It was behind her back?' I asked.

Georgiana looked down into her lap.

'She helped me plan the elopement.'

I felt myself grow grim.

'Did she indeed?'

Georgiana nodded miserably. I was cut to the heart by the sight of it. For my sister's happiness to be destroyed by such a worthless man!

I put my hand on her shoulder.

'Never fear, Georgie,' I said, overcome with tenderness. 'When you are older you will meet a man who will love you for yourself. A good-natured, charming, respectable man who is liked by your family. A man who will ask me for your hand in the proper manner. There will be no need for an elopement. You will have a grand wedding, with splendid wedding clothes and a honeymoon wherever you wish.'

She tried to smile, and she put her hand on mine.

'I have been a sore trial to you,' she said.

'Never,' I told her gently.

I wanted to find something to distract her thoughts from their unhappy path. I glanced around the room and my eye came to rest on one of her sketches.

'This is well done,' I said. 'I see you have caught the fishing boats just coming in from the sea.'

'Yes, I had to get up very early to catch them. The fishermen were surprised to see me sitting there,' she said.

I was pleased to see that she put aside my handkerchief as she took the sketch, and to hear that her voice was stronger.

'Perhaps you would like to finish it. Can you do so indoors, or would you need to go out again?'

'No, I can do it here. I have done enough to show me what is needed.'

'Good. Then I will leave you for a few minutes whilst I talk to Mrs Younge.'

'You will not be angry with her?' asked Georgiana.

'I will be very angry with her. She will pack her bags and leave this house within the hour.'

My conversation with Mrs Younge was not pleasant. First of all she denied all knowledge of a friendship between my sister and Wickham, saying she had never admitted him to the house and indeed that she did not know such a man.

To hear her call my sister a liar made me more angry than I have ever been and she shrank, admitting at last that she had encouraged Georgiana's friendship with him. Upon further enquiry I found that Mrs Younge had known Wickham previously, and had planned the first meeting between him and Georgiana. She had then told him where they would be every day, so that he could arrange several further 'chance' encounters. After this she had encouraged Georgiana to invite him to the house, and had taught her to see him, first as a friend and then as a lover.

'And why shouldn't I?' she asked when I berated her. 'After he's been so badly dealt with by you. Why shouldn't he have what's owing to him, and a little bit of fun besides?'

I had been going to allow her an hour in which to pack, but I changed my mind.

'You will leave this house immediately,' I said to her coldly. 'I will send your boxes on.'

She seemed about to refuse, when one glance at my face told her it would be unwise. She muttered curses under her breath, but put on her cloak and bonnet, then gathering up her basket she left the house.

When my anger had cooled, I wrote to Wickham, Mrs Younge having given me his address, telling him that he must leave Ramsgate at once. Furthermore, I told him that if he ever attempted to see or speak to Georgiana again I would ruin him.

I am still angry as I write. That he could have done anything so underhand. That he could have used Georgiana in his schemes, his playmate of gentler times....He is lost to all decency. I am almost tempted to expose him, but if I do so, Georgiana's reputation will suffer. I must hope that his experiences in this matter will prevent him from ever doing anything like it again.

August

Thursday 1st August

I have brought Georgiana back to London. She will stay with me until I can find a new companion for her. After the trouble with Mrs Younge, I am afraid to leave her, but I know it must be done. I cannot be always in London, and she cannot be always travelling with me. She must attend to her studies. However, I mean to make sure I am not deceived in a companion again. I will not only follow up references, I will visit former employers and satisfy myself as to their honesty, and the prospective companion's suitability, before leaving Georgiana in her charge.

It is a comfort to me to know that as long as Georgiana is in London, she will have the protection of a faithful butler and housekeeper. They have been with the family for many years, and will soon alert me if anything is amiss. I do not mean to send Georgiana away from the city again, unless I can go with her.

Wednesday 14th August

'I have discovered a lady who might suit Georgiana,' said Colonel Fitzwilliam when he dined with me this evening.

As he is joined with me in Georgiana's guardianship, I had told him what had happened in Ramsgate.

'Who is she?'

'A Mrs Annesley. She comes from a good family, and her time with my friends, the Hammonds, is coming to an end.'

'Have you met her?'

'Yes, on a number of occasions. I know the Hammonds have been very pleased with her.'

'Then I will call on the Hammonds tomorrow and see what can be arranged.'

Thursday 15th August

I called on the Hammonds and found Mrs Annesley to be a genteel, agreeable-looking woman who impressed me favourably with her breeding and her discourse. She will take up her position with Georgiana next week. I will remain in town for a few weeks to make sure she is as suitable as she appears, and then I intend to make several unexpected visits over the next few months to satisfy myself that everything is in order.

In the meantime, Georgiana's school friend will be arriving soon. It will do her good to have some company of her own age.

Friday 23rd August

Mrs Annesley arrived this morning. She and Georgiana have discovered a liking for each other and I think the relationship will prove to be a happy one. She is delighted to know that one of Georgiana's school friends is to visit, and she has arranged a variety of outings for the girls. I hope this will complete Georgiana's recovery from her affair with Wickham. I am persuaded that by Christmas she will have put the whole incident out of her mind.

Friday 30th August

Now that Georgiana is settled I feel confident about leaving her whenever Bingley has need of me. It is fortunate, for if I let him choose his own estate he will choose one with a flooding river, or rats, or an exorbitant rent. He will declare it capital and close with the agent before he has realized what he is about, and then he will ask me how he is to extricate himself from his predicament. It is far better that I help him to begin with, rather than having to rescue him at a later date.

I must confess I am looking forward to seeing him again. I am tired of London, and looking forward to a visit to the country.

September

Monday 2nd September

I have had a letter from Bingley.

> *My dear Darcy,*
> *I have found an estate in Hertfordshire that*
> *sounds just the thing. Well placed, so that I can*
> *travel to London when the mood takes me, or*
> *to the north of England to visit my family, and*
> *it is not too far from Pemberley so that I can*
> *visit you easily, too. The agent recommends it*
> *highly, but I know very little about this sort of*
> *thing and I would like your advice. Will you*
> *meet me there?*

Monday 9th September

I left London today and met Bingley at Netherfield Park.
I had forgotten what good company he is; always ready
to be pleased and always cheerful. After my difficult summer, it is good to be with him again.

'Darcy! I knew I could rely on you. How was your
summer? Not as trying as mine, I'll wager.'

I said nothing, which he took to be an assent.

'Caroline has been plaguing me these last three
months, but now that I have found an estate I hope she
will be satisfied.'

Bingley was, of course, delighted with everything he
saw. He said how splendid it was and asked no sensible
questions, but instead walked around with his hands
behind his back as though he had lived there for the last

twenty years. He was pleased with the situation and the principal rooms, and satisfied with what the agent, Mr Morris, said in its praise. He asked nothing about the chimneys, or the game, or the lake, or indeed anything at all.

'Is it sound?' I asked Mr Morris.

He assured me it was, but I inspected it carefully all the same.

'Will it be easy to find servants in the neighbourhood? My friend will be bringing some of his own, but he will need maids, gardeners and stable-hands from the local area.'

'He will not find any difficulty in procuring them from Meryton.'

'What do you think, Darcy?' asked Bingley, when we had completed our tour.

'The price is far too high.'

Mr Morris insisted it was fair, but he was soon brought to realize that it was excessive, and a far lower sum was settled on.

'Upon my honour, Darcy, I would not like to try and stand against you when your mind is made up. Poor Mr Morris might as well have agreed with you straight away, and saved himself the effort of trying to argue with you!' said Bingley, when he had closed with the agent.

He might laugh, but he will thank me for my care when he is well settled.

'When do you mean to take possession?' I asked him.

'As soon as possible. Before Michaelmas, certainly.'

'You should send some of your servants down before you, then they can make sure that the house is ready for your arrival.'

'You think of everything! I will have them here by the end of next week.'

I was glad he had taken my advice. If not, he would have arrived at the same time as his servants, and then wondered why there was no dinner waiting for him.

Tuesday 24th September

'Darcy, welcome to my estate!' said Bingley when I joined him at Netherfield Park this afternoon. His sisters, Caroline and Louisa, were with him, as was Louisa's husband, Mr Hurst. 'The house, the neighbourhood, everything is exactly as I would wish it to be.'

'The estate is well enough, but the neighbourhood is small, with very few families,' I pointed out. 'I warned you of it at the time.'

'There are plenty of families,' he said. 'Enough for us to dine with, and what more do we want?'

'Superior company?' asked Caroline satirically. 'Entertaining conversation?'

'I am sure we will find plenty of it,' said Bingley.

'You should have let me help you choose the house,' said Caroline.

'I did not need your help, I had Darcy's,' said Bingley.

'And a good thing, too. I was only saying to Louisa this morning that you could not have found a better one,' said Caroline, smiling at me.

'Upon my honour, I can think of no finer country than Hertfordshire,' said Bingley.

He is delighted with the neighbourhood at the moment, but I think he will find it dull if he settles here for any length of time. It is unlikely, however. He is so capricious he will probably be off again in a month. I said as much to Caroline after dinner.

'Very likely,' she said. 'Until then, we must be thankful we have each other's company.'

Wednesday 25th September

This has been our first full day at Netherfield Park. Caroline has managed things well, and she was particularly pleased when I commented that no one would guess it was a rented house. She has had some trouble with the servants hired from the surrounding neighbourhood, but it is to her credit that the household is running smoothly.

Thursday 26th September

The neighbourhood visits have begun. It is a bore, but it was only to be expected. Sir William and Lady Lucas called this morning. Bingley thought them very civil, on account of Sir William bowing every two minutes and mentioning that he had been presented at St James's. Caroline suspected that their haste in calling marked them out as the parents of an elderly, unattractive spinster whom they wished to see married, and she told Bingley so as soon as they had departed.

'Depend upon it, they have a daughter nearing thirty

and intend to pass her off as one-and-twenty!' she warned him.

Bingley laughed.

'I am sure they do not have a daughter at all, and if they do, I am sure she is positively charming!'

'Caroline is right,' said Louisa. 'One of the housemaids told me the Lucases have a daughter named Charlotte. Charlotte is unmarried, and is seven-and-twenty.'

'That does not stop her being charming. I am sure she is a delightful young lady,' protested Bingley.

'And I am sure she is a homely body who is always helping her mother about the pies,' said Caroline in a droll voice.

'Well, I think it was very good of the Lucases to call, and even better of them to invite us to the Meryton assembly,' said Bingley stoutly.

'The Meryton assembly! God save me from country assemblies!' I remarked.

'You have been spoilt by superior company,' said Caroline.

'I have indeed. The London assemblies are full of the most elegant people in the country.'

For some reason she did not smile at this remark. I cannot think why. She smiles at everything else I say, and she must surely have been thinking of my London acquaintance, for whom else could she have meant?

Sir William and Lady Lucas were not our only callers today. They were followed by a Mr Bennet. He seems to be a gentlemanlike man.

'He has five daughters,' said Caroline, when he had gone.

'Pretty girls,' said Mr Hurst, rousing himself from his stupor. 'Saw 'em in Meryton. Handsome, the lot of 'em.'

'There you are!' said Bingley. 'I knew I had chosen well in settling at Netherfield. There will be plenty of pretty girls to dance with.'

'I know what you are thinking,' Caroline remarked, on seeing my expression. 'You are thinking it would be a bore to be forced to stand up with a country wench. But you need not do so. Charles will make a spectacle of himself, no doubt, but you need not. No one will expect you to dance.'

'I hope not,' I said. 'The idea of standing up with people I do not know is insupportable to me.'

Bingley laughed.

'Come now, Darcy, this is not like you. You are not usually so stiff-necked. It is the weather. Only let the rain stop and you will be as eager to dance as I am.'

Bingley is an optimist.

Monday 30th September

Bingley and I rode round part of the estate this morning. It has been kept in good order, and if he means to buy it, I think it might be suitable. But I will wait to see if he settles. He is just as likely to decide he wants to buy an estate in Kent, or Cheshire, or Suffolk next week.

He soon suggested we turn back.

'I thought I might pay the Bennets a visit,' he said nonchalantly, as we trotted back to the house.

'Eager to see the Misses Bennet?' I asked him.

He took it in good part.

'I know you think I fall in and out of love every few weeks, but it is simply that I feel it would be polite to return Mr Bennet's call.'

We parted company, he to ride to Longbourn, and I to return to Netherfield. He was not gone long.

'Well, did you see the five beautiful daughters you have heard so much about?' I asked when he returned.

'No,' he said gloomily. 'I sat in Mr Bennet's library for about ten minutes but never had a glimpse of the girls.'

October

Tuesday 1st October

Bingley's spirits were restored by an invitation from Mrs Bennet, asking him to join the family for dinner.

'But I cannot go!' he said, crestfallen. 'They ask me for tomorrow, and I have to be in town.'

'My dear Bingley, both they and you will survive. Besides, you will see them at the Meryton assembly.'

He brightened at this. 'Yes, I will.'

Wednesday 2nd October

Bingley went to town today. It is as I thought. He will never settle in the country. Already he is growing restless. I will not be surprised if he quits Netherfield before Christmas.

Saturday 12th October

We have been to the Meryton assembly, and it was even worse than I had expected. We had not been there five minutes before I heard one woman – I hesitate to call her a lady – whispering to another that I had ten thousand a year. It is of all things the one I hate the most, to be courted for my wealth. The whisper ran round the room, and I found myself being looked at as though I was a pot of gold. It did nothing to improve my enjoyment of the evening. Luckily, I did not need to mix with the local people. Though we were a small party, Caroline, Mr and Mrs Hurst and I endeavoured to entertain each other.

Bingley threw himself into the affair as he always does. He, of course, was well liked. He always is. He has an ease of manner which recommends him everywhere he goes. I heard a number of comments on his fine person and his handsome face. I, too, was described as a handsome man, until I snubbed Mrs Carlisle. She made a presumptuous remark and I was irritated into giving her a set-down: not two minutes before, she had been whispering to her neighbour that she meant to get my ten thousand a year for her daughter, and then, when she introduced her daughter, she had the audacity to say to my face that she thought wealth was immaterial in marriage, and that what mattered was mutual affection.

Bingley danced every dance, much to Caroline's amusement.

'He will be in love again before the evening is out,' she said.

I agreed. I have never known a man fall in and out of love so easily. Let him see a pretty face and pretty manners, and he looks no further.

I danced once with Mrs Hurst, but the musicians were so poor that once was enough. I declined to be introduced to any other young ladies and contented myself with walking around the room until Bingley should have danced himself to a standstill. Not that it was easy to avoid partners. There were several young ladies sitting around the sides of the room. One of them was a sister of the lady who had taken Bingley's fancy, and Bingley decided he wanted to see me dance with her.

'Come, Darcy,' said he, 'I must have you dance. I hate to see you standing about by yourself in this stupid manner. You had much better dance.'

'I certainly shall not. Your sisters are engaged, and there is not another woman in the room, whom it would not be a punishment to me to stand up with,' I said, not in a mood to be pleased with anything.

'I would not be as fastidious as you are for a kingdom! Upon my honour, I never met with so many pretty girls in my life.'

'You are dancing with the only handsome girl in the room,' I reminded him, looking at the eldest Miss Bennet.

'Oh! she is the most beautiful creature I ever beheld! But there is one of her sisters sitting down just behind you, who is very pretty, and I dare say, very agreeable. Do let me ask my partner to introduce you.'

'Which do you mean?' I asked him, looking round. I noticed Miss Elizabeth Bennet, then, catching her eye, I was forced to look away. 'She is tolerable,' I admitted, 'but not handsome enough to tempt me, and I am in no humour at present to give consequence to young ladies who are slighted by other men.'

Caroline understood my feelings very well.

'These people!' she said to me. 'They have no style and no fashion, and yet they are all so pleased with themselves! Do you know I was forced to smile politely whilst Mary Bennet was described to me as the most accomplished girl in the neighbourhood? If she was half, nay one tenth, as accomplished as Georgiana I should be very surprised.'

'But then that would be difficult,' I said. 'Georgiana is unusually gifted.'

'Indeed she is. I dote on her,' said Caroline. 'I declare, she is quite like a sister to me.'

Perhaps in time she will really be a sister to Caroline. Not that I said anything of this to her, but Bingley is a good-natured man with an adequate fortune, and will make a good husband. I had not thought to arrange a marriage for Georgiana before she was one-and-twenty, but after the affair with George Wickham, I have begun to think that it would not be a bad thing to marry her sooner. Once wed to Bingley, she would be safe from scoundrels of Wickham's stamp. I am not sure that Meryton would suit her, though. If Bingley shows any inclination to leave, I will encourage it. I would like to have her closer to me, in Derbyshire, or in Cheshire, perhaps. Then she could visit me in a few hours if she had a mind to.

We returned home at last.

'I have never met with pleasanter people or prettier girls in my life,' said Bingley, as we retired to the drawing-room. 'Everyone was most kind and attentive. There was no formality, no stiffness. I soon felt myself acquainted with everyone in the room. As to Miss Bennet, I cannot conceive of an angel more beautiful.'

Caroline cast me a satirical glance. In Brighton, Bingley had told us that Miss Hart was the most entrancing creature he had ever seen. In London it had been Miss Pargeter. It seems that in Meryton, Miss Bennet is to be his choice.

'She is a very sweet girl,' Caroline allowed.

'She is pretty,' I said. It is always better to humour Bingley in these moods. 'But she smiles too much.'

'To be sure, she does smile too much,' agreed Louisa, 'but she is still a sweet girl. I believe we may make a friend of her whilst we are here, Caroline?'

'By all means,' said Caroline, adding, 'We must have someone to help us while away the tedious hours, and to amuse us whilst the gentlemen are out.'

The only thing that lingers in my mind as I write is the look I caught in Miss Elizabeth Bennet's eye when I remarked that she was not handsome enough to tempt me to dance. If I did not know better, I would think it had been satirical. I am not quite easy that she should have overheard me, but it was not my intention that the words should reach her ears. Besides, it would be foolish to worry about her feelings. Her temperament is not delicate, and if she takes after her mother she will suffer no hurt. That abominable woman roundly condemned me for my chance remark, describing me to anyone who would listen as the most proud, disagreeable man in the world, and saying she hoped I would never come there again.

I never thought I would agree with a woman of her stamp, but on this occasion I find that our minds are as one.

Tuesday 15th October

Bingley and I examined the woods today. Whilst we were out, the Misses Bennet waited on Caroline and Louisa.

Friday 18th October

Whilst Bingley and I were out riding, Caroline and Louisa took the carriage to Longbourn and called on the Bennets. I believe they mean to make friends of the two eldest girls. God knows, there is little enough company for them here.

Saturday 19th October

A wet day. After being confined within doors it was almost a relief to go out to a dinner-party this evening. It was no better than the assembly, the people no more elegant and the conversation no more stimulating, but it had the advantage of providing novelty.

Bingley once again sat with Miss Jane Bennet. He has made her his flirt, and as her manners are as easy-going as his own, they make a good pair. She is not likely to be wounded by his attention, taking it in good part and seeing it as the agreeable diversion it is.

'It is a shame the other Bennet girls do not have their eldest sister's face or manner,' remarked Caroline after dinner.

'It is,' I agreed.

'I am not surprised you could not support the idea of standing up with Miss Elizabeth Bennet. She has none of her sister's beauty.'

'She has hardly a good feature in her face,' I replied, turning my eyes on her and studying her closely.

'No, indeed,' said Caroline.

'Oh, come now, Darcy,' said Bingley, who had joined

us as he had relinquished Miss Bennet to one of her sisters. 'She is a very pretty girl.'

'She is unremarkable in every way,' I replied.

'Very well, have it your own way. She has not one tolerable thing about her.'

He laughed, and returned to Jane Bennet.

Caroline continued to criticize our neighbours. As she did so, my eyes were drawn again to Miss Elizabeth Bennet, and I began to feel that I had not done her justice. Though she had not one good feature in her face, it was rendered uncommonly intelligent by the beautiful expression of her dark eyes. They gave her an animation which I thought very agreeable. I found myself watching her, and as she stood up to leave the table I further discovered that her figure was light and pleasing.

She is still not handsome enough to tempt a man of my worth, but she has more beauty than I at first thought.

November

Monday 4th November

Another party. It was unavoidable, but I find I am not as
ill-disposed to outings as I was. They provide a change
from our usual intimate circle. Tonight's party was at Sir
William Lucas's house, Lucas Lodge.

'Be prepared to be bowed to every ten minutes,' said
Caroline, as we went into the house.

'Every five minutes,' said Louisa.

'Sir William is a very agreeable person,' said Bingley.

'Dear Charles, you would think anyone agreeable if
they allowed you to flirt with Miss Bennet at one of their
gatherings,' I said.

'She is an angel,' said Bingley, not in the least discom-
posed.

He soon found Miss Bennet. Mr Hurst danced with
Caroline, and Louisa fell into conversation with Lady
Lucas.

I noticed that Miss Elizabeth Bennet was there, talking to Colonel Forster. Without knowing what I was
doing I drew close, and I could not help overhearing her
conversation. There was that in her manner which rendered it playful, and when she is being playful there is a
certain lustre to her eyes. I remarked it, as I remarked the
flush of animation that added beauty to her cheek. Her
complexion is a healthy one, and her skin is lightly
bronzed. It is perhaps not as fashionable as Caroline's pallor, but it is pleasing all the same.

She soon left Colonel Forster's side and sought out
Miss Lucas. The two of them appeared to be friends. I

was about to speak to her, feeling an urge to see the sparkle in her eye once again, when the lady herself challenged me.

'Did you not think, Mr Darcy, that I expressed myself uncommonly well just now, when I was teasing Colonel Forster to give us a ball at Meryton?'

'With great energy,' I replied, surprised, but not displeased, to be spoken to. 'But it is a subject which always makes a lady energetic,' I added.

'You are severe on us.'

This was said with such a saucy look that I was compelled to smile. Her manners would not do in London, but there is something to be said for being in the country. One needs variety, after all.

'It will be her turn soon to be teased,' said Miss Lucas, turning to me. 'I am going to open the instrument, Eliza, and you know what follows.'

She refused at first, saying that she did not want to play in front of those who must be used to hearing the very best musicians, but Miss Lucas teased her until she gave way.

Her performance was surprisingly good. Not by way of notes; I believe a great many of them were wrong. But there was a sweetness to the tone that sounded well to my ears.

I was beginning to warm towards her, indeed I was intending to continue our conversation, when she relinquished the pianoforte and by some chance – lucky or unlucky, I do not quite know which – her younger sister took her place. My smile froze on my face. I have never heard a more disastrous performance in my life, and I could not believe Miss Mary Bennet was exhibiting her lack of talent for so many people to hear. If I had had to listen to it one minute longer I believe I would have told her so.

Matters were made worse when the two youngest girls got up a dance with some of the officers. Their mother looked on, all smiles, as the youngest flirted with every officer in turn. How old is he? She does not look to be more than fifteen. She should still be in the school-room, not out in public where she can disgrace herself and her family.

Her behaviour banished any warm feelings I had been entertaining towards Miss Elizabeth Bennet, and I did not speak to her again.

'What a charming amusement for young people this is, Mr Darcy!' said Sir William Lucas, coming up beside me. 'There is nothing like dancing, after all. I consider it one of the first refinements of polished societies.'

'Certainly sir,' I replied, as my gaze rested on Miss Lydia Bennet, who was dancing without the least shred of decorum, 'and it has the advantage also of being in vogue amongst the less polished societies of the world. Every savage can dance.'

Sir William only smiled, and tormented me with a long conversation on the subject of dancing, asking me if I had ever danced at St James's. I replied politely enough, but I thought that if he mentioned St James's once more,

I should be tempted to strangle him with his own garter. As my gaze travelled round the room, I saw Miss Elizabeth Bennet moving towards me. Despite her sisters' shortcomings, I was struck once again by the grace of her movement, and I thought that, if there was one person in the room I should like to see dancing, it was she.

'My dear Miss Eliza, why are you not dancing?' asked Sir William, as though reading my thoughts. 'Mr Darcy, you must allow me to present this young lady to you as a very desirable partner. You cannot refuse to dance, when so much beauty is before you.'

He took her hand, and surprised me by almost giving it to me. I had not thought of dancing with her myself, I had only thought of watching her, but I would have taken her hand if she had not surprised me by drawing back.

'Indeed, sir, I have not the slightest intention of dancing. I entreat you not to suppose that I moved this way in order to beg for a partner,' she said.

I found that I did not want to give up the unlooked-for treat.

'Will you give me the honour of your hand?' I asked, interested rather than otherwise by her reluctance to dance with me.

But again she refused.

Sir William tried to persuade her.

'Though this gentleman dislikes the amusement in general, he can have no objection, I am sure, to oblige us for one half hour.'

A smile lit her eyes, and turning towards me, she said: 'Mr Darcy is all politeness.'

It was a challenging smile; there was no doubt about it. Although she said that I was all politeness, she meant the reverse. I felt my desire to dance with her grow. She had set herself up as my adversary, and I felt an instinct to conquer her rise up inside me.

Why had she refused me? Because she had overheard me saying that she wasn't handsome enough to tempt me at the Meryton ball? Of course! I found myself admiring her spirit. My ten thousand pounds a year meant nothing to her when compared with her desire to be revenged on me.

I watched her walk away from me, noticing the lightness of her step and the trimness of her figure, and trying to remember the last time I had been so well pleased.

'I can guess the subject of your reverie,' said Caroline, coming up beside me.

'I should imagine not,' I said.

'You are considering how insupportable it would be to pass many evenings in this manner, in such society; and indeed I am quite of your opinion. I was never more annoyed! The insipidity and yet the noise; the nothingness and yet the self-importance of all these people! What would I give to hear your strictures on them!'

'Your conjecture is totally wrong, I assure you. My mind was more agreeably engaged. I have been meditating on the very great pleasure which a pair of fine eyes in the face of a pretty woman can bestow.'

Caroline smiled.

'And what lady has the credit of inspiring such reflections?' she asked, turning her gaze to my face.

'Miss Elizabeth Bennet,' I replied, as I watched her cross the room.

'Miss Elizabeth Bennet!' exclaimed she. 'I am all astonishment. How long has she been such a favourite? And pray when am I to wish you joy?'

'That is exactly the question which I expected you to ask,' I told her. 'A lady's imagination is very rapid; it jumps from admiration to love, from love to matrimony, in a moment. I knew you would be wishing me joy.'

'Nay, if you are so serious about it, I shall consider the matter as absolutely settled. You will have a charming mother-in-law, indeed, and of course she will be always at Pemberley with you.'

I let her speak. It is matter of perfect indifference to me what she says. If I wish to admire Miss Elizabeth Bennet, I shall do so, and not all Caroline's sallies on fine eyes and mothers-in-law will prevent me.

Tuesday 12th November

Bingley and I dined with the officers this evening. There is a regiment stationed here, and they are for the most part well-educated and intelligent men. When we returned to Netherfield we found Miss Bennet at the house. Caroline and Louisa had invited her to dine. She had ridden over on horseback, and an unlucky downpour had soaked her through. Not surprisingly, she had taken a chill.

Bingley was at once alarmed, insisting she should stay the night. His sisters concurred. She retired to bed early, and Bingley was distracted for the rest of the evening.

I was reminded of the fact that he is still only three-and-twenty, and so he is still at an unsettled age. He is presently concerned for Miss Bennet's health, and yet by Christmas he will be in London, where he will no doubt forget all about her.

Wednesday 13th November

Miss Bennet was still unwell this morning, and Caroline and Louisa insisted she stay at Netherfield until she is full recovered. Whether they would have insisted quite so vehemently if they had not been bored is doubtful, but as the weather is poor, and there is nothing for them to do but stay indoors, they were eager to persuade her to remain.

Bingley insisted on sending for Mr Jones, the apothecary, as soon as he knew she was no better.

'Is it really necessary?' I asked him. 'Your sisters seem to think it is nothing more than a sore throat and a headache.'

'There is no telling where a sore throat and a headache might lead,' said Bingley.

A note was dispatched to Mr Jones, and another to Miss Bennet's family, and we settled down to breakfast.

We were still in the breakfast parlour some time later when there was a disturbance in the hall. Caroline and Louisa looked up from their cups of chocolate, turning enquiring glances on each other and then on their brother.

'Who would come calling at this hour, and in this weather?' asked Caroline.

Her question was soon answered as the door opened and Miss Elizabeth Bennet was shown in. Her eyes were bright and her cheeks were flushed. Her clothes showed signs of her walk, and her stout boots were covered in mud.

'Miss Bennet!' exclaimed Mr Hurst, looking at her as though she were an apparition.

'Miss Bennet!' echoed Caroline. 'You have not come on foot?' she asked, appalled, staring at her boots, and at her petticoats, which were six inches deep in mud.

'Yes,' she said, as if it was the most natural thing in the world.

'To walk three miles so early in the day!' said Caroline, with a horrified glance towards Louisa.

'And in such dirty weather!' exclaimed Louisa, returning her look.

Bingley was troubled by no such astonishment.

'Miss Elizabeth Bennet, how good of you to come,' he said, jumping up and shaking her by the hand. 'Your sister is very ill, I fear.'

Caroline had by now recovered from her astonishment.

'Really, Charles, do not distress her,' she said. She turned to Miss Bennet. 'It is nothing but a headache and a sore throat. She did not sleep very well, but she has risen this morning. She is feverish, though, and she is not well enough to leave her room.'

'You must be cold and wet,' said Bingley, glancing at Elizabeth with concern.

'It is nothing. I often walk out in the morning. The cold and the wet do not trouble me. Where is Jane? Can I see her?'

'Of course,' said Bingley. 'I will take you to her at once.'

I could not help thinking of the brilliance the exercise had given to her complexion, although I wondered whether she should have walked so far alone. If her sister had been dangerously ill, perhaps, but for a cold?

Charles left the room with Miss Bennet. Caroline and Louisa, feeling it incumbent upon them as hostesses to go too, followed them. Bingley soon returned, leaving his sisters in the sick room.

'We ought to be leaving,' I said, glancing at the clock.

We had arranged to meet some of the officers for a game of billiards. I could tell that Bingley did not want to go, but I persuaded him that he would make himself ridiculous if he remained indoors because his sister's friend had a cold. He looked as though he was about to protest, but he has a habit of listening to me and took my advice. I am glad of it. Colonel Forster would have thought it very odd if he had cancelled the engagement on so slight a pretext.

We returned home later that afternoon and at half past six we all sat down to dinner. Miss Elizabeth Bennet was one of our party. She looked tired. The colour had gone from her cheeks and her eyes were dim. But as soon as Bingley asked about her sister she became more animated.

'How is your sister?' Bingley asked.

'I'm afraid she is no better.'

'Shocking!' said Caroline.

'I am grieved to hear it,' said Louisa.

Mr Hurst grunted.

'I dislike being ill excessively,' said Louisa.

'So do I. There is nothing worse,' said Caroline.

'Is there anything I can do for her?' asked Bingley.

'No, thank you,' she replied.

'There is nothing she needs?'

'No, she has everything.'

'Very well, but you must let me know if there is anything I can give her which will ease her suffering.'

'Thank you, I will,' she said, touched.

'You look tired. You have been sitting with her all day. You must let me help you to a bowl of soup. I do not want you to grow ill with nursing your sister.'

She smiled at his kindness, and I blessed him. He has an ease of manner which I do not possess, and I was glad to see him use it to help her to the best of the dishes on the table.

'I must return to Jane,' she said, as soon as dinner was over.

I would rather she had stayed. As soon as she left, Caroline and Louisa began abusing her.

'I shall never forget her appearance this morning. She really looked almost wild,' said Louisa.

'She did indeed, Louisa,' returned Caroline.

'I hope you saw her petticoat, six inches deep in mud,' said Louisa.

At this Bingley exploded.

'Her dirty petticoat quite escaped my notice,' he said.

'You observed it, I am sure, Mr Darcy,' said Caroline. 'I am afraid that this adventure has rather affected your admiration of her fine eyes.'

'Not at all,' I retorted. 'They were brightened by the exercise.'

Caroline was silenced. I will not have her abusing Miss Elizabeth Bennet to me, though I am sure she will abuse her the moment my back is turned.

'I have an excessive regard for Jane Bennet, she is really a very sweet girl, and I wish with all my heart she were well settled. But with such a father and mother, and such low connections, I am afraid there is no chance of it,' said Louisa.

'I think I have heard you say, that their uncle is an attorney in Meryton,' remarked Caroline.

'Yes; and they have another, who lives somewhere near Cheapside,' said Louisa.

'If they had uncles enough to fill all Cheapside, it would not make them one jot less agreeable,' cried Bingley.

'But it must very materially lessen their chance of marrying men of any consideration in the world,' I remarked.

It does no harm to remind Bingley of reality. He was almost carried away last year, and nearly proposed to a young lady whose father was a baker. There is nothing wrong with bakers, but they do not belong in the family, and neither do attorneys or people who live in Cheapside.

'How well you put it, Mr Darcy,' said Caroline.

'Couldn't have put it better myself,' chimed in Mr Hurst, rousing himself momentarily from his stupor.

'Cheapside!' said Louisa.

Bingley said nothing, but sank into gloom.

His sisters presently visited the sick room, and when they came down, Miss Elizabeth Bennet was with them.

'Join us for cards?' asked Mr Hurst.

'No, thank you,' she said, seeing the stakes.

To begin with, she took up a book, but by and by she walked over to the card-table and attended to the game. Her figure was displayed to advantage as she stood behind Caroline's chair.

'Is Miss Darcy much grown since spring?' asked Caroline. 'Will she be as tall as I am?'

'I think she will. She is now about Miss Elizabeth Bennet's height, or rather taller.'

'How I long to see her again! Such a countenance, such manners! And so extremely accomplished for her age!'

'It is amazing to me how young ladies can have patience to be so very accomplished, as they all are,' said Bingley.

'All young ladies accomplished! My dear Charles, what do you mean?' asked Caroline.

'Yes, all of them, I think. They all paint tables, cover screens and net purses.'

'Your list of the common extent of accomplishments has too much truth,' I said, amused. I have been told that dozens of young ladies are accomplished, only to find that they can do no more than paint prettily. 'I cannot boast of knowing more than half a dozen.'

'Nor I, I am sure,' said Caroline.

'Then you must comprehend a great deal in your idea of an accomplished woman,' said Miss Bennet.

Did I imagine it, or was she laughing at me? Perhaps, but perhaps not. I was stung to retort: 'Yes; I do comprehend a great deal in it.'

'Oh! certainly,' said Caroline.

Miss Bennet was not abashed, as I had intended her to be. Indeed, as Caroline listed the accomplishments of a truly accomplished woman, I distinctly saw a smile spreading across Miss Bennet's face. It started at her eyes, when Caroline began by saying: 'A woman must have a thorough knowledge of music, singing, drawing, dancing and the modern languages...' and had spread to her mouth by the time Caroline ended: 'She must possess a certain something in her air and manner of walking, the tone of her voice, her address and expressions.'

Miss Bennet's amusement annoyed me, and I added severely: 'To all this she must yet add something more substantial, in the improvement of her mind by extensive reading.'

'I am no longer surprised at your knowing only six

accomplished women. I rather wonder at your knowing any,' said Miss Bennet with a laugh.

I should have been angered by her sauciness, but somehow I felt an answering smile spring into my eyes. It seemed absurd, all of a sudden, that I should expect so much from the opposite sex, when a pair of fine eyes was all that was needed to bestow true happiness. It is a happiness I have never felt when listening to a woman sing or play the piano, and I doubt if I ever will.

'Are you so severe upon your own sex, as to doubt the possibility of all this?' asked Caroline.

'I never saw such a woman,' Miss Bennet replied. 'I never saw such capacity, and taste, and application, and elegance, as you describe, united.'

I began to wonder if I had ever seen it myself.

Caroline and Louisa rose to the challenge, declaring they knew many women who answered this description. Miss Bennet bent her head, but not in acknowledgement of defeat. She did it so that they would not see the smile that was widening about her mouth.

It was only when I saw her smile that I realized they were contradicting their own earlier professions, when they had said that few such women existed. They were now saying that such women were commonplace. As I watched Miss Bennet's smile spread to her eyes, I thought I had never liked her better, nor enjoyed a discussion more.

Mr Hurst called his wife and her sister to order, drawing their attention back to the game, and Miss Bennet returned to her sister's sick room.

I realized that there is a strong bond of affection between her and her sister. I could not help thinking that Caroline and Louisa would not have been so eager to wait upon each other, if one of them had been ill; though they, too, are sisters, there seems to be very little affection between them. It is a pity. The affection of my sister is one of the greatest joys of my life.

'Eliza Bennet,' said Caroline, when Miss Bennet had left the room, 'is one of those young ladies who seek to recommend themselves to the other sex, by undervaluing their own; and with many men, I dare say, it succeeds. But, in my opinion, it is a paltry device, a very mean art.'

'Undoubtedly, there is a meanness in all the arts which ladies sometimes condescend to employ for captivation. Whatever bears affinity to cunning is despicable.'

She retired from the lists, and retreated into her game.

I returned to my room at last, feeling dissatisfied with the day. My usual peace of mind had deserted me. I found myself thinking, not of what I was going to do tomorrow, but of Elizabeth Bennet.

Thursday 14th November

I have had a timely reminder of the folly of being carried away by a pair of fine eyes. Elizabeth sent a note to her mother this morning, requesting her to come and make her own judgement on Miss Bennet's state of health. After sitting a little while with her sick daughter, Mrs Bennet and her two younger daughters, who had accompanied her, accepted an invitation to join the rest of the party in the breakfast parlour.

'I hope Miss Bennet is not worse than you expected,' said Bingley.

He has been upset by the whole business, and nothing would comfort him but a constant string of instructions to the housekeeper, with the intention of increasing Miss Bennet's comfort.

'Indeed I have, sir,' said Mrs Bennet. 'She is a great deal too ill to be moved. Mr Jones says we must not think of moving her. We must trespass a little longer on your kindness.'

'Removed!' cried Bingley. 'It must not be thought of.'

Caroline did not seem pleased with his remark. I think the presence of an invalid in the house is beginning to irk her. She has spent very little time with her guest, and if Elizabeth had not come, her sister would have spent a very lonely time in a house of strangers.

Caroline replied civilly enough, however, saying that Miss Bennet would receive every attention.

Mrs Bennet impressed upon us all how ill her daughter was, and then, looking about her, remarked that Bingley had chosen well in renting Netherfield.

'You will not think of quitting it in a hurry, I hope, though you have but a short lease,' she said.

'Whatever I do is done in a hurry,' he said.

This led to a discussion of character, whereupon Elizabeth confessed herself to be a student of it.

'The country can in general supply but few subjects for such a study,' I said.

'But people themselves alter so much that there is something new to be observed in them for ever,' she returned.

Talking to Elizabeth is like talking to no one else. It is not a commonplace activity; rather it is a stimulating exercise for the mind.

'Yes, indeed,' said Mrs Bennet, startling us all. 'I assure you there is quite as much of that going on in the country as in the town. I cannot see that London has any great advantage over the country for my part, except the shops and public places. The country is a vast deal pleasanter, is it not, Mr Bingley?'

Bingley, as easy-going as ever, said that he was equally happy in either.

'That is because you have the right disposition. But that gentleman,' she said, looking at me, 'seemed to think the country was nothing at all.'

Elizabeth had the goodness to blush, and tell her mother she was quite mistaken, but I was forcibly reminded of the fact that no amount of blushes, however pleasing, can overcome the disadvantage of such a mother.

Mrs Bennet grew worse and worse, praising Sir William Lucas's manners, and making veiled references to 'persons who find themselves very important and never open their mouths' by which, I suppose, she meant me.

Worse was to come. The youngest girl stepped forward and begged Bingley for a ball. He is so good-humoured that he readily agreed, after which Mrs

Bennet and her two youngest daughters departed. Elizabeth returned to her sister's sick room.

Caroline was merciless once she had left.

'They dine with four-and-twenty families!' she said. 'I don't know how I stopped myself from laughing! And the poor woman thinks that is a varied society.'

'I never heard anything more ridiculous in all my life,' said Louisa.

'Or vulgar,' said Caroline. 'And the youngest girl! Begging for a ball. I cannot believe you encouraged her, Charles.'

'But I like giving balls,' protested Bingley.

'You should not have rewarded her impertinence,' said Louisa.

'No, indeed. You will only make her worse. Though how she could become any worse I do not know. Kitty was dreadful enough, but the youngest girl – what was her name?'

'Lydia,' supplied Louisa.

'Lydia! Of course, that was it! To be so forward. You would not like your sister to be so forward, I am persuaded, Mr Darcy.'

'No, I would not,' I said, ill pleased.

To compare Georgiana to such a girl was beyond anything I could tolerate.

'And yet they are the same age,' went on Caroline. 'It is incredible how two girls can be so different, the one so elegant and refined, and the other so brash and noisy.'

'It is their upbringing,' said Louisa. 'With such a low

mother, how could Lydia be anything but vulgar?'

'Those poor girls,' said Caroline, shaking her head. 'They are all touched with the same vulgarity, I fear.'

'Not Miss Bennet!' protested Bingley. 'You said yourself she was a sweet girl.'

'And so she is. Perhaps you are right. Perhaps she has escaped the taint of mixing with such people. But Elizabeth Bennet is inclined to be pert, even though she does have fine eyes,' said Caroline, turning her gaze towards me.

I had been about to dismiss Elizabeth from my thoughts, but I changed my mind. I will not do so to please Miss Bingley, however satirical she may be.

In the evening, Elizabeth joined us in the drawing-room. I took care to say no more than a brief, 'Good evening', and then I took up a pen and began writing to Georgiana. Elizabeth, I noticed, took up some needle-work at the far side of the room.

I had hardly begun my letter, however, when Caroline began to compliment me on the evenness of my handwriting and the length of my letter. I did my best to ignore her, but she was not to be dissuaded and continued to praise me at every turn. Flattery is all very well, but a man may tire of it as soon as curses. I said nothing, however, as I did not wish to offend Bingley.

'How delighted Miss Darcy will be to receive such a letter!' Caroline said.

I ignored her.

'You write uncommonly fast.'

I was unwise enough to retaliate with, 'You are mistaken. I write rather slowly.'

'Pray tell your sister that I long to see her.'

'I have already told her so once, by your desire.'

'How can you contrive to write so even?' she asked.

I swallowed my frustration and resumed my silence. A wet evening in the country is one of the worst evils I know, especially in restricted company, and if I replied I feared I would be rude.

'Tell your sister I am delighted to hear of her improvement on the harp...'

Pray, whose letter is it? I nearly retorted, but stopped myself just in time.

'...and pray let her know that I am quite in raptures with her beautiful little design for a table, and I think it infinitely superior to Miss Grantley's.'

'Will you give me leave to defer your raptures till I write again? At present I have not room to do them justice.'

I saw Elizabeth smile at this, and bury her head in her needlework. She smiles readily, and I am beginning to find it infectious. I was almost tempted to smile myself. Caroline, however, was not to be quelled.

'Do you always write such charming long letters to her, Mr Darcy?'

'They are generally long,' I replied, not being able to avoid answering her question. 'But whether always charming, it is not for me to determine.'

'It is a rule with me, that a person who can write a long letter, with ease, cannot write ill,' she said.

'That will not do for a compliment to Darcy,' broke in Bingley, 'because he does not write with ease. He studies too much for words of four syllables. Do you not, Darcy?'

'My style of writing is very different from yours,' I agreed.

'My ideas flow so rapidly that I have not time to express them, by which means my letters sometimes convey no ideas at all to my correspondents,' said Bingley.

'Your humility must disarm reproof,' said Elizabeth, laying her needlework aside.

'Nothing is more deceitful than the appearance of humility,' I said, laughing at Bingley's comments, but underneath I was conscious of a slight irritation that she was praising him. 'It is often only carelessness of opinion, and sometimes an indirect boast.'

'And which of the two do you call my little recent piece of modesty?' asked Bingley.

'The indirect boast,' I said with a smile. 'The power of doing anything with quickness is always much prized by the possessor, and often without any attention to the imperfection of performance. When you told Mrs Bennet this morning that if you ever resolved on quitting Netherfield you should be gone in five minutes, you meant it to be a sort of compliment to yourself, but I am by no means convinced. If, as you were mounting your horse, a friend were to say, "Bingley, you had better stay till next week," you would probably do it.'

'You have only proved by this that Mr Bingley did not do justice to his own disposition. You have shown him off now much more than he did himself,' said Elizabeth with a laugh.

'I am exceedingly gratified by your converting what my friend says into a compliment on the sweetness of my temper,' said Bingley merrily.

I smiled, but I was not so gratified, though why this should be I do not know. I am sure I like Bingley very well, and I am always pleased when other people value him, too.

'But Darcy would think the better of me, if under such a circumstance I were to give a flat denial, and ride off as fast as I could!' he added.

'Would Mr Darcy then consider the rashness of your original intention as atoned for by your obstinacy in adhering to it?' asked Elizabeth playfully.

'Upon my word, I cannot explain the matter. Darcy must speak for himself.'

I laid down my quill, all thoughts of my letter forgotten.

'You expect me to account for opinions which you choose to call mine, but which I have never acknowledged,' I said with a smile.

'To yield readily to the persuasion of a friend is no merit with you,' said Elizabeth.

Despite myself, I was drawn into her banter.

'To yield without conviction is no compliment to the understanding of either,' I returned.

'You appear to me, Mr Darcy, to allow nothing for the influence of friendship and affection.'

I saw Caroline looking horrified at our exchange, but I was enjoying Elizabeth's stimulating conversation.

'Will it not be advisable to arrange the degree of intimacy subsisting between the parties before we decide?' I asked her.

'By all means,' cried Bingley. 'Let us have all the particulars, not forgetting their comparative height and size, for I assure you that if Darcy were not such a great tall fellow I should not pay him half so much deference. I declare I do not know a more awful object than Darcy, at his own house especially, and of a Sunday evening when he has nothing to do.'

I smiled, but I was offended nonetheless. I feared there was a grain of truth in what Bingley said, and I did not want Elizabeth to know it.

Elizabeth looked as though she would like to laugh, but did not. I hope she is not afraid of me. But no. If she was afraid of me, she would not laugh at me so much!

'I see your design, Bingley,' I said, turning his remark aside. 'You dislike an argument, and want to silence this.'

'Perhaps I do,' Bingley admitted.

The liveliness had gone out of the conversation, and an awkwardness prevailed. Elizabeth returned to her needlework, and I returned to my letter. The clock ticked on the mantelpiece. I finished my letter and put it aside. The silence continued.

To break it, I asked the ladies to favour us with some music. Caroline and Louisa sang, and I found my gaze wandering to Elizabeth. She is like no woman I have ever met before. She is not beautiful, and yet I find I would rather look at her face than any other. She is not gracious, and yet her manners please me better than any I have met with. She is not learned, and yet she has an intelligence that makes her a lively debater, and renders her conversation stimulating. It is a long time since I have had to fence with words, indeed I am not sure I have ever done it before, and yet with her I am frequently engaged in a duel of wits.

Caroline began to play a lively Scotch air, and moved by a sudden impulse I said, 'Do not you feel a great inclination, Miss Bennet, to seize such an opportunity of dancing a reel?'

She smiled, but did not answer. I found her silence enigmatic. Is she a sphinx, sent to torment me? She must be, for my thoughts are not usually so poetic.

Instead of disgusting me, however, her silence only inflamed me more, and I repeated my question.

'Oh,' she said, 'I heard you before; but could not immediately determine what to say in reply. You wanted me, I know, to say "Yes", that you might have the pleasure of despising my taste; but I always delight in overthrowing those kind of schemes. I have therefore made up my mind to tell you, that I do not want to dance a reel at all – and now despise me if you dare.'

Did I really seem so perverse to her? I wondered. And

yet I could not help smiling at her sally, and her bravery in uttering it.

'Indeed I do not dare,' I said.

She looked surprised, as though she had expected a cutting retort, and I was glad to have surprised her, the more so because she is forever surprising me.

I find her quite bewitching, and if it were not for the inferiority of her station in life I believe I might be in some danger, for I have never been so captivated by a woman in my life.

It was Caroline's intervention that broke my train of thought and prevented me from saying something I might later have regretted.

'I hope your sister is not feeling too poorly,' said Caroline. 'I think I must go up to her room and see how she does.'

'I will come with you,' said Elizabeth. 'Poor Jane. I have left her alone too long.'

They went upstairs, and I was left to wonder whether Caroline had turned Elizabeth's attention to her sister deliberately, and to think how close I had come to betraying my feelings.

Friday 15th November

It was a fine morning, and Caroline and I took a walk in the shrubbery.

'I wish you very happy in your marriage,' she said as we strolled along the path.

I wish she would leave the subject, but I fear there is

little chance of that. She has been teasing me about my supposed marriage for days.

'I hope, though, that you will give your mother-in-law a few hints, when this desirable event takes place, as to the advantage of holding her tongue; and if you can compass it, do cure the younger girls of running after the officers.'

I smiled, but I was annoyed. She had hit on the very reason I could not pursue my feelings. I could never have Mrs Bennet for a mother-in-law. It would be insupportable. And as for the younger girls, to make them sisters to Georgiana – no, it could not be done.

'Have you anything else to propose for my domestic felicity?' I asked, not letting her see my irritation, for it would only make her worse.

'Do let the portraits of your uncle and aunt Philips be placed in the gallery at Pemberley. As for your Elizabeth's picture, you must not attempt to have it taken, for what painter could do justice to those beautiful eyes?' she said in a droll voice.

I ignored her drollery, and imagined a portrait of Elizabeth hanging at Pemberley. I imagined another portrait hanging next to it, of Elizabeth and myself. The thought was pleasing to me and I smiled.

'It would not be easy, indeed, to catch their expression, but their colour and shape, and the eyelashes, so remarkably fine, might be copied,' I mused.

Caroline was not pleased, and I found that I was glad to have vexed her. She was about to reply, when we were met from another walk by Louisa and Elizabeth herself.

Caroline was embarrassed, and well she might be. I, too, was uncomfortable. I did not think Elizabeth had overheard Caroline, but even if she had, it would not have disturbed her. She had not been perturbed when she had heard an uncharitable remark from me at the assembly.

As I looked at her, I was suddenly conscious of the fact that she was a guest in the house. I had been so busy thinking of her in another way that I had forgotten that she was staying with Bingley. I felt an uncomfortable pang as I realized that she had not met with any warmth or friendship during her stay. To be sure, she had met with politeness to her face, but even politeness had been lacking as soon as her back was turned. I had never felt so out of sympathy with Caroline…or in sympathy with Louisa, for she at least had taken the trouble to ask Elizabeth if she cared for a walk, which I had not. I berated myself for it. I was not averse to admiring her eyes, but I had done little to make her stay at Netherfield more enjoyable.

Louisa's next words undid my charitable feelings towards her, however. Saying: 'You used us abominably ill in running away without telling us that you were coming out,' she took my free arm and left Elizabeth to stand alone.

I was mortified, and said at once: 'The walk is not wide enough for our party. We had better go into the avenue.'

But Elizabeth, who was not in the least mortified at being used so ill, merely smiled mischievously and said that we looked so well together the group would be spoilt by a fourth. Then wishing us goodbye she ran off gaily, like a child who suddenly finds herself free of the schoolroom. As I watched her run, I felt my spirits lift. I felt as though I, too, was suddenly free, free of the trammelled dignity of my life, and I longed to run after her.

'Miss Eliza Bennet behaves as badly as her younger sisters,' said Caroline mockingly.

'She does not behave as badly as we do, however,' I returned, annoyed. 'She is a guest in your brother's house, and as such she is entitled to our respect. She should not have to suffer our neglect, nor suffer our abuse the minute her back is turned.'

Caroline looked astonished and then displeased, but my expression was so forbidding that she fell silent. Bingley might complain about my awful expressions, but they have their uses.

I turned back to look at Elizabeth, but she had already passed out of sight. I did not see her again until dinnertime. She disappeared immediately afterwards, to see to her sister, but when Bingley and I joined the ladies in the drawing room we found her with them.

Caroline's eyes turned to me straight away. I could see that she was apprehensive. I had spoken to her sharply earlier in the day, and had not said a word to her since. I gave her a cool glance and then turned my attention to Miss Bennet, who was well enough to be downstairs, and who was sitting next to her sister.

Bingley was delighted to see that Miss Bennet was feeling better. He fussed around her, making sure the fire was high enough and that she was not in a draught. My expression softened. I could feel it doing so. He was treating her with all the care and attention she deserved, and I was reminded of why I like him so much and am happy to call him a friend. His manners might be so easy-going as to make him a target for anyone who wishes to sway him, but those same compliant manners make him an agreeable companion and a warm host. It was evident that Elizabeth thought so, too. I felt that, after our sparring, we had found common ground.

Caroline pretended to pay attention to the invalid, but in fact was more interested in my book, which I had taken up when we had decided not to play cards.

'I declare there is no enjoyment like reading a book!' she said, ignoring her own in favour of mine.

I did not reply. I was out of sympathy with her. Instead, I studiously applied myself to my book; which was a pity, as I would have liked to watch Elizabeth. The firelight playing on her skin was a sight I found mesmerizing.

Discovering that she could not make me talk, Caroline then disturbed her brother with talk of his ball, before taking a turn around the room. She was restless, and longing for attention. I, however, did not give it to her. She had offended me, and I was not ready to forgive her her offence.

'Miss Eliza Bennet, let me persuade you to follow my example, and take a turn about the room.'

I could not help myself. I looked up. I saw a look of surprise cross Elizabeth's face, and I wondered if my words to Caroline had affected her behaviour, pricking her conscience about her treatment of her brother's guest. But no such thing. She simply wanted my attention, and she had been clever enough to realize that this was the way to achieve it. Unconsciously, I closed my book.

'Mr Darcy, will you not join us?' said Caroline.

I declined.

'There are only two reasons why you would wish to walk together, and my presence would interfere with both,' I said.

My smile was not directed at Caroline, but at Elizabeth.

'What can you mean?' asked Caroline, amazed. 'Miss Eliza Bennet, do you know?'

'Not at all,' was her answer. 'But depend upon it, he means to be severe on us, and our surest way of disappointing him, will be to ask nothing about it.'

I felt my blood stir. She was fencing with me, even though she was speaking to Caroline, and I was enjoying the experience.

Caroline, however, could not fence. Caroline could only say: 'I must know what he means. Come, Mr Darcy, explain yourself.'

'Very well. You are either in each other's confidence and have secret affairs to discuss, or you are conscious that your figures appear to the greatest advantage in walking; if the first, I should be completely in your way; and if the second, I can admire you much better as I sit by the fire.'

'Oh, shocking!' exclaimed Caroline. 'How shall we punish him for such a speech?'

'Nothing so easy, if you have but the inclination,' said Elizabeth with a gleam in her eye. 'Tease him – laugh at him. Intimate as you are, you must know how it is to be done.'

'Tease calmness of temper and presence of mind! And as to laughter, we will not expose ourselves, if you please, by attempting to laugh without a subject. Mr Darcy may hug himself.'

'Mr Darcy is not to be laughed at!' cried Elizabeth. 'That is an uncommon advantage. I dearly love a laugh.'

And so do I. But I do not like to be laughed at. I could not say so, however.

'Miss Bingley has given me credit for more than can be,' I said. 'The wisest of men may be rendered ridiculous by a person whose first object in life is a joke.'

'I hope I never ridicule what is wise or good,' she returned. 'Follies and nonsense do divert me, but these, I suppose, are precisely what you are without.'

'Perhaps that is not possible for anyone. But it has been the study of my life to avoid those weaknesses which often expose a strong understanding to ridicule.'

'Such as vanity and pride.'

'Vanity, yes. But where there is a real superiority of mind, pride will always be under good regulation,' I said.

Elizabeth turned away to hide a smile.

I did not know why it should be, but her smile hurt me. I believe it made me short-tempered, for when she said: 'Mr Darcy has no defect. He owns it himself without disguise,' I was stung to reply: 'I have faults enough, but they are not, I hope, of understanding. My temper I dare not vouch for. It would perhaps be called resentful. My good opinion once lost is lost for ever.'

As I spoke, I thought of George Wickham.

'That is a failing indeed,' said Elizabeth. 'Implacable resentment is a shade in a character. But you have chosen your fault well. I really cannot laugh at it. You are safe from me.'

But I am not safe from you, I thought.

'Do let us have a little music,' said Caroline, tired of having no part in the conversation.

The pianoforte was opened, and she begged Elizabeth to play.

I was annoyed with her at the time, but after a few minutes I began to be glad of it.

I am paying Elizabeth far too much attention. She beguiles me. And yet it would be folly to find myself falling in love with her. I mean to marry quite a different sort of woman, one whose fortune and ancestry match my own. I will pay Elizabeth no more attention.

Saturday 16th November

Bingley and I rode to the east this morning and examined more of the estate. He was pleased with everything he saw and pronounced it all capital. I pointed out that the fences were broken and the land needed draining, but he said only: 'Yes, I suppose it does.' I know he has an easy nature, but there was something more than his usual compliance in his manner. I suspected he was not really paying attention, but was worried about Miss Bennet. It is unfortunate that she should have been taken ill whilst visiting his sisters. It has set the household by the ears. It has also brought me too much into contact with Elizabeth.

True to my resolve, I paid Elizabeth no notice when she walked into the drawing-room with her sister later this morning, when Bingley and I had returned from our ride. After greetings had been exchanged, Miss Bennet begged the loan of Bingley's carriage.

'My mother cannot spare our carriage until Tuesday, but I am much recovered and we cannot trespass on your hospitality any longer,' she said.

I felt a mixture of emotions: relief that Elizabeth would soon be removing from Netherfield, and regret that I would not be able to talk to her any longer.

Bingley did not share Miss Bennet's view.

'It is too soon!' he cried. 'You might seem better when you are sitting by the fire, but you are not yet well enough to withstand the journey. Caroline, tell Miss Bennet that she must stay.'

'Dear Jane, of course you must stay,' said Caroline. I detected a coolness in her voice, and was not surprised when she added: 'We cannot think of letting you leave before tomorrow.'

A stay of more than one extra day did not please her.

Bingley looked surprised, but Miss Bennet agreed to this suggestion.

'Even tomorrow is far too soon,' protested Bingley.

'It is very kind of you, but we really must leave then,' said Miss Bennet.

She is a sweet girl but she can also be firm, and nothing Bingley could say would shake her resolve.

I was conscious of a need to be on my guard during this last day. I had paid Elizabeth too much attention during her stay, and I was belatedly aware that it could have given rise to expectations. I resolved to crush them, if any such expectations had been formed. I scarcely spoke ten words to her throughout the course of the day, and when I was unfortunately left alone with her for half an hour, I applied myself to my book and did not look up once.

Sunday 17th November

We all attended morning service, and then the Miss Bennets took their leave.

'Dear Jane, the only thing that can resign me to your leaving is the knowledge that you are well at last,' said Caroline, taking an affectionate leave of her friend.

'I am a selfish man. If it were not for the fact that you had suffered, I would almost have been glad that you had a cold,' said Bingley warmly, clasping Jane's hand. 'It has allowed me to be with you every day for almost a week.'

He, at least, has made her stay agreeable, and has taken the trouble to entertain her whenever she was downstairs. It is easy to see why Bingley has made her his flirt. She has a sweetness and openness of manner that makes her agreeable, whilst her feelings are not the sort to be deeply touched. No matter how charming or lively Bingley is, he need have no fear of his intentions being misunderstood.

'And Miss Eliza Bennet,' said Caroline, with a wide smile. 'It has been so…charming to have you here.'

Elizabeth noticed the hesitation and her eyes sparkled with mirth. She replied politely enough, however.

'Miss Bingley. It has been good of you to have me here.'

To Bingley, she gave a warmer farewell.

'Thank you for all you have done for Jane,' she said. 'It made a great difference to me to see that she was so well cared for. Nothing could have been kinder than your banking up of the fires, or your moving of screens to prevent draughts, or your instructing your housekeeper to make some tasty dishes to tempt Jane to eat.'

'I was only sorry I could not do more,' he said. 'I hope we will soon see you at Netherfield again.'

'I hope so, too.'

She turned to me.

'Miss Bennet,' I said, making her a cold bow.

She looked surprised for a moment, then a smile appeared in her eyes, and she dropped me a curtsy, replying in stately tones: 'Mr Darcy.'

She almost tempted me to smile. But I schooled my countenance into an expression of severity and turned away.

The party then broke up. Bingley escorted the two young ladies to the carriage and helped them inside. My coldness had not damped Elizabeth's spirits for one minute. I was glad of it – before reminding myself that Elizabeth's spirits were not my concern.

We returned to the drawing-room.

'Well!' said Caroline. 'They have gone.'

I made no reply.

She turned to Louisa and immediately began talking of household matters, forgetting all about her supposed friend.

As I write this, I find I am glad that Elizabeth has gone. Now, perhaps I can think of her as Miss Elizabeth Bennet again. I mean to indulge in more rational thoughts, and I will not have to suffer any more of Caroline's teasing.

Monday 18th November

At last, a rational day. Bingley and I examined the south corner of his land. He seems interested in purchasing the estate, and says he is ready to settle. However, he has not been here very long and I shall not believe his intentions are fixed until he has spent a winter here. If he likes it after that, I believe it might be the place for him.

Caroline was charming this evening. Without Miss Elizabeth Bennet in the house she did not tease me, and we passed a pleasant evening playing at cards. I did not miss Elizabeth at all. I believe I scarcely thought of her half a dozen times all day.

Tuesday 19th November

'I think we should ride round the rest of the estate today,' I said to Bingley this morning.

'Later, perhaps,' he said. 'I mean to ride over to Longbourn this morning to ask after Miss Bennet's health.'

'You saw her only the day before yesterday,' I remarked with a smile; Bingley in the grip of one of his flirtations is most amusing.

'Which means I did not see her yesterday. It is time I made up for my neglect!' he replied, matching my tone. 'Will you come with me?'

'Very well,' I said.

A moment later I regretted it, but I was then annoyed with myself for my cowardice. I can surely sit with Miss Elizabeth Bennet for ten minutes without falling prey to a certain attraction, and besides, there is no certainty that I will see her. She might very well be from home.

We rode out after breakfast. Our way took us through Meryton, and we saw the object of our ride in the main street. Miss Bennet was taking the air with her sisters. On hearing our horses' hoofs she looked up.

'I was riding over to see how you did, but I can see you are much better. I am glad of it,' said Bingley, touching his hat.

'Thank you,' she said, with a charming, easy smile.

'You have lost your paleness, and have some colour in your cheeks.'

'The fresh air has done me good,' she said.

'You walked into Meryton?' he asked.

'Yes.'

'You have not tired yourself, I hope?' he added with a frown.

'No, thank you, the exercise was beneficial. I have spent so much time indoors that I am glad to be outside again.'

'My feelings are exactly the same. If ever I am ill, I cannot wait to be out of doors as soon as I am well enough.'

Whilst they went on in this manner, with Bingley looking as happy as though Miss Bennet had escaped the clutches of typhus rather than a trifling cold, I studiously avoided looking at Elizabeth. I let my eyes drift over the rest of the group instead. I saw the three younger Bennet girls, one of them carrying a book of sermons and the other two giggling together, and a heavy young man whom I had not seen before. By his dress he was a clergyman, and he appeared to be in attendance on the ladies. I was just reflecting that perhaps his presence explained why Miss Mary Bennet was clutching a book of sermons when I received an unwelcome surprise, nay a terrible shock. At the edge of the group there were two further gentlemen. One was Mr Denny, an officer whom Bingley and I had already met. The other was George Wickham.

George Wickham! That odious man, who betrayed my father's belief in him and almost ruined my sister! To be forced to meet him again, at such a time and in such a place....It was abominable.

I thought I had done with him. I thought I would never have to see him again. But there he was, talking to Denny as though he had not a care in the world. And I suppose he had not, for he has never cared about anything in his life, unless it is himself.

He turned his head towards me. I felt myself grow white, and saw him grow red. Our eyes met. Anger, disgust and contempt shot from mine. But, recovering himself quickly, a damnable impertinence shot from his. He had the audacity to touch his hat. To touch his hat! To me! I would have turned away, but I had too much pride to create a scene, and I forced myself to return his salute.

My courtesy was for nothing, however. Catching a glimpse of Miss Elizabeth Bennet out of the corner of my eye, I saw that she had noticed our meeting, and she was not deceived for an instant. She knew that something was badly wrong between us.

'But we must not keep you,' I heard Bingley saying.

I felt, rather than saw, him turn towards me.

'Come, Darcy, we must be getting on.'

I was only too willing to fall in with his suggestion. We bade the ladies goodbye and rode on.

'She is feeling much better, and believes herself to be quite well again,' said Bingley.

I did not reply.

'She looked well, I thought,' said Bingley.

Again, I did not reply.

'Is something wrong?' asked Bingley, at last catching my mood.

'No, nothing,' I said shortly.

'Nay, Darcy, this will not do. Something has troubled you.'

But I would not be drawn. Bingley knows nothing of the trouble I had with Wickham over the summer, and I do not want to enlighten him. Georgiana's foolishness would cast a shadow over her reputation if it was known, and I am determined Bingley shall never hear of it.

Wednesday 20th November

I rode out early this morning, without asking Bingley if he chose to go with me, for I wanted to be on my own. George Wickham, in Meryton!

It has robbed my visit of its pleasure. Even worse, I am haunted by a glimpse of memory, something so slight I can hardly be sure if it is real. But it will not leave me, and fills my dreams. It is this: when I rode up to the ladies yesterday, I thought I saw an expression of admiration on Elizabeth's face as she looked at Wickham.

Surely she cannot prefer him to me!

What am I saying? Her feelings for me are unimportant. As are her feelings for George Wickham. If she wishes to admire him, it is her concern.

I cannot believe she will still admire him when she finds him out, and find him out she will. He has not changed. He is still the wastrel he has always been, and she is too intelligent to be deceived for long.

And yet he has a handsome face. The ladies have always admired it. And he has an ease of manner and style of address which make him well liked amongst those who do not know him, whereas I...

I cannot believe I am comparing myself to George Wickham! I must be mad. And yet if Elizabeth...I must not think of her as Elizabeth.

If she chooses to compare us, then so be it. It will prove she is beneath my notice, and I will no longer be troubled by thoughts of her.

Thursday 21st November

Bingley declared his intention of going to Longbourn to give the Bennets an invitation to his ball. Caroline and Louisa eagerly agreed to go with him, but I declined, saying I had some letters to write. Caroline immediately declared that she had some letters to write, too, but Bingley told her they could wait until she returned. I was pleased. I did not want company today. I cannot keep my thoughts from George Wickham. From the local talk, I gather he is thinking of joining the regiment. No doubt he thinks he will look well in a scarlet coat.

Worse still, Bingley has included all the officers in his invitation to Netherfield, and I fear Wickham might join them. I have no wish to see him, and yet I will not avoid the ball. It is not up to me to avoid him. He is a scoundrel and a villain but I will not upset Bingley by refusing to attend his ball.

Friday 22nd November

A wet day. I was able to ride out with Bingley this

morning, but then the rain poured down and we were obliged to stay indoors. We whiled away the time by talking of the estate and Bingley's plans for it. His sisters gave us the benefit of their views on necessary alterations to the house and the time passed pleasantly enough, though I missed Elizabeth's lively company.

Saturday 23rd November

Another wet day. Caroline was in a provoking mood. I am glad Elizabeth was not here, or she would have surely borne the brunt of Caroline's ill-humour. Bingley and I retired to the billiard-room. It is a good thing the house possesses one, or I believe we should have been terribly bored.

Sunday 24th November

I received a letter from Georgiana this morning. She is doing well with her studies, and is happy. She is beginning a new concerto with her music master, a man who I am happy to say is almost in his dotage, and she is enjoying herself.

The rain continued. Caroline and Louisa amused themselves by deciding what they will wear for the ball, whilst Bingley and I discussed the war. I am beginning to find the country tiresome. At home, at Pemberley, I have plenty to occupy me, but here there is little to do beyond reading or playing billiards when the weather is poor.

I will be interested to see if this spell of wet weather dissuades Bingley from buying Netherfield. A country estate in the sunshine is a very different thing from a country estate in the rain.

Monday 25th November

I am glad of the ball. At least, if we have another wet day tomorrow, we will have something to occupy us.

Tuesday 26th November

The morning was wet, and I spent it writing letters. This afternoon, Bingley and his sisters were involved in final preparations for the ball. I had little to do and was vexed to find myself thinking of Miss Elizabeth Bennet, so much so that when the party from Longbourn arrived this evening I found myself looking for her. I thought I had put her out of my mind, but I am not as impervious to her as I had supposed.

'Jane looks charming,' said Caroline, as her brother moved forward to greet Miss Bennet.

'It is a pity the same cannot be said for her sister,' said Louisa. 'What is Miss Elizabeth Bennet wearing?'

Caroline regarded her with a droll eye.

'Miss Eliza Bennet scorns fashion, and is wearing a dress that is three inches too long and uses a great deal too much lace. Do you not think so, Mr Darcy?'

'I know nothing about ladies' fashions,' I said, 'but she looks very well to me.'

Caroline was silenced, but only for a moment.

'I wonder who she can be looking for. She is certainly looking for someone.'

'She is probably looking for the officers,' said Louisa.

'Then she is not as quick as her sisters, for they have already found them,' said Caroline.

The younger girls had run noisily across the ballroom, and were greeting the officers with laughs and squeals.

'If they move any closer to Mr Denny, they will suffocate him!' remarked Louisa.

'You would not like to see your sister behaving in such a way with the officers, I am persuaded,' said Caroline, turning to me.

She did not mean to wound me, and yet her remark could not have been less well chosen. It sent my thoughts to Georgiana, and from thence to Wickham, who was to don a red coat. No, I would not like to see it, but I was uncomfortably aware that if I had not arrived in Ramsgate without warning, it could almost have come to pass.

Caroline looked alarmed as my face went white, but I managed to reply coolly enough: 'Are you comparing my sister to Lydia Bennet?'

'They are the same age!' said Louisa, with a trill of laughter.

'No, of course not,' said Caroline quickly, realizing she had made a mistake. 'There can be no comparison. I meant only that the Bennet girls are allowed to run wild.'

I gave a cool nod and then moved away from her, hoping that Elizabeth's glances round the room had been for me. As I drew close to the officers, I heard Denny saying to Miss Lydia Bennet that Wickham was not there as he had been forced to go out of town for a few days.

'Oh!' she said, her face dropping.

Elizabeth had joined them and she, too, looked disappointed. I remembered the look she had bestowed on Wickham in Meryton and I felt my hands clench as I realized with an unpleasant shock that when she had entered the ballroom she had been looking for Wickham, and not for me.

'I do not imagine his business would have called him away just now if he had not wished to avoid a certain gentleman here,' I overheard Mr Denny saying.

So he had turned coward, had he? I could not wonder at it. Courage was never a part of Wickham's character. Imposing on the gullible, deceiving the innocent and seducing young girls, that was his strength.

But surely Elizabeth was not gullible? No. She was not to be so easily taken in. She might not have found him out yet, but I was confident she would do so. In the meantime, I did not want to miss the opportunity of speaking to her.

I continued walking towards her.

'I am glad to see you here. I hope you had a pleasant journey?' I asked. 'This time, I hope you did not have to walk!'

'No, I thank you,' she said stiffly. 'I came in the carriage.'

I wondered if I had offended her. Perhaps she felt I had meant my remark as a slight on her family's inability to keep horses purely for their carriage. I tried to repair the damage of my first remark.

'You are looking forward to the ball?'

She turned and looked at me directly.

'It is the company that makes a ball, Mr Darcy. I enjoy any entertainment at which my friends are present.'

'Then I am sure you will enjoy your evening here,' I said.

She turned away with a degree of ill-humour that shocked me. She did not even manage to overcome it when speaking to Bingley, and I resolved I had done with her. Let her turn her shoulder when I spoke to her. Let her prefer Wickham to me. I wanted nothing more to do with her.

She left her sisters and crossed the room to speak to her friend, Miss Lucas, and then her hand was sought by the heavy young clergyman I had seen with her at Meryton. Despite my anger, I could not help but feel sorry for her. I had never seen a display of more mortifying dancing in my life. From her expression, I could tell she felt the same. He went left when he should have gone right. He went back when he should have gone forward. And yet she danced as well as if she had had an expert partner.

When I saw her leaving the floor, I was moved to ask for the next dance. I was frustrated in this by her dancing with one of the officers, but then I moved forward and asked for the next dance. She looked surprised, and I felt it, for as soon as I had asked for her hand I wondered what I was about. Had I not decided to take no further notice of her? But it was done. I had spoken, and I could not unspeak my offer.

She accepted, though out of surprise more than anything else, I think. I could find nothing to say to her, and walked away, determined to spend my time with more rational people until it was time for the dance to begin. We went out on to the floor. There were looks of amazement all around us, though I am sure I do not know why. I might not have chosen to dance at the assembly, but that is a very different situation from a private ball.

I tried to think of something to say, but I found that I was speechless. It surprised me. I have never been at a loss before. To be sure, I do not always find it easy to talk to those I do not know very well, but I can generally think of at least a pleasantry. I believe the hostility I felt coming from Elizabeth robbed me of my sense.

At last she said: 'This is an agreeable dance.'

Coming from a woman whose wit and liveliness delight me, it was a dry remark, and I made no reply.

After a few minutes, she said: 'It is your turn to say something now, Mr Darcy. I talked about the dance, and you ought to make some kind of remark on the size of the room, or the number of couples.'

This was more like Elizabeth.

'I will say whatever you wish me to say,' I returned.

'Very well. That reply will do for the present. Perhaps by and by I may observe that private balls are much pleasanter than public ones. But now we may be silent.'

'Do you talk by rule then, while you are dancing?' I asked.

'Sometimes. One must speak a little, you know, and yet for the advantage of some, conversation ought to be so arranged as that they may have the trouble of saying as little as possible.'

'Are you consulting your own feelings in the present case, or do you imagine that you are gratifying mine?'

'Both,' she replied archly.

I could not help smiling. It is that archness that draws me. It is provocative without being impertinent, and I have never come across it in any woman before. She lifts her face in just such a way when she makes one of her playful comments that I am seized with an overwhelming urge to kiss her. Not that I would give in to such an impulse, but it is there all the same.

'I have always seen a great similarity in the turn of our minds,' she went on. 'We are each of an unsocial, taciturn disposition, unwilling to speak, unless we expect to say something that will amaze the whole room, and be handed down to posterity with all the éclat of a proverb.'

I was uneasy, not sure whether to laugh or feel concerned. If it was part of her playfulness, then I found it amusing, but if she thought it was the truth? Had I been so taciturn when I had been with her? I thought back to the Meryton assembly, and the early days at Netherfield. I had perhaps not set out to charm her, but then I never did. I had, perhaps, been abrupt to begin with, but I thought I had repaired matters towards the end of her stay at Netherfield. Until the last day. I remembered my silence, and my determination not to speak to her. I remembered congratulating myself on not saying more than ten words to her, and remaining determinedly silent when I was left alone with her for half an hour, pretending to be absorbed in my book.

I had been right to remain silent, I thought. Then immediately afterwards I thought I had been wrong. I had been both right and wrong: right if I wished to crush any expectations that might have arisen during the course of her visit, but wrong if I wished to win her favour, or to be polite. I am not used to being so confused. I never was, before I met Elizabeth.

I became aware of the fact that again I was silent, and I knew I must say something if I was not to confirm her in the suspicion that I was deliberately taciturn.

'This is no very striking resemblance of your own character, I am sure,' I said, my uneasiness reflected in my tone of voice, for I did not know whether to be amused or hurt. 'How near it may be to mine, I cannot pretend to say. You think it a faithful portrait, undoubtedly.'

'I must not decide on my own performance.'

We lapsed into an uneasy silence. Did she judge me? Did she despise me? Or was she playing with me? I could not decide.

At length, I spoke to her about her trip to Meryton, and she replied that she and her sisters had made a new acquaintance there.

I froze. I knew whom she meant. Wickham! And the way she spoke of him! Not with contempt, but with liking. I feared she meant to go on, but something in my manner must have kept her silent.

I knew I should ignore the matter. I did not have to explain myself to her. And yet I found myself saying: 'Mr Wickham is blessed with such happy manners as may ensure his making friends. Whether he may be equally capable of retaining them is less certain.'

'He has been so unlucky as to lose your friendship, and in a manner which he is likely to suffer from all his life.'

What has he said to her? What has he told her? I longed to tell her the truth of the matter, but I could not do so for fear of hurting Georgiana.

Once more a silence fell. We were rescued from it by Sir William Lucas who let slip a remark that drove Wickham out of my mind. For that, at least, I must thank him. He complimented us on our dancing, and then, glancing at Miss Bennet and Bingley, he said he hoped to have the pleasure of seeing it often repeated when a certain desirable event took place.

I was startled. But there could be no mistaking his meaning. He thought it possible, nay certain, that Miss Bennet and Bingley would wed. I watched them dancing, but I could see nothing in the demeanour of either to lead to this conclusion. Yet if it was being talked of then I knew the matter was serious. I could not let Bingley jeopardize a woman's reputation, no matter how agreeable his flirtation. Recovering myself, I asked Elizabeth what we had been talking about.

She replied, 'Nothing at all.'

I began to talk to her of books. She would not admit that we might share the same tastes, so I declared that then, at least, we would have something to talk about. She claimed she could not talk of books in a ballroom, but I thought that was not what was troubling her. The trouble was that her mind was elsewhere.

Suddenly she said to me, 'I remember hearing you once say, Mr Darcy, that you hardly ever forgave, that your resentment once created was unappeasable. You are very cautious, I suppose, as to its being created?'

Was she thinking of Wickham? Had he told her of the coldness between us? She seemed genuinely anxious to hear my answer, and I reassured her.

'I am,' I said firmly.

More questions followed, until I asked where these questions tended.

'Merely to the illustration of your character,' said she, trying to shake off her gravity. 'I am trying to make it out.'

Then she was not thinking of Wickham. I was grateful.

'And what is your success?' I could not help asking.

She shook her head. 'I do not get on at all. I hear such different accounts of you as puzzle me exceedingly.'

'I can readily believe it,' I said, thinking with a sinking feeling of Wickham. I added on impulse, 'I could wish that you were not to sketch my character at the present moment, as there is reason to fear that the performance would reflect no credit on either.'

'But if I do not take your likeness now, I may never have another opportunity.'

I had begged for clemency. I would not beg again. I replied coldly, stiffly: 'I would by no means suspend any pleasure of yours.'

We finished the dance as we had begun it, in silence. But I could not be angry with her for long. She had been told something by George Wickham, that much was clear, and as he was incapable of telling the truth, she had no doubt been subjected to a host of lies. As we left the floor, I had forgiven Elizabeth, and turned my anger towards Wickham instead.

What had he told her? I wondered. And how far had it damaged me in her esteem?

I was saved from these unsettling reflections by the sight of a heavy young man bowing in front of me and begging me to forgive him for introducing himself. I was about to turn away when I remembered having seen him with Elizabeth, and I found myself curious as to what he might have to say.

'It is not amongst the established forms of ceremony amongst the laity to introduce themselves, I am well aware, but I flatter myself that the rules governing the clergy are quite different, indeed I consider the clerical office as equal in point of dignity with the highest rank in the kingdom, and so I have come to introduce myself to you, an introduction which, I am persuaded, will not be deemed impertinent when you learn that my noble benefactor, the lady who has graciously bestowed on me a munificent living, is none other than your estimable aunt, Lady Catherine de Bourgh. It was she who preferred me to the valuable rectory of Hunsford, where it is my duty, nay my pleasure, to perform the ceremonies that must, by their very nature, devolve upon the incumbent,' he assured me with an obsequious smile.

I looked at him in astonishment, wondering if he could be quite sane. It seemed that he did indeed believe a clergyman to be the equal of the King of England, though not of my aunt, for his speech was littered with effusions of gratitude and praise of her nobility and condescension. I found him an oddity; but my aunt, however, had evidently found him worthy of the living, and as she knew him far better than I did I could only suppose he had virtues I knew nothing of.

'I am certain my aunt could never bestow a favour unworthily,' I said politely, but with enough coldness to prevent him saying anything further. He was not deterred, however, and began a second speech which was even lengthier and more involved than the first. As he opened his mouth to draw breath, I made him a bow and walked away. Absurdity has its place, but I was not in the mood to be diverted by it, so soon after quitting Elizabeth.

'I see you have met the estimable Mr Collins,' said Caroline to me as we went into supper. 'He is another of the Bennet relatives. Really, they seem to have the most extraordinary collection. I think this one surpasses even the uncle in Cheapside. What do you think, Mr Darcy?'

'We may all have relatives we are not proud of,' I said.

It gave Caroline pause. She likes to forget that her father made his fortune in trade.

'Very true,' she answered. I thought she had acquired some sense, but a moment later she said, 'I have just been speaking to Eliza Bennet. She seems to have developed the most extraordinary liking for George Wickham. I do not know if you realized, but he is to attach himself to the militia here. It is of all things the most vexing, that you should be plagued with a man like George Wickham. My brother did not wish to invite him, I know, but he felt he could not make an exception of him when inviting the other officers.'

'It would have looked particular,' I conceded.

Bingley could not be blamed for the situation.

'I know that Charles was very pleased when Wickham took himself out of the way. Charles would not wish to disconcert you in any way. Knowing Wickham was not a man to be trusted, I warned Eliza Bennet against him, telling her that I knew he had behaved infamously to you, though I did not have all the particulars...'

She paused, but if she was expecting me to enlighten her, she was to be disappointed. My dealings with Wickham will never be made public, nor told to anyone who does not already know of them.

'...but she ignored my warning and leapt to his defence in the wildest way.'

I was about to put an end to her conversation, as it was causing me no small degree of pain, when another voice penetrated the chatter. I recognized the strident tones at once. They were those of Mrs Bennet. I had no wish to listen to her conversation, but it was impossible not to hear what she was saying.

'Ah! She is so beautiful I knew she could not be so beautiful for nothing. My lovely Jane. And Mr Bingley! What a handsome man. What an air of fashion. And such pleasing manners. And then, of course, there is Nether-field. It is just the right distance from us, for she will not like to be too close, not with her own establishment to see to, and yet it will take no time at all for her to come and visit us in the carriage. I dare say she will have a very fine carriage. Probably two fine carriages. Or perhaps three. The cost of a carriage is nothing to a man with five thousand pounds a year.'

I found myself growing rigid as I listened to her running on.

'And then his sisters are so fond of her.'

I was glad that Caroline's attention had been claimed by a young man to her left, and that she did not hear. Her fondness for Jane would evaporate in a moment if she knew where Mrs Bennet's thoughts were tending. But it was not just Mrs Bennet's thoughts. Sir William's thoughts had been running in the same direction.

I looked along the table, and saw Bingley talking to Miss Bennet. His manner was as open as ever, but I thought I detected something of more than usual regard. In fact, the longer I watched him, the more I became sure that his feelings were engaged. I watched Miss Bennet, and although I could tell that she was pleased to talk to him, she gave no signs that her feelings were in any way attached. I breathed more easily. If I could but remove Bingley from the neighbourhood, I felt sure that he would soon forget her, and she would forget him.

If it had only been a matter of Miss Bennet, I might not have been so concerned at the thought of Bingley marrying her, but it was not only a matter of Miss Bennet, it was a matter of her mother, who was an unbridled gossip, and her indolent father, and her three younger sisters who were either fools or common flirts, and her uncle in Cheapside, and her uncle the attorney, and on top of all this, her strange connection, the obsequious clergyman....

As I listened to Mrs Bennet, I felt the time was fast approaching when I must take a hand. I could not abandon my friend to such a fate, when a little effort on my part would extricate him from his predicament.

I was sure that with a few weeks in London, he would soon find a new flirt.

'I only hope you may be so fortunate, Lady Lucas,' Mrs Bennet continued, though evidently believing there was no chance of her neighbour sharing her fortune. 'To have a daughter so well settled – what a wonderful thing!'

Supper was over. It was followed by a display from Mary Bennet, whose singing was as bad as her playing. To make matters worse, when her father finally removed her from the pianoforte, he did so in such a way as to make any decent person blush.

'That will do extremely well, child. You have delighted us long enough. Let the other young ladies have time to exhibit.'

Was there ever a more ill-judged speech?

The evening could not be over too soon, but by some coincidence or contrivance, I know not which, the Bennet carriage was the last to arrive.

'Lord, how tired I am!' exclaimed Lydia Bennet, giving a violent yawn that set Caroline and Louisa exchanging satirical glances.

Mrs Bennet would not be quiet, and talked incessantly. Mr Bennet made no effort to check her, and it was one of the most uncomfortable quarter-hours of my life. To save Bingley from such company became uppermost in my mind.

'You will come to a family dinner with us, I hope, Mr Bingley?' said Mrs Bennet.

'Nothing would give me greater pleasure,' he said. 'I have some business to attend to in London, but I will wait upon you as soon as I return.'

The knowledge delighted me. It means I will not have to think of a way of removing him from the neighbourhood, for if he happens to remain in London, then the contact with Miss Bennet will be broken and he will not think of her any more.

I intend to speak to Caroline, to make sure that Jane's affections are not engaged, and if I find, as I suspect, that they are not, then I shall suggest that we remove to London with Bingley and persuade him to remain there. A winter in town will cure him of his affections, and leave him free to bestow them on a more deserving object.

Wednesday 27th November

Bingley left for London today.

'Caroline, I wish to speak to you,' I said, when he had departed.

Caroline looked up from her book and smiled.

'I am at your disposal.'

'It is about Miss Bennet that I wish to speak.'

Her smile dropped, and I felt I was right in thinking that her affection for her friend was on the wane.

'There were several allusions made at the ball, suggesting that some of Bingley's new neighbours were expecting a marriage to take place between him and Miss Bennet.'

'What!' cried Caroline.

'I thought it would distress you. I can see nothing in Miss Bennet's manner that makes me think she is in love, but I want your advice. You know her better than I do. You have been in her confidence. Does she entertain tender feelings for your brother? Because, if so, those feelings must not be trifled with.'

'She has none at all,' said Caroline, setting my mind at rest.

'You are sure of this?'

'I am indeed. She has talked of my brother a number of times, but only in the terms she uses for every other young man of her acquaintance. Why, I am sure she has never thought of Charles in that light. She knows he does not mean to settle at Netherfield, and she is simply amusing herself whilst he is here.'

'It is as I thought. But Bingley's feelings are in a fair way to being engaged.'

'I have had the same fear. If he should be foolish enough to ally himself with that family, he will regret it for ever.'

'He will. I think we must separate them, before their behaviour gives rise to even more expectations. If it does, there will come a time when those expectations must be fulfilled, or the lady's reputation will suffer irreparable harm.'

'You are quite right. We must not damage dear Jane's reputation. She is such a sweet girl. Louisa and I quite dote on her. She must not be harmed.'

Mr Hurst interrupted us at that moment.

'Coming to dine with the officers?' he asked. 'They invited me to go along. Sure you'd be welcome.'

'No,' I said. I wanted to finish my conversation with Caroline.

Hurst managed an idle shrug and called for the carriage.

'I propose we follow Bingley to London. If we stay with him there, he will have no reason to return,' I said.

'An excellent plan. I will write to Jane tomorrow. I will say nothing out of the ordinary, but I will let her know that Charles will not be returning this winter, and I will wish her enjoyment of her many beaux this Christmas.'

Thursday 28th November

Caroline's letter was written and sent this morning, shortly before we departed for London.

'Heard the damnedest thing in Meryton last night,' said Mr Hurst as the coach rattled along on its way to London.

I did not pay much attention, but on his continuing I found myself attending to him.

'The Bennet girl – what was her name?'

'Jane,' supplied Louisa.

'No, not her, the other one. The one with the petticoat.'

'Ah, you mean Elizabeth.'

'That's the one. Had an offer from the clergyman.'

'An offer? From the clergyman? What do you mean?' asked Caroline and Louisa together.

'An offer of marriage. Collins. That was his name.'

'Mr Collins! How delicious!' said Louisa.

'It seems that Mr Collins is another admirer of fine eyes,' said Caroline, looking at me satirically. 'I think they will deal well together. One is all impertinence, and the other is all imbecility.'

I had not known, till I heard this, how far my feelings had gone. The idea of Elizabeth marrying Mr Collins was mortifying, and painful in a way I had not imagined. I quickly rallied. Hurst must be mistaken. She could not lower herself so far. To be tied to that clod for the rest of her life...

'You must be mistaken,' I said.

'Not mistaken at all,' said Hurst. 'Had it from Denny.'

'It is not a bad match,' said Louisa, considering. 'In fact, it is a good one. There are five daughters, all unmarried, and their estate is entailed, I believe.'

'Entailed on Collins,' said Mr Hurst.

'All the better,' said Louisa. 'Miss Eliza Bennet will not have to leave her home, and her sisters will have somewhere to live when her father dies.'

'And so will her mother,' said Caroline gaily. 'How charming to be confined with Mrs Bennet for the rest of their lives!'

I had never liked Caroline less. I would not wish such a fate on anyone, and certainly not on Elizabeth. She suffers for her mother. I have seen it. She blushes every time her mother reveals her foolishness. To be forced to endure such humiliation for the rest of her life…

'But I wonder why he did not ask Jane,' said Louisa.

'Jane?' enquired Caroline.

'Yes. She is the eldest.'

Caroline looked at me. I knew what she was thinking. Mr Collins had not asked Jane, because Mrs Bennet had led him to believe that Jane was shortly to be married to Bingley.

'I dare say, with the estate entailed, he thought he could have his choice,' Caroline said. 'Miss Eliza Bennet's pertness must have appealed to him, though I am not sure she will make a suitable wife for a clergyman. What say you, Mr Darcy?'

I said nothing, for fear of saying something I should regret. I could not possibly allow myself to admire Elizabeth, so what did it matter if another man did? But I found that my hands were clenched and, looking down, perceived my knuckles had grown white.

She looked at me, expecting an answer, however, and at last I said, more to satisfy my own feelings than hers: 'It might come to nothing. Denny might be mistaken.'

'I do not see how,' said Caroline. 'He is as thick as thieves with Lydia. He knows everything that goes on in that household I dare say.'

'Lydia is a child, and might have been wrong,' I heard myself saying.

'Denny did not have it from Lydia,' said Mr Hurst. 'Had it from the aunt. Aunt lives in Meryton. Told Denny herself. Whole house was in an uproar, she said. First Mr Collins offers for Elizabeth, then Elizabeth tells him she will not have him.'

'Will not have him?'

I heard the hope in my voice.

'Refused him. Mother in hysterics. Father on her side,' said Mr Hurst.

God bless Mr Bennet! I thought, prepared to forgive him every other instance of neglect.

'If she doesn't change her mind and have him, he will have the Lucas girl,' said Mr Hurst.

'How do you know?' asked Caroline in surprise.

'Aunt said so. "If Lizzy doesn't look sharp, Charlotte will have him," she said. "He has to marry, his patroness has told him so, and one girl is as good as another in the end." '

I breathed again. It was only when I did so that I realized how deeply I had been attracted by Elizabeth. It was a good thing I was going to London. I had saved Bingley from an imprudent match, I could do no less for myself. Once out of Elizabeth's neighbourhood, I would cease to think about her. I would engage in rational conversation with rational women, and think no more of her saucy wit.

We arrived in London in good time. Bingley was surprised to see us.

'We did not want you to be alone here, and to have to spend your free hours in a comfortless hotel,' said Caroline.

'But my business will only take a few days!' he said in surprise.

'I hope you will not go before seeing Georgiana,' I said. 'I know she would like to see you.'

'Dear Georgiana,' said Caroline. 'Do say we can stay in town for a week, Charles.'

'I do not know why I should not stay an extra day or two,' he conceded. 'I should like to see Georgiana myself. Tell me, Darcy, is she much grown?'

'You would not recognize her,' I said. 'She is no longer a girl. She is well on the way to becoming a woman.'

'But still young enough to enjoy Christmas?' Caroline asked.

I smiled. 'I believe so. You must stay and celebrate it with us.'

'We will not be staying so long,' said Bingley.

'What, and miss Christmas with Darcy and Georgiana?' asked Caroline.

'But I promised to dine with the Bennets,' he said. 'Mrs Bennet asked me particularly, and in the kindest manner.'

'Are you to abandon old friends for new?' cried Caroline. 'Mrs Bennet said you could dine with her family at any time. I heard her say so myself. The Bennets will still be there after Christmas.'

Bingley looked uncertain, but then he said: 'Very well. We will stay in town for Christmas.' He began to look more cheerful. 'I dare say it will be good fun. It is always better to celebrate Christmas when there are children in the house.'

This did not bode well for his feelings towards Georgiana, but I comforted myself with the fact that he had not seen her for a long time, and that although she might have seemed like a child the last time they met, she was now clearly becoming a young woman.

'And once it is over, we will go to Hertfordshire for the New Year,' he said. 'I will write to Miss Bennet and tell her of our plans.'

'There is no need for that,' said Caroline. 'I will be writing to her today. I will tell her so myself.'

'Send her my best wishes,' said Bingley.

'Indeed I will.'

'And tell her we will be in Hertfordshire in January.'

'I will make sure I do so.'

'Commend me to her family.'

'Of course.'

He would have gone on, but I broke in with: 'Then it is settled.'

Caroline left the room in order to write her letter. Louisa and her husband went, too, and Bingley and I were left alone.

'A Christmas to look forward to, and a New Year to look forward to even more,' said Bingley.

'You like Miss Bennet,' I observed.

'I have never met a girl I liked half so well.'

I sat down, and Bingley sat down opposite me.

'And yet I am not sure she would make you a good wife,' I said pensively.

'What do you mean?' he asked, surprised.

'Her low connections – '

'I do not intend to marry her connections!' said Bingley with a laugh.

'An uncle who is an attorney, another who lives in Cheapside. They can add nothing to your consequence, and will, in the end, diminish it.'

Bingley's smile faded.

'I cannot see that it matters. What need have I of consequence?'

'Every gentleman needs consequence. And then there are the sisters.'

'Miss Elizabeth is a charming girl.'

He had hit me at my weakest spot, but I was firm with myself and rallied.

'Her sisters are, for the most part, ignorant and vulgar. The youngest is a hardened flirt.'

'There will be no need for us to see them,' said Bingley.

'My dear Bingley, you cannot live at Netherfield and not see them. They will always be there. So will her mother.'

'Then we will not live at Netherfield. I have not yet
bought the estate. It is only rented. We will settle elsewhere.'

'But would Jane consent to it?'

His face fell.

'If she felt a strong attachment to you, perhaps she
might be persuaded to leave her neighbourhood,' I said.

'You think she does not feel it?' asked Bingley uncer-
tainly.

'She is a delightful girl, but she showed no more pleasure in your company than in any other man's.'

He chewed his lip.

'I thought...she seemed pleased to talk to
me...seemed pleased to dance with me...I rather
thought she seemed more pleased with me than any
other man. When we danced together – '

'You danced but twice at each ball, and she danced
twice with other men.'

'She did,' he admitted, 'but I thought that was just
because it would have been rude to refuse.'

'Perhaps it would have been rude of her to refuse
you.'

'You think she only danced with me to be polite?' he
asked in consternation.

'I would not go so far. I think she enjoyed dancing
with you, and talking to you, and flirting with you. But
I think she enjoyed it no more than with other men, and
now that you are not in Hertfordshire – '

'I must go back,' he said, standing up. 'I knew it.'

'But if she is indifferent, you will only give yourself pain.'

'If she is indifferent. You do not know that she is.'

'No, I do not know it, but I observed her closely, and I could see no sign of particular regard.'

'You observed her?' he asked in surprise.

'Your singling her out was beginning to attract attention. Others had noticed besides myself. If it had been gone on much longer, you would have been obliged to have made her an offer.'

'I would have liked to have made her an offer,' he corrected me, then faltered. 'Do you think she would have accepted?'

'Of course. It would have been a good match for her. You have a considerable income, and a beautiful house. She would have been settled near her family. There is no question of her refusing. But should you like to be married for those reasons?'

He looked doubtful.

'I would rather be married for myself,' he conceded.

'And so you will be, one day.'

He sat down again.

'She was too good for me,' he said morosely.

'Hardly that, but if her affections are not engaged, what is the point of marriage? You will meet another girl, as sweet as Miss Bennet, but one who can return your feelings in full measure. London is full of young ladies.'

'But I have no interest in other young ladies.'

'In time, you will have.'

Bingley said nothing, but I was easy in my mind. He will have forgotten her before the winter is over.

I am pleased he has expressed a desire to see Georgiana again. He has known her very much longer than he has known Miss Bennet, and a new acquaintance cannot be expected to hold the same place in his affections as an old, particularly when he sees how much Georgiana has grown. The match would be welcome on both sides, and I flatter myself that it would be a happy one.

December

Thursday 5th December

Bingley came to dine with me today. He has been busy this last week, but he arrived punctually this evening and was very much taken with Georgiana.

'She is turning into a beauty,' he said to me. 'And she is so accomplished,' he added, when she played for us after dinner.

She is. I had almost forgotten what it is to listen to excellent playing, and I could not help an inward shudder when I thought of Mary Bennet's playing and compared it to Georgiana's. Elizabeth's playing was sweet, it is true, though it was not so accomplished as my sister's, but there was still a quality about it that made me want to listen.

Friday 6th December

Caroline called to see Georgiana this morning, and I entertained her until my sister's music lesson was over.

'Charles was very taken with Georgiana last night,' she remarked. 'He said that Georgiana was one of the most beautiful and accomplished young women of his acquaintance.'

I was well pleased. Caroline seemed pleased, too. I think she would not be averse to a marriage between them.

'Are you going to visit your aunt in Kent before Christmas?' she asked.

'No, I think not, though I will probably visit her at Easter.'

'Dear Lady Catherine,' said Caroline, removing her

gloves. 'How I long to meet her. Rosings is a fine house, by all accounts.'

'Yes, it is, very fine indeed.'

'Such a pleasant part of the country.'

'It is.'

'I suggested to Charles that he should look for a house there. I would be happy to live in Kent. But he felt Hertfordshire was better placed. A pity. He would have avoided certain entanglements if he had settled elsewhere.'

'He is free of them now, however.'

'Yes, thanks to your intervention. He is lucky to have such a friend. I would find it a great comfort to know that such a friend was looking after me,' she said, looking up at me.

'You have your brother.'

She smiled. 'Of course, but Charles is still a boy. One does so need a man at times, someone of depth and maturity, who is used to the ways of the world and knows how to live in it.'

'Have you no plans to marry?'

'I would, if I met the right gentleman.'

'Now that you are in London you will have more chance of meeting people. Bingley means to arrange some balls, I know. I have encouraged it. The more pretty faces he sees over the next few weeks the better. And for you, it will extend your social circle.'

'It is not so very constrained. We dine with more than four-and-twenty families, you know,' she remarked satirically.

I was reminded of the Bennets, as she intended I should be, but if she knew the exact form of my thoughts I doubt she would have been so pleased. No matter what I do, every conversation seems to remind me of them in some fashion. It is fortunate that I have stopped thinking about Elizabeth, otherwise the Bennets would never be out of my mind.

Saturday 7th December

Bingley occupies himself with business and is in good spirits, though now and then I catch a wistful look in his eye.

'You are sure she felt nothing for me?' he asked this evening, when the ladies had withdrawn after dinner.

I did not need to ask whom he meant.

'I am sure of it. She enjoyed your company, but nothing more.'

He nodded.

'I thought she could not...such an angel...still, I hoped...but it is as you say. She will marry someone from Meryton, I expect. Someone she has known all her life.'

'Very probably.'

'Not someone she has only just met.'

'No.'

'She will not miss me, now I am gone.'

'No.'

He was silent.

'There is a great deal to be said for marrying someone one has known all one's life, or at least for a long time,' I said.

'Yes, I suppose there is,' he said, but without any real enthusiasm.

'Their defects are already known, and there can be no unpleasant surprises,' I continued.

'It is as you say.'

'And it is as well to know, and like, their family. Georgiana will marry someone she knows, I hope,' I said.

'Yes, it would be a good thing,' said Bingley, but without real interest.

A pity. I thought his affections were turning in that direction. However, I have made the point, and in the future he may remember it.

Tuesday 10th December

I have had my mother's pearls restrung for Georgiana, and mean to give them to her as a present. She is old enough for them now, and I think she will look well in them. Whilst I was at Howard & Gibbs, I enquired about having the rest of my mother's jewellery remodelled. It is of good quality, and much of it has been in the family for generations. I have arranged for the pearl brooch and earrings to be reset at once, and I will give them to Georgiana for her next birthday. I have arranged to take in the other pieces of jewellery so that they can be examined and sketches for new settings made. The sketches can be altered to accommodate any changing fashions and the pieces can be reset as Georgiana becomes old enough to wear them.

Thursday 12th December

I dined with Bingley and his sisters. During the course of the evening we talked of the Christmas festivities. There will be some large parties for us to attend, but in the days immediately proceeding Christmas I would like to arrange a few small private parties with no one but the Bingleys, so that Georgiana can attend.

'I thought I would have a small dance on the twenty-third,' I said, 'and then charades on Christmas Eve.'

'An excellent idea,' said Caroline.

'I have invited Colonel Fitzwilliam, which will make us four gentlemen and three ladies. Do you think I should invite any more ladies?' I asked Caroline.

'No,' she said emphatically. 'Mr Hurst never dances, which leaves us with three couples.'

My thoughts went back to Bingley's ball at Netherfield, where I danced with Elizabeth.

'Have you decided when Georgiana will make her come out?' asked Caroline, as if reading my mind.

'Not until she is eighteen, perhaps later.'

'Eighteen is a good age. She will have left the schoolroom behind her and overcome her shyness, but will have the fresh bloom of youth. She will break a great many hearts.'

'I hope she will not break any. I want her to be happy, and if she should happen to find a good man in her first season, I will be glad to see her settled.'

Caroline glanced at Bingley.

'In two years, then, we must hope she finds someone

worthy of her. Someone with an easy temper, who is generous and kind.'

'That would be the very thing.'

'In the meantime, it will be good for her to have the company of a personable young man, so that she is used to male company and does not become tongue-tied when in gentlemen's presence. She is never tongue-tied with Charles, but seems to enjoy his company,' said Caroline.

'What is that you are saying?' asked Bingley, who had been talking to Louisa, but who looked up when he heard his name.

'I was saying that Georgiana is always easy with you. Darcy wants her to enjoy some adult entertainments this Christmas, and I am sure he can rely on you to dance with her.'

'Nothing would give me greater pleasure. She is becoming a beauty, Darcy.'

I was gratified.

Monday 16th December

The house is looking festive. Georgiana has been helping Mrs Annesley to decorate it with holly, tucking pieces of the greenery behind the pictures and around the candlesticks. She has always liked doing this, ever since she was a young child. When I arrived, I found her adorning the window in the drawing-room with more greenery.

'I thought we would have a dance in a few days' time,' I said.

She flushed.

'Just a small one, with our intimate friends,' I reassured her.

'Perhaps you would like some new ribbon to trim your muslin,' said Mrs Annesley to Georgiana.

'Oh, yes,' she said, looking at me hopefully.

'You must buy whatever you need,' I replied.

I was about to say she should buy herself a new fan when I thought better of it. I will buy one for her myself, and surprise her with it.

Wednesday 18th December

Today we had snow. Georgiana was as excited as a child, and I took her into the park. We walked along the white paths and returned to the house with flushed faces and hearty appetites.

I could not help remembering how flushed Elizabeth had looked after her walk to Netherfield. Her eyes had been sparkling, and her complexion had been brightened by the exercise.

Where is she now? Is she walking along the country lanes around her home in the snow? Is she at home, arranging holly, even as Georgiana is arranging it here? Is she looking forward to Christmas? If I had not kept Bingley from Netherfield, we could all be there now...which would have been a very grave mistake. It is better for all of us that we are in London.

Monday 23rd December

We had our dance this evening, and I was gratified to see Georgiana enjoying herself. She danced twice with Bingley, once with Colonel Fitzwilliam and once with myself.

'Georgiana moves with extraordinary grace,' said Caroline.

It was a subject that could not fail to please me.

'You think so?'

'I do. It was an excellent idea to hold a private dance. It is good for her to practise at these sorts of occasions. You dance very well, Mr Darcy. You and I together can set her an example. Charles and I are at your disposal if you should wish to hold another such evening. It can do Georgiana nothing but good to see others dancing, and it will help her achieve confidence and poise.'

I was reminded of another time when she had praised me, saying how well I wrote my letters. I recalled the scene exactly. It had been at Netherfield, and Elizabeth had been with us. I felt a stirring of something inside me as I thought of her. Anger, perhaps, that she had so bewitched me?

Our dance broke up. Our guests left, and I had the satisfaction of seeing Georgiana retiring to bed, tired but happy.

She has completely forgotten George Wickham, I am sure of it. As long as nothing reminds her of him, I do not believe she will think of him again.

Tuesday 24th December

We had our game of charades after dinner this evening. I was pleased when Caroline thought of suggesting that Georgiana and Bingley work on their charade together. They retreated into a corner of the room, their heads close enough to be almost touching. It was a most pleasing sight.

The charades were very enjoyable, and after we had all performed, we went in to supper.

'Do you know, Darcy, I thought we would be spending Christmas at Netherfield this year,' said Bingley with a sigh. 'That had been my plan when I took the house. I wonder what they are all doing now.'

I thought it wiser to turn his thoughts away from this direction.

'Much the same as we are doing here. Take some more of the venison.'

He did as I suggested, and said no more about Netherfield.

Wednesday 25th December

I have never enjoyed a Christmas day more. We went to church this morning and this evening we played at bullet pudding and snapdragon. As we did so I noticed a change in Georgiana. Last year she played as a child, enjoying the novelty of putting her hands into the flames to snatch a burning raisin, and blowing on her fingers when she was not quick enough to emerge unscathed. This year, she played to please me. I could see it in her eyes.

I wonder if Elizabeth plays at bullet pudding and snapdragon. I wonder if she burnt her fingers as she snatched the raisins out of the flames.

Saturday 28th December

'I wonder you do not think of marrying Miss Bingley,' I said to Colonel Fitzwilliam as we rode out together this morning.

'Miss Bingley?'

'She is a wealthy young woman, and you are in need of an heiress.'

He shook his head.

'I do not wish to marry Miss Bingley.'

'She is charming and elegant, gracious and well bred.'

'She is all those things, but I could not marry her. She is a cold woman. When I marry, I would like a wife with more warmth. I would also like someone who will look up to me, rather than someone who will look up to my family name.'

'I never knew you wanted that from a wife,' I said in surprise.

'As a younger son, I have had to look up to others all my life. I would like to experience the situation from another side!'

He spoke lightly, but I think there was some truth in what he said.

We rode on in silence for some way, enjoying the snow-covered scenery.

'How long will you be in town?' I asked him.

'Not long. I have business which requires my attention in Kent. I mean to pay my respects to Lady Catherine whilst I am there. Shall I tell her you will be visiting her at Easter?'

'Yes, I will visit her as usual. When will you be returning to town?'

'Soon, I hope. Before Easter, certainly.'

'Then you must dine with me when you do.'

January

Friday 3rd January

There has been a most unwelcome incident. Caroline has had a letter from Miss Bennet.

'She writes that she is coming to London,' cried Caroline. 'She will be staying with her aunt and uncle in Gracechurch Street. From the date of her letter, I believe she must already be here.'

'It is not something I would have wished to happen,' I said. 'Bingley seems to have forgotten her. If he sees her again, his admiration might be rekindled.'

'He does not need to know of her visit,' Caroline said.

I agreed to this. 'I doubt they will ever come across each other,' I said.

'I think I shall not reply to her letter. She will not be in town long, and she will think only that the letter was lost. Better that, than that she thinks she is not welcome here. She is a sweet girl, and I have no wish to wound her feelings, but my love for my brother runs deeper, and I must do what I can to save him from an unsuitable match.'

I applaud her sentiments, but I find I am not easy in my mind. Anything devious or underhand is abhorrent to me. But Caroline is right. We cannot allow Bingley to sacrifice his life on the altar of a vulgar family, and it is but a small deception after all.

Monday 6th January

Georgiana is developing just as I could wish. Her accomplishments, her deportment, her manners are all those I like to see. I did not know how to proceed when she was left in my care, but I flatter myself she is turning into the young woman my mother would wish her to be.

Tuesday 7th January

I had a shock when visiting Caroline and her sister today, in order to give them a note from Georgiana. As I approached the house, I saw Jane Bennet leaving it.

'What has happened here?' I asked when I was admitted.

Caroline looked out of spirits.

'The most unfortunate thing. Jane Bennet has been here. I thought she would have gone back to the country by now, but it seems she means to make an extended visit.'

'This is most unlucky. What did you say to her?'

'I scarcely know what I said. She took me by surprise. She told me she had written to me and I said I had never received her letter. She enquired after Charles. I told her that he was well, but that he was so often with you I scarcely saw him. I told her how much Georgiana was grown, and how we were seeing her for dinner this evening. Then I intimated that Louisa and I were on the point of going out. After that she could not stay.'

'You will have to return the call,' I said.

'It cannot be avoided. But I shall not stay long, and I hope by my manner she will see that any further intimacy is not to be expected. Charles has almost forgotten her. In another few weeks he will be out of danger.'

Of that I am not so sure. He speaks of her sometimes still. He checks himself when he sees my expression, but

it is not safe for him to think of either Miss Bennet or
Hertfordshire yet.

Tuesday 21st January

Caroline paid her call on Miss Bennet this morning. It
was of a short duration, and she used her time to tell Miss
Bennet that Bingley is not certain of returning to Hert–
fordshire, and may give up Netherfield. When she left she
made no mention of seeing Jane again, and she tells me
she is now perfectly satisfied that Miss Bennet will not
call again.

One day Bingley will be glad of our care. It is only this
thought that reconciles me to the duplicity we have been
forced to employ.

February

Saturday 1st February

'Caroline has suggested we go to Bath for the spring,' said Bingley this morning. 'Perhaps I might take a house there,' he added nonchalantly.

I thought it was an encouraging sign that he has forgotten Hertfordshire.

'That is an excellent idea,' I said.

'Would you like to come with us?' he asked.

'I have to go to Pemberley and make sure Johnson has everything well in hand. There are a number of changes I wish to make to the running of the home farm, and some further improvements I should like to make on the estate.'

'Then I will see you again in the summer.'

Friday 7th February

Colonel Fitzwilliam has returned to town and he dined with me this evening, bringing me all the news from Rosings. He told me that Mr Collins has taken a wife. I held my breath, hoping that Hurst had been right when he had said that Elizabeth had refused Mr Collins.

'She seems a very good sort of girl, although I should say woman. She appears to be approaching thirty,' said my cousin.

I let go of my breath.

'But this is a good thing,' he went on. 'A younger woman might have been intimidated by my aunt's – '

'Interference?'

'Helpfulness,' he said with a wry smile. 'But Mrs Collins accepts Lady Catherine's advice without a fuss.'

'I believe I might have known her in Hertfordshire. What was her maiden name?'

'Lucas. Miss Charlotte Lucas.'

'Yes, I met her and her family. I am glad she is well settled. Mr Collins might not be the most sensible husband, but he can provide her with a comfortable life.'

And I could provide Elizabeth with so much more. But I will not think of it. I am resolved never to think of her again.

March

Friday 28th March

I received a letter from Lady Catherine, this morning, telling me that she was looking forward to seeing me. I was surprised to read the following passage in her letter.

> *Mrs Collins has her sister, Maria, to stay with her, and a friend, Miss Elizabeth Bennet.*

It was a shock to learn that Elizabeth is at the parsonage.

> *I believe they are both of them known to you. Sir William Lucas was also here, but he has since returned home. Miss Elizabeth Bennet has a great deal to say for herself but as she has never had the benefit of a governess it is not to be wondered at. A governess is necessary in a family of girls, and so I told her. Mr Collins was in full agreement with me. I have had the pleasure of introducing many governesses to their employers. Four nieces of Mrs Jenkinson are delightfully situated through my means.*
>
> *Miss Bennet's sisters are all out. I do not know what her mother can be thinking of. Five sisters, all out! It is very odd. And the younger sisters are out before the older are married. A very ill-regulated household. If Mrs Bennet lived nearer, I would tell her so. I would find her a governess, and she would no doubt be*

grateful to me for the recommendation. She
manages her household ill.

Miss Bennet gives her opinions very decid-
edly for one so young. Her view of her family is
extraordinary. She declared it would be very
hard upon the younger sisters to wait until their
sisters were married before they had their share
of society.

I found myself smiling at this. I have never heard anyone, man or woman, trifle with Lady Catherine before,
and to trifle with her in such a way! For it is undoubtedly hard on younger girls to have to wait their turn to
come out, though I have never thought of it in this way
before.

Perhaps I am wrong to be shocked that Elizabeth is at
the parsonage. Perhaps I should be pleased. It will give
me the perfect opportunity to demonstrate that she no
longer has any hold over me. It will be a delight to me
to know that I can meet her in company without any
improper feelings, and I will be able to congratulate
myself on having saved myself, as well as Bingley, from a
most imprudent attachment.

April

Thursday 3rd April

I dined with Colonel Fitzwilliam at my club today. We have decided that we will travel to Rosings together.

Monday 7th April

My cousin and I had an enjoyable journey into Kent, and after generalities the conversation turned to marriage again.

'I am of an age now when I feel I should be settled, and yet marriage is a dangerous venture,' he said. 'It is so easy to make a false step and then be forced to live with it.'

'It is,' I agreed, thinking of Bingley. 'I have recently saved one of my friends from just such a false step.'

'Really?'

'Yes. He took a house in the country, where he met a young lady of low connections. He was much taken with her, but fortunately business compelled him to return to London for a time. Perceiving his danger, his sisters and I followed him to London and persuaded him to remain.'

'Then you have saved him from a most imprudent marriage.'

'I have.'

'He will thank you for it when it has done. It is not pleasant to wake from a dream and find oneself trapped in a nightmare.'

I am heartened by his opinion. I respect his judgement, and it is reassuring to know that he feels as I do on the matter.

We arrived at Rosings this afternoon, and the beauty of the park struck me anew. It is not as fine as Pemberley, but it looks very well in the spring. We passed Mr Collins on our way to the house, and I believe he had been looking for us. He bowed as we passed, and then hurried off in the direction of the parsonage to share the news with its inmates. I found myself wondering if Elizabeth was within doors, and how she would feel at the news of our arrival.

Tuesday 8th April

Mr Collins called this morning to pay his respects. He found me with Colonel Fitzwilliam. My aunt was taking a drive with my cousin, Anne.

'Mr Darcy, it is an honour to meet you again. I had the good fortune to make your acquaintance in Hertfordshire, when I was staying with my fair cousins. I was not married then, as my dear Charlotte had not yet consented to be my wife. From the first moment I saw her I knew she would not disgrace the parsonage at Hunsford, and would delight my esteemed patroness, Lady Catherine de Bourgh, who has the honour and distinction of being your most revered aunt, with her humility and sympathy. Indeed, Lady Catherine herself was kind enough to say – '

'Are you returning to the parsonage?' I asked, cutting short his effusions.

He paused momentarily, then said, 'Indeed I am.'

'It is a fine morning. We will walk with you. What do you say?' I asked Colonel Fitzwilliam.

'By all means.'

We set out. Mr Collins recounted the beauties of the park to us, interspersed with expressions of humble gratitude for our condescension in visiting his poor home. I found my mind wandering. Would Elizabeth have changed since the autumn? Would she be surprised to see me? No. She knew of my visit. Would she be pleased or otherwise? Pleased, of course. To reacquaint herself with a man of my standing must be desirable for her.

Our arrival was announced by the door-bell, and shortly afterwards we entered the room. I paid my compliments to Mrs Collins, and she bade me welcome. Elizabeth dropped a curtsy.

She is much as she ever was, but the pleasure I experienced on seeing her took me by surprise. I thought I had conquered my feelings for her, and of course, I have. It was just that the first instant of seeing her took me aback.

'The house is to your liking, I hope?' I asked Mrs Collins.

'Yes, indeed it is,' she said.

'I am glad. My aunt has made some improvements of late, I know. And the garden? Do you like the aspect?'

'It is very pleasant.'

'Good.'

I would have said more, but I found my attention straying to Elizabeth. She was conversing with Colonel Fitzwilliam in her usual free and easy manner. I could not decide whether I liked it or not. She was at liberty to talk to my cousin, of course, and to charm him if she would, but I felt dissatisfied to see how much he enjoyed her company, and even worse, to see how much she enjoyed his. At length I realized I was lost in my thoughts, and I made an effort to be civil.

'Your family are well, I hope, Miss Bennet?' I asked.

'Yes, thank you,' she replied. She paused, then said, 'My sister Jane has been in town these three months. Have you never happened to see her?'

I was disconcerted, but I replied calmly enough.

'No, I have not been so fortunate.'

I relapsed into silence, dissatisfied with the turn the conversation had taken, and soon afterwards my cousin and I took our leave.

Easter Day, Sunday 13th April

I had seen nothing of Elizabeth since my visit to the parsonage, but I saw her this morning at church. She was looking very well. The early sun had put colour in her cheeks, and brightened her eyes.

After the service, Lady Catherine stopped to speak to the Collinses. Mr Collins beamed as she walked towards him.

'Your sermon was too long,' said Lady Catherine. 'Twenty minutes is ample time in which to instruct your flock.'

'Yes, Lady Catherine, I – '

'You made no mention of sobriety. You should have done. There has been too much drunkenness of late. It is a rector's business to tend to the body of his parishioners as well as their souls.'

'Of course, Lady – '

'There were too many hymns. I do not like to have above three hymns in an Easter service. I am very musical and singing is my joy, but three hymns are enough.'

She began to walk to the carriage, and Mr Collins followed her.

'Yes, Lady Catherine, I – '

'One of the pews has woodworm. I noticed it as I walked past. You will see to it.'

'At once, Lady – ' he said.

'And you will come to dinner with us tonight. Mrs Collins will come with you, as will Miss Lucas and Miss Elizabeth Bennet. We will make up a card-table.'

'So good – ' he said, bowing and rubbing his hands together.

'I will send the carriage for you.'

I followed her into the carriage and the footman closed the door.

I found myself looking forward to Elizabeth's arrival at Rosings, but quickly crushed the feeling.

Her party arrived punctually, and because I knew the danger of speaking to her, I passed the time in conversation with my aunt. We talked of our various relations, but I could not help my eyes straying to Elizabeth. Her conversation was of a more lively kind. She was speaking to Colonel Fitzwilliam, and as I saw the animation of her features, I found it hard to take my eyes away.

My aunt, too, kept looking towards them, until at last she said: 'What is it you are talking of? What are you telling Miss Bennet? Let me hear what it is.'

Colonel Fitzwilliam replied that they were speaking of music. My aunt joined in the conversation, praising Georgiana's abilities on the pianoforte, then mortifying me by inviting Elizabeth to practise on the pianoforte in Mrs Jenkinson's room. To invite a guest to play on the pianoforte in the companion's room? I had not thought my aunt could be so ill-bred.

Elizabeth looked surprised, but said nothing, only her smile showing what she thought.

When coffee was over, Elizabeth began to play, and remembering the pleasure I had had in her playing before, I walked over to her side. Her eyes were brightened by the music, and I placed myself in a position from which I could see the play of emotion over her countenance.

She noticed. At the first pause in the music she turned to me with a smile and said: 'You mean to frighten me, Mr Darcy, by coming in all this state to hear me. But I will not be alarmed, though your sister does play so well. There is a stubbornness about me that never can bear to be frightened at the will of others. My courage always rises with every attempt to intimidate me.'

'I shall not say you are mistaken,' I replied, 'because you could not really believe me to entertain any design of alarming you; and I have had the pleasure of your acquaintance long enough to know that you find great enjoyment in occasionally professing opinions which in fact are not your own.'

Where this speech came from I do not know. I am not used to making playful exchanges, but there is something in Elizabeth's character which lightens mine.

Elizabeth laughed heartily, and I smiled, knowing that we were both enjoying the exchange. So well was I enjoying it that I forgot my caution and gave myself over to an appreciation of the moment.

'Your cousin will give you a very pretty notion of me,' she said to Colonel Fitzwilliam. Turning to me, she said: 'It is very ungenerous of you to mention all that you knew to my disadvantage in Hertfordshire – and, give me leave to say, very impolitic too – for it is provoking me to retaliate, and such things may come out, as will shock your relations to hear.'

I smiled. 'I am not afraid of you.'

Her eyes brightened at my remark.

Colonel Fitzwilliam begged to be told how I behave amongst strangers.

'You shall hear all then,' said Elizabeth. 'But prepare yourself for something very dreadful. The first time of my ever seeing him in Hertfordshire, you must know, was at a ball – and at this ball, what do you think he did? He danced only four dances!'

In her eyes, my refusal to dance became ridiculous, and I saw it so myself, for the first time. To stride about in all my pride, instead of enjoying myself as any well-regulated man would have done. Absurd! I would not ordinarily have tolerated any such teasing, and yet there was something in her manner that removed any sting, and instead made it a cause for laughter.

It was at this moment I realized there had been little laughter in my life of late. I had taken on the responsibilities of a man when my father died, and had prided myself on discharging them well, as my father would have done. I had tended my estate, looked to the welfare of my tenants, provided for my sister's health, happiness and education, seen to the livings in my patronage and discharged my business faithfully. Until meeting Elizabeth that had been enough, but now I saw how dull my life had been. It had been too ordered. Too well-regulated. Only now did I begin to see it, and to feel it, for the feelings inside me were wholly different from any I had known. When I laughed, my disposition lightened.

'I had not at that time the honour of knowing any lady in the assembly beyond my own party,' I pointed out, catching her tone.

'True: and nobody can ever be introduced in a ballroom.'

'Perhaps I should have judged better, had I sought an introduction, but I am ill-qualified to recommend myself to strangers.'

She teased me, wondering how it was that a man of sense and education could not do so, and Colonel Fitzwilliam joined her, saying I would not give myself the trouble.

'I certainly have not the talent which some people possess, of conversing easily with those I have never seen before. I cannot catch their tone of conversation, or appear interested in their concerns, as I often see done,' I agreed.

'My fingers do not move over this instrument in the masterly manner which I see so many women's do, but then I had always supposed it to be my own fault – because I would not take the trouble of practising.'

I smiled.

'You are perfectly right.'

At this moment, Lady Catherine interrupted us.

'What are you talking about, Darcy?'

'Of music,' I said.

Lady Catherine joined us at the pianoforte.

'Miss Bennet would not play amiss, if she practised more, and could have the advantage of a London master,' declared my aunt. 'She has a very good notion of fingering, though her taste is not equal to Anne's. Anne would have been a delightful performer, had her health allowed her to learn.'

I scarcely heard her. I was watching Elizabeth. She bore with my aunt's comments with remarkable civility, and at the request of Colonel Fitzwilliam and myself, she remained at the instrument until the carriage was ready to take the party home.

I thought I had rid myself of my admiration for her. I thought I had forgotten her. But I was wrong.

Monday 14th April

I was taking a walk round the grounds this morning when my steps led me unconsciously to the parsonage.

Finding myself outside I could not, in all politeness, pass by, and I called in to pay my respects. To my horror, I found Elizabeth there alone. She seemed as surprised as I was, but she was not, I think, displeased. Why should she be? It must be satisfying for her to think that she has captivated me. She bid me take a seat, and I had no choice but to sit down.

'I am sorry for this intrusion,' I said, feeling the awkwardness of the situation, and wanting to make sure she knew it had not been by design. 'I understood all the ladies to be within.'

'Mrs Collins and Maria have gone on business to the village,' she replied.

'Ah.'

'Lady Catherine is well?' she said at last.

'Yes, I thank you. She is.'

Silence fell.

'And Miss de Bourgh? She, too, is well?'

'Yes, I thank you. She is.'

'And Colonel Fitzwilliam?' she asked.

'Yes, he too is well.'

Another silence fell.

'How very suddenly you all quitted Netherfield last November, Mr Darcy!' she began at last. 'It must have been a most agreeable surprise to Mr Bingley to see you all after him so soon; for, if I recollect right, he went but the day before. He and his sisters were well, I hope, when you left London?'

'Perfectly so, I thank you.'

'I think I have understood that Mr Bingley has not much idea of ever returning to Netherfield again?'

'I have never heard him say so; but it is probable that he may spend very little of his time there in future. He has many friends, and he is at a time of life when friends and engagements are continually increasing.'

'If he means to be but little at Netherfield, it would be better for the neighbourhood that he should give up the place entirely, for then we might possibly get a settled family there. But perhaps Mr Bingley did not take the house so much for the convenience of the neighbourhood as for his own, and we must expect him to keep it or quit it on the same principle.'

I did not like the subject, but replied evenly enough.

'I should not be surprised if he were to give it up, as soon as any eligible purchase offers.'

I should have left the parsonage then. I knew it. And yet I could not tear myself away. There was something about the shape of her face that invited my eye to follow it, and something about the way her hair fell that made me want to touch it.

She said nothing, and once more there was silence.

I could not say what was in my mind, and yet I found I could not leave.

'This seems a very comfortable house,' I said.

'Yes, it is.'

'It must be agreeable for Mrs Collins to be settled within so easy a distance of her own family and friends.'

'An easy distance do you call it?' she asked in surprise. 'It is nearly fifty miles.'

'And what is fifty miles of good road? Little more than half a day's journey.'

'I should never have considered the distance as one of the advantages of the match,' cried Elizabeth.

'It is a proof of your own attachment for Hertford-shire. Anything beyond the very neighbourhood of Longbourn, I suppose, would appear far,' I said.

'I do not mean to say that a woman may not be set-tled too near her family.'

Ah. She knew the evils of her relations and would not be sorry to escape them. When she married, she would leave them behind.

'But I am persuaded my friend would not call herself near her family under less than half the present distance,' she continued.

'You cannot have a right to such very strong local attachments,' I said, pulling my chair forward a little as I spoke, for I felt an overwhelming urge to be near her. 'You cannot have always been at Longbourn.'

She looked surprised, and I was halted. I had almost been carried away by admiration and tempted into say-ing that she could have no objection to living at Pem-berley, but I had gone too quickly and I was thankful for it. Her look of surprise saved me from committing myself to a course of action I would surely regret. I drew my chair back, and picking up a newspaper, I glanced over it.

'Are you pleased with Kent?' I asked, with enough coolness to depress any hope she might have been entertaining from my ill-judged manner.

'It is very pleasant,' she said, looking at me in perplexity.

I embarked on a discussion of its attractions, until we were saved from the need of further conversation by the return of Mrs Collins and Maria. They were surprised to see me there, but explaining my mistake I stayed only a few minutes longer and then returned to Rosings.

Tuesday 15th April

Elizabeth has bewitched me. I am in far more danger here than I ever was in Hertfordshire. There, I had her family constantly before me, reminding me how impossible a match between us would be. Here, I have only her. Her liveliness, her gaiety, her good humour, all tempt me to abandon self-restraint and declare myself; but I must not do it. I do not only have myself to consider. I have my sister.

To expose Georgiana to the vulgarity of Mrs Bennet would be an act of cruelty no brotherly devotion could allow. And to present to Georgiana, as sisters, Mary, Kitty and Lydia Bennet would be repulsive. To have her influenced by them, to force her into company with them – for it could not be otherwise if I were to make Elizabeth my wife – would be unforgivable. Worse still, she might be forced to hear of George Wickham, who is a favourite of the younger girls. No. I cannot do it. I will not do it.

I must beware, then, lest I let slip a word in Elizabeth's company. I must not let her know how I feel. She suspects my partiality I am sure. Indeed, by her lively nature she has encouraged it, and no doubt she is waiting for me to speak. If she married me she would be lifted out of her sphere and elevated to mine. She would be joined in matrimony to a man of superior character and understanding, and she would be the mistress of Pemberley. A man of my character and reputation, wealth and position would tempt any woman. But it must never be.

Thursday 17th April

I do not know what has come over me. I should be avoiding Elizabeth, but every day when Colonel Fitzwilliam goes to the parsonage, I go with him. I cannot deny myself the pleasure of looking at her. Her face is not beautiful but it haunts me.

I have had enough resolution to say nothing, for fear of saying too much, but my silence has begun to be noticed.

'Why are you silent when we go to the parsonage?' asked Colonel Fitzwilliam as we returned home today. 'It is not like you, Darcy.'

'I have nothing to say.'

'Come now! I have seen you talk to bishops and ploughmen. You can always think of something to say to them, however much you protest you find it difficult to converse with strangers. And yet when you go to the parsonage, you do not open your mouth. It is most uncivil of you. The least you could do is ask after Mrs Collins's chickens, and ask Mr Collins how his sermons are coming along, and if you cannot think of anything to say to the young ladies, you can always fall back on the weather.'

'I will endeavour to do better next time.'

But as I said it, I realized I must not go to the parsonage again. If I talk to Elizabeth, there is no telling where it will lead. She looks at me archly sometimes, and I am sure she is expecting me to declare myself.

Would a marriage between us really be so impossible? I ask myself, but even as I wonder, an image of her family rises up before me, and I know it would. And so I am determined to remain silent, for if I give in to a moment of weakness, I will regret it for the rest of my life.

Saturday 19th April

I have remained true to my resolve not to visit the parsonage, but my good intentions have been thwarted by my tendency to walk in the park, and three times now I have come upon Elizabeth. The first time was by chance; the second and third times, I seemed to find myself there whether I would or not. From doing nothing more than doffing my hat and asking after her health on the first occasion, I have come to say more, and this morning I betrayed my thoughts to an alarming degree.

'You are enjoying your stay at Hunsford, I hope?' I asked her when I met her.

It was an innocent question.

'Yes, I am, thank you.'

'You find Mr and Mrs Collins in good health?'

'I do.'

'And happy, I trust?'

'I believe so.'

'Rosings is a fine house.'

'It is, though it is difficult to find my way about. I have become lost on one or two occasions. When I tried to find the library, I walked into the parlour instead.'

'It is not to be expected that you would find your way round it all at once. Next time you visit Kent you will have a better opportunity to become acquainted with it.'

She looked astonished at this, and I berated myself inwardly. I had almost betrayed my feelings, which in that incautious sentence had suggested the idea that the next time she visited Kent she would be staying at Rosings, and how could she do that unless she was my wife? But indeed, it grows harder and harder to be circumspect. I ought to leave at once, and put myself out of harm's way. But if I do, it will arouse comment, so I must endure a little while longer. Colonel Fitzwilliam and I will be leaving soon, and then I will be safe.

Tuesday 22nd April

I am in torment. After all my promises to myself. After all my resolutions, this – this! – is the result.

I cannot believe the events of the last few hours. If only I could put them down to a fever of the brain, but there is no doubt they happened. I have offered my hand to Elizabeth Bennet.

I should not have gone to see her. I had no need to do it, merely because she did not join us for tea. She had a headache. What lady does not suffer from headaches?

At first I drank my tea with my aunt, my cousins and Mr and Mrs Collins, but all the time my thoughts were on Elizabeth. Was she suffering? Was she really ill? Could I do anything to help her?

At last I could contain myself no longer. Whilst the others talked of the parish, I declared I needed some fresh air and expressed my intention of taking a walk. I scarce know whether I meant to visit the parsonage or not when I left Rosings. My heart drove me on but my reason urged me back, and all the while my feet carried on walking until at last I found myself outside the parsonage door.

On enquiring if Miss Bennet was in I was shown into the parlour, where she looked up in surprise as she saw me enter. I was surprised myself.

I began rationally enough. I asked after her health, and she replied that she was not too poorly. I sat down. I stood up. I walked about the room. At last I could contain it no longer.

'In vain have I struggled.' The words were out before I could stop them. 'It will not do,' I went on. 'My feelings will not be repressed. You must allow me to tell you how ardently I admire and love you.'

There. It was out. The secret I had carried so long had found voice, and pushed its way into the light of day.

She stared, she coloured, and was silent. How could she not be? There was nothing for her to say. She had only to listen to my declaration and then accept me. Knowing that I had fallen beneath her spell, she knew full well that the door of Pemberley would be open to her, and the world of society would be hers.

'I do not pretend to be ignorant of the low nature of your connections, of their inferiority and lack of worth,' I said, scarcely believing that I had allowed my love for her to overcome such natural feelings, but driven onwards by emotions that were impossible to control. 'Having spent many weeks in Hertfordshire, it would be folly to pretend that it would not be a degradation to ally myself to such a family, and only the force of my passion has allowed me to put such feelings aside.'

As I spoke, a picture of the Bennets rose before my eyes, and I found that I was not so much speaking to Elizabeth as to myself, thinking aloud all the thoughts that had plagued me over the last few weeks and months.

'Your mother, with her vulgarity and prattling tongue; your father with his wilful refusal to curb the wild excesses of your younger sisters. To be joined to such girls!' I said, as I recalled Mary Bennet singing at the assembly. 'The best of them a dull, plodding girl with neither taste nor sense, and the worst of them silly, spoilt and selfish, finding nothing better to do with their time than to run after officers,' I continued, as I remembered Lydia and Kitty at the Netherfield ball. 'One uncle an attorney and another living in Cheapside,' I went on, my feelings pouring forth with a torrent. 'I have felt all the impossibility of such a match these many weeks. My reason revolts against it, nay, my very nature revolts against it. I know that I am lowering myself in making such an offer. I am wounding both family connections and family pride. That I should entertain such feelings for someone so far beneath me is a weakness I despise, and yet I cannot conquer my feelings. I took myself to London and immersed myself in both business and pleasure, but none of it would remove the memory of you from my mind,' I said, turning to look at her and letting my eyes linger on her face. 'My attachment has outlived all my reasoned arguments, it has outlived a lengthy separation, which, instead of curing it, has only made it stronger, and it has resisted my determination to root it out. No matter what my more rational feelings, it will not be denied. It is so strong that I am prepared to overlook the faults of your family, the lowness of your connections and the pain I know I must inflict on my friends and family, by asking you to marry me. I only hope my struggles will now be rewarded,' I said. 'Relieve me from my apprehension. Still my anxieties. Tell me, Elizabeth, that you will be my wife.'

My speech had been impassioned. I had done what I had never done for any other human being; I had bared my soul. I had shown her all my fears and anxieties, my arguments and wrestling, and now I waited for her answer. It could not be long in coming. She had been waiting for my declaration; expecting it; I was sure of it. She could not be unaware of my attraction, and any woman would be elated to have won the hand of Fitzwilliam Darcy. It only remained for her to say the word that would unite us and the thing would be done.

And yet, to my amazement, the smile I had expected to see on her face did not appear. She did not say: 'You do me too much honour, Mr Darcy. I am flattered, nay gratified by your professions, and I am grateful to you for your condescension. My relatives' situation in life, their follies and vices, cannot be expected to bring you pleasure, and I am sensible of the honour you do me in overlooking their inadequacies in order to ask me to be your wife. It is therefore with a humble sense of obligation that I accept your hand.'

She did not even say a simple 'Yes.'

Instead, the colour rose to her cheeks, and in the most indignant voice possible she said: 'In cases such as this, it is, I believe, the established mode to express a sense of obligation for the sentiments avowed, however unequally they may be returned. It is natural that obligation should be felt, and if I could feel gratitude, I would now thank you. But I cannot. I have never desired your good opinion, and you have certainly bestowed it most unwillingly. I am sorry to have occasioned pain to anyone. It has been most unconsciously done, however, and I hope will be of short duration. The feelings which, you tell me, have long prevented the acknowledgement of your regard, can have little difficulty in overcoming it after this explanation.'

I looked at her in astonishment. She had refused me!
Never once had I imagined she might do so. Not once
in all those nights when I had lain awake, telling myself
how impossible such a union would be, had I pictured
this outcome.

This was to be the end of all my struggles? To be
rejected? And in such a manner! I! A Darcy! To be
answered as though I was a fortune-hunter or an undesirable suitor. My astonishment quickly gave way to
resentment. So resentful did I feel that I would not open
my lips until I believed I had mastered my emotion.

'And this is all the reply which I am to have the honour of expecting!' I said at last. 'I might, perhaps, wish to
be informed why, with so little endeavour at civility, I am
thus rejected. But it is of small importance.'

'I might as well enquire,' replied she heatedly, 'why
with so evident a design of offending and insulting me,
you chose to tell me that you liked me against your will,
against your reason and even against your character? Was
not this some excuse for incivility, if I was uncivil? But I
have other provocations. You know I have. Had not my
own feelings decided against you, had they been indifferent, or had they even been favourable, do you think that
any consideration would tempt me to accept the man
who has been the means of ruining, perhaps for ever, the
happiness of a most beloved sister?'

I felt myself change colour. So she had heard of that.
I hoped she had not. It could not be expected to make
her think well of me. But I had nothing to be ashamed

of. I had acted in the best interests of my friend.

'I have every reason in the world to think ill of you. No motive can excuse the unjust and ungenerous part you acted there,' she went on.

I felt my expression hardening. Unjust? Ungenerous? No indeed.

'You dare not, you cannot deny that you have been the principal, if not the only means of dividing them from each other, of exposing one to the censure of the world for caprice and instability, the other to its derision for disappointed hopes, and involving them both in misery of the acutest kind.'

I could not believe what I was hearing. Caprice and instability? Who would judge Bingley capricious for removing to London when he had business to attend to?

Derision for disappointed hopes? Miss Bennet had had no hopes, unless they had been planted in her mind by her mother, who could see no further than Bingley's five thousand pounds a year.

Misery of the acutest kind? Yes, that was what Bingley would have suffered if he had voiced his feelings. He would have been joined to a woman who was beneath him.

'I have no wish to deny that I did everything in my power to separate my friend from your sister, or that I rejoice in my success. Towards him I have been kinder than towards myself.'

Elizabeth ignored my remark and said, 'But it is not merely this affair on which my dislike is founded. Long before it had taken place my opinion of you was decided. Your character was unfolded in the recital which I received many months ago from Mr Wickham. On this subject, what can you have to say? In what imaginary act of friendship can you here defend yourself? Or under what misrepresentation can you here impose upon others?'

Wickham! She could not have found a name more calculated to wound and, at the same time, disgust me.

'You take an eager interest in that gentleman's concerns,' I remarked in agitation.

I regretted the words as soon as they were spoken. What was it to me if she showed an interest in George Wickham? After her refusal of my hand, nothing about Elizabeth had any right to interest me ever again.

And yet the mortification I felt intensified, and I found a new emotion in my breast, a most unwelcome one. Jealousy. I found it intolerable that she should prefer George Wickham to me! That she should be unable to see through his smiling exterior to the black heart beneath.

'Who that knows what his misfortunes have been, can help feeling an interest in him?'

'His misfortunes!' I repeated. What tale had he been spinning her? Wickham, who had had everything. Who had been spoilt and petted in childhood and, despite that, had turned into one of the most dissolute, profligate young men of my acquaintance.

As I thought of the money my father had lavished on him, the opportunities he had had and the help I myself had given him, I could not help my lip's curling. 'Yes, his misfortunes have been great indeed.'

'And of your infliction,' she said angrily. 'You have reduced him to his present state of poverty, comparative poverty. You have withheld the advantages, which you must know to have been designed for him. You have deprived the best years of his life, of that independence which was no less his due than his desert. You have done all this! And yet you can treat the mention of his misfortunes with contempt and ridicule.'

'And this,' I cried, as, goaded beyond endurance, I began to pace the room, 'is your opinion of me! This is the estimation in which you hold me! I thank you for explaining it so fully. My faults, according to this calculation, are heavy indeed! But perhaps these offences might have been overlooked, had not your pride been hurt by my honest confession of the scruples that had long prevented my forming any serious design. But disguise of every sort is my abhorrence. I am not ashamed of the feelings I related. They were natural and just. Could you expect me to rejoice in the inferiority of your connections? To congratulate myself on the hope of relations, whose condition in life is so decidedly beneath my own?'

She was growing as angry as I was, yet she controlled her temper sufficiently to reply.

'You are mistaken, Mr. Darcy, if you suppose that the mode of your declaration affected me in any other way, than as it spared me the concern which I might have felt

in refusing you, had you behaved in a more gentleman-
like manner.'

I felt an intense shock. *If I had behaved in a more
gentleman-like manner?* When had I ever been anything
but a gentleman?

'You could not have made me the offer of your hand
in any possible way that would have tempted me to
accept it,' she said.

I could not believe it. She could never have accepted
my hand? Never accept a connection with the Darcy
family? Never accept all the benefits that would accrue
to her as my wife? It was madness. And to blame it, not
on my manner, but on my person! I looked at her with
open incredulity. I, who had been courted in drawing-
rooms the length and breadth of the land!

But she had not finished.

'From the very beginning, from the first moment I
may almost say, of my acquaintance with you, your manners impressing me with the fullest belief of your arrogance, your conceit and your selfish disdain of the
feelings of others, were such as to form that ground-
work of disapprobation on which succeeding events have
built so immoveable a dislike; and I had not known you
a month before I felt that you were the last man in the
world whom I could ever be prevailed on to marry.'

I felt incredulity give way to anger, and anger to
humiliation. My mortification was now complete.

'You have said quite enough, madam,' I told her curtly.
'I perfectly comprehend your feelings, and have now

only to be ashamed of what my own have been. Forgive me for having taken up so much of your time' – and to prove that I was, even now after such base insults, a gentleman, I added – 'and accept my best wishes for your health and happiness.'

Then, having delivered myself of my final proud utterance, I left the room.

I returned to Rosings, walking blindly, seeing nothing of my surroundings, seeing only Elizabeth. Elizabeth telling me I had ruined her sister's happiness. Elizabeth telling me I had ruined George Wickham's hopes. Elizabeth telling me I had not behaved like a gentleman. Elizabeth, Elizabeth, Elizabeth.

I said not a word at dinner. I saw nothing, heard nothing, tasted nothing. I thought only of her.

Try as I might, I could not put her accusations out of my mind. The charge that I had ruined her sister's happiness might have some merit, though I had acted for the best. The accusation that I had ruined Wickham's hopes was of another order. It impugned my honour, and I could not let it rest.

'A game of billiards, Darcy?' asked Colonel Fitzwilliam, when Lady Catherine and Anne retired for the night.

'No. Thank you. I have a letter to write.'

He looked at me curiously but said nothing. I retired to my room and took up my quill. I had to exonerate myself. I had to answer her accusation. I had to show her she was wrong. And yet how?

My dear Miss Bennet

I scored through the lines as soon as I had written them. She was not my dear Miss Bennet. I had not the right to call her dear.

I crushed my piece of paper and threw it away.

Miss Bennet

The name conjured up an image of her sister. It would not do.

I threw away a second sheet of paper.

Miss Elizabeth Bennet

No.

I tried again.

Madam, you have charged me with

She will not read it.

> *Be not alarmed, Madam, on receiving this letter, by the apprehension of its containing any repetition of those sentiments, or renewal of those offers which were last night so disgusting to you.*

Better.

I write without any intention of paining you,
or humbling myself by dwelling on wishes
which, for the happiness of both, cannot be too
soon forgotten.

Yes. The manner was formal but, I prided myself, not
stiff. It should relieve her immediate concerns and persuade her to read on. But what to write next? How to
put into words what I had to say?

I threw down my quill and walked over to the win
dow. I looked out over the parkland as I gathered my
thoughts. The night was still. There were no clouds, and
the moon could be seen glistening in the sky. Beneath
that same moon, within the parsonage, was Elizabeth.

What was she thinking? Was she thinking about me?
About my proposal? About my sins?

My sins! I had no sins. I returned to my desk and read
over what I had written. I picked up my quill and continued. My words flowed easily.

Two offences of a very different nature, and by
no means of equal magnitude, you last night
laid to my charge. The first mentioned was that,
regardless of the sentiments of either, I had
detached Mr Bingley from your sister: and the
other, that I had, in defiance of various claims,
in defiance of honour and humanity, ruined the
immediate prosperity and blasted the prospects
of Mr Wickham.

Blasted the prospects of that scoundrel! I had given him every benefit, and he had repaid me by seeking to ruin my sister. But the first charge must be answered first.

I thought back to the autumn, when I had first arrived in Hertfordshire. It was a few months ago only, and yet it seemed a lifetime away.

> *I had not been long in Hertfordshire, before I saw, in common with others, that Bingley pre-ferred your eldest sister, to any other young woman in the country. I observed my friend's behaviour attentively; and I could then perceive that his partiality for Miss Bennet was beyond what I had ever witnessed in him.*

Let there be no deception. I had done with deceit. I had seen a partiality in Bingley, and I did not disguise it.

> *Your sister I also watched. Her look and man-ners were open, cheerful and engaging as ever, but without any symptom of peculiar regard, and I remained convinced from the evening's scrutiny, that though she received his attentions with pleasure, she did not invite them by any participation of sentiment. If you have not been mistaken here, I must have been in an error. Your superior knowledge of your sister must make the latter probable. If it be so, if I have*

been misled by such error, to inflict pain on her,
your resentment has not been unreasonable.

I was charitable, allowing Elizabeth her feelings, and her natural defensiveness on behalf of her sister, but I must also be charitable to myself.

...the want of connection could not be so great
an evil to my friend as to me. But there were
other causes of repugnance.

I hesitated. I had expressed these feelings before, in person. Elizabeth's words came back to me. 'Had you behaved in a more gentleman-like manner.' Was it ungentleman-like to list her family's failings? My anger stirred. No, it was nothing but the truth. And I would tell the truth. I had already given her a disgust of me. I had nothing left to fear.

These causes must be stated, though briefly.
The situation of your mother's family, though
objectionable, was nothing in comparison of
that total want of propriety so frequently, so
almost uniformly betrayed by herself, by your
three younger sisters, and occasionally even by
your father. Pardon me. It pains me to offend
you.

Ungentleman-like? I thought, as I wrote the words. I

had begged her pardon. What could be more gentleman-
like than that?

> *...let it give you consolation to consider that, to*
> *have conducted yourselves so as to avoid any*
> *share of the like censure, is praise no less gener-*
> *ally bestowed on you and your eldest sister,*
> *than it is honourable to the sense and disposi-*
> *tion of both.*

Not only gentleman-like but magnanimous, I thought,
well pleased.

> *Bingley left Netherfield for London, on the day*
> *following, as you, I am certain, remember, with*
> *the design of soon returning.*

I paused for a moment. Here my conscience troubled
me. I had behaved in an underhand manner. It had worried me at the time, for deceit is repugnant to me, and
yet I had done it.

> *The part which I acted is now to be explained.*

I paused again. But the letter must be written, and the
night was drawing on.

> *His sisters' uneasiness had been equally excited*
> *with my own; our coincidence of feeling was*

soon discovered, and, alike sensible that no time was to be lost in detaching their brother, we shortly resolved on joining him directly in London. We accordingly went, and there I readily engaged in the office of pointing out to my friend the certain evils of such a choice. I described, and enforced them earnestly. But, however this remonstrance might have staggered or delayed his determination, I do not suppose that it would ultimately have prevented the marriage, had it not been seconded by the assurance, which I hesitated not in giving, of your sister's indifference. He had before believed her to return his affection with sincere, if not with equal regard. But Bingley has great natural modesty, with a stronger dependence on my judgement than on his own. To convince him, therefore, that he had deceived himself, was no very difficult point. To persuade him against returning into Hertfordshire, when that conviction had been given, was scarcely the work of a moment. I cannot blame myself for having done thus much.

No, indeed I cannot. I spared him a fate which I did not spare myself, and yet I was not easy. I had acted badly, I must confess it. My honour demanded it.

There is but one part of my conduct in the whole affair, on which I do not reflect with

*satisfaction; it is, that I condescended to adopt
the measures of art so far as to conceal from him
your sister's being in town. I knew it myself, as
it was known to Miss Bingley; but her brother
is even yet ignorant of it. That they might have
met without ill consequence, is perhaps probable; but his regard did not appear to me enough
extinguished for him to see her without some
danger. Perhaps this concealment, this disguise
was beneath me; it is done, however, and it was
done for the best. On this subject I have nothing more to say, no other apology to offer. If I
have wounded your sister's feelings, it was
unknowingly done: and though the motives
which governed me may to you very naturally
appear insufficient, I have not yet learnt to con-
demn them.*

I had written the easy part of the letter. The difficult
part was still to come. Had I the right to go further? The
incidents I had to relate did not only concern myself,
they concerned my sister, my dear Georgiana. If they
should ever be made public…but I found I had no
apprehension of it. Elizabeth would not speak of them to
anyone, certainly not if I asked her to keep silence, and
she had to know.

But did she have to know all? Did she have to know
of my sister's weakness? I wrestled with myself. I returned
once more to the window. I watched the moon sailing

over the cloudless sky. If she did not know of my sister's weakness, then she could not know of Wickham's perfidy, I reflected, and it was to tell her of this that I had begun the letter.

I could pretend it was to answer the charge of being the cause of her sister's unhappiness, but I knew in my heart it was because I wanted to exonerate myself of all blame in my conduct towards George Wickham.

I could not bear the thought of him being her favourite, or the thought of my being valued at nothing by his side.

I resumed my letter.

> *With respect to that other, more weighty accusation, of having injured Mr Wickham, I can only refute it by laying before you the whole of his connection with my family. Of what he has particularly accused me I am ignorant; but of the truth of what I shall relate, I can summon more than one witness of undoubted veracity.*

'Colonel Fitzwilliam will vouch for me,' I said under my breath.

But how to tell the tale? How to arrange the incidents of Wickham's life into some coherent whole? And how to write it in such a way that my animosity did not colour every word? For I meant to be fair, even to him.

I thought. At last I continued to write.

Mr Wickham is the son of a very respectable man, who had for many years the management of all the Pemberley estates, and whose good conduct in the discharge of his trust naturally inclined my father to be of service to him, and on George Wickham, who was his godson, his kindness was therefore liberally bestowed. My father supported him at school, and afterwards at Cambridge. Hoping the church would be his profession, he intended to provide for him in it. As for myself it is many, many years since I first began to think of him in a very different manner. The vicious propensities, the want of principle, which he was careful to guard from the knowledge of his best friend, could not escape the observation of a young man of nearly the same age with himself. Here again I shall give you pain...

How deep do her feelings go? I wondered. I stabbed the paper with my quill and blotted the page. It was so scored through with crossings out and additions, however, that I knew I would have to rewrite it before presenting it to Elizabeth, and I paid the blot no heed.

...to what degree you only can tell. But whatever may be the sentiments which Mr Wickham has created, a suspicion of their nature shall not prevent me from unfolding his real character. It adds even another motive.

A motive of keeping you safe, dear Elizabeth.

I found myself thinking of what could have been. If she had accepted me, I could be sleeping soundly, with the expectation of rising to a happy morning spent in her company. As it was, I was unable to sleep, writing by the light of a candle and the glow of the moonlight that came in at the window.

I took up my quill, telling her how my father, in his will, had desired me to give Wickham a valuable living, that Wickham had decided he did not want to enter the church and that he had asked for money instead.

> He had some intention, he added, of studying the law, and I must be aware that the interest of one thousand pounds would be a very insufficient support therein. I rather wished, than believed him to be sincere; but, at any rate, was perfectly ready to accede to his proposal. I knew that Mr Wickham ought not to be a clergyman; the business was therefore soon settled, he resigned all claim to assistance in the church, were it possible that he could ever be in a situation to receive it, and accepted in return three thousand pounds. All connection between us seemed now dissolved. I thought too ill of him to invite him to Pemberley, or admit his society in town.

Rationally put. She could not take exception to such

moderation, though I had had to write it five times to achieve such a result.

> *For about three years I heard little of him; but on the decease of the incumbent of the living which had been designed for him, he applied to me again by letter for the presentation. His circumstances, he assured me, and I had no difficulty in believing it, were exceedingly bad. You will hardly blame me for refusing to comply with this entreaty, or for resisting every repetition of it. His resentment was in proportion to the distress of his circumstances, and he was doubtless as violent in his abuse of me to others as in his reproaches to myself. After this period every appearance of acquaintance was dropped. How he lived I know not. But last summer he was again most painfully obtruded on my notice.*

Yes. Last summer. I went over to the side of the room. I had brought a decanter with me, and a glass. I poured myself a whisky and drank it off. The fire had been lit against the Easter chill, but it had long since gone out, and I needed the whisky to warm me.

I did not want to write the next part of the letter but it had to be done. I tried to put it off, but the clock on the mantelpiece was ticking and I knew I must finish what I had begun. I must, however, ask her for secrecy. That she would grant it I had no doubt. She had a sister whom she loved dearly. She would understand the love and affection I had for mine.

I told her of Georgiana's meeting with Wickham in Ramsgate, and of the way he had played upon her affections, persuading her to agree to an elopement.

> *Mr Wickham's chief object was unquestionably my sister's fortune, which is thirty thousand pounds; but I cannot help supposing that the hope of revenging himself on me, was a strong inducement. His revenge would have been complete indeed.*

I sat back, tired. I had come to the end. Now all that remained was for me to wish her well.

> *This, madam, is a faithful narrative of every event in which we have been concerned together; and if you do not absolutely reject it as false, you will, I hope, acquit me henceforth of cruelty towards Mr Wickham. I know not in what manner, under what form of falsehood he has imposed on you; but his success is not perhaps to be wondered at. Ignorant as you previously were of everything concerning either, detection could not be in your power, and suspicion certainly not in your inclination. You may possibly wonder why all this was not told you last night. But I was not then master*

*enough of myself to know what could or ought
to be revealed. For the truth of everything here
related, I can appeal more particularly to the
testimony of Colonel Fitzwilliam; and that
there may be the possibility of consulting him,
I shall endeavour to find some opportunity of
putting this letter in your hands in the course of
the morning. I will only add, God bless you.*

> *Fitzwilliam Darcy.*

It was done.

I glanced at the clock. It was half past two. I had to copy the letter into a fair hand, one she could read, but I was tired. I decided to rest.

I undressed slowly and went to bed.

Wednesday 23rd April

This morning I woke with the dawn. I slept again, until my valet wakened me. I rose quickly, then made a fair copy of my letter. I made my way to Colonel Fitzwilliam's room. He was in his dressing-gown when I arrived, about to have his valet shave him.

'I need to speak to you,' I said.

'At this hour?' he asked, laughing.

'I need your help.'

His look changed. He dismissed his valet.

'You have it,' he said.

'I need you to do something for me.'

'Name it.'

'I need you to bear witness to the events related in this letter.'

He looked at me in surprise.

'They contain particulars of Wickham's relations with my sister.'

He frowned. 'I do not think you should divulge them to anyone.'

'Events have made it imperative that I do so.'

In the briefest of terms I told him of what had passed; that I had proposed to Elizabeth and been refused.

'Refused?' He broke in at that. 'Good God, what can you have said to her to make her refuse you?'

'Nothing. I said only what any sensible man would have said,' I replied. 'I told her of the struggle I had had in overlooking the inferiority of her connections, the objectionable behaviour of her family, the lowness of her situation in life – '

'Only what any sensible man would have said?' he asked in surprise. 'Darcy, this is not like you. You cannot have so mismanaged it. To insult a woman and then to expect her to marry you?'

I was surprised at his reaction.

'I spoke nothing but the truth.'

'If we all spoke the truth there would be a great deal of unhappiness in the world, and particularly at such a time. Some things are better left unsaid.'

'I abhor deception,' I said.

'And I abhor a blockhead!' he returned, half-smiling, half-exasperated. Then he became serious. 'But to offer

for Miss Bennet…I confess you have taken me by surprise. I had no idea your affections were engaged.'

'I took care you should not know. I did not want anyone to know. I thought I could vanquish them.'

'But they were too strong for you?'

I nodded, and though I would not have admitted it to
anyone but myself, they still were. No matter. I would
conquer them. I had no choice.

'Will you stand witness for me? Will you make yourself available to her, should she wish it?' I asked him.

'You are sure she will say nothing of it to anyone?'

'I am sure.'

'Very well. Then yes, I will.'

'Thank you. And now I must leave you. I hope to put
this letter into her hand this morning. She walks in the
park after breakfast. I hope to find her there.'

I left him to his valet and went out into the park. I had
not long to wait. I saw Elizabeth and walked towards her.
She hesitated, and I believe she would have turned away
if she could, but she knew that I had seen her. I walked
towards her purposefully.

'I have been walking in the grove some time in the
hope of meeting you. Will you do me the honour of
reading that letter?'

I put it into her hand. And then, before she could
hand it back to me, I made her a slight bow and walked
away.

Of my feelings as I returned to Rosings I will say
nothing. I scarcely know what they were. I imagined her

reading the letter. Would she believe me? Would she think better of me? Or would she dismiss it as a fabrication?

I had no way of knowing.

My visit to my aunt is drawing to an end. I leave tomorrow with my cousin. I could not go without taking my leave of those at the parsonage, but I was apprehensive about the visit. How would Elizabeth look? What would she say? What would I say?

As chance should have it, Elizabeth was not there. I said all that was proper to Mr and Mrs Collins and then took my leave.

Colonel Fitzwilliam went later, remaining an hour so that Elizabeth might have a chance of speaking to him if she wished it, but she did not return. I can only hope she has accepted that I have told her the truth, and that her feelings towards me are now less hostile. But any other kind of feelings…such hopes are over.

Thursday 24th April

I am in London again. After all the unforeseeable events at Rosings I find that here, at least, things are still the same. Georgiana has learnt a new sonata and netted a purse. She has also made a very good sketch of Mrs Annesley. But although London has not changed, I find that I have. I am no longer happy here. My house seems lonely. I had never realized how large it is, or how empty. If things had gone otherwise…but they did not.

I have much to do, and I will soon be too busy to think of the past. During the days, I have business which must be attended to, and at night I mean to attend every party and ball to which I have been invited. I will not allow the events of the last few weeks to discompose me. I have been a fool, but I will be a fool no more. I am determined to forget Elizabeth.

Friday 25th April

'Mr Darcy! How good of you to attend our little gathering!' said Lady Susan Wigham as I entered her house this evening.

It was comfortable to be back in a world of elegance and taste, with not one vulgar person to mortify me. The ballroom was full of refined people, many of whom I had known all my life.

'Do let me introduce you to my niece, Cordelia. She is visiting me from the country. She is a charming girl, and a graceful dancer.'

She presented Miss Farnham, a blonde beauty of some nineteen or twenty years of age.

'Would you care to dance, Miss Farnham?' I asked.

She blushed prettily and whispered: 'Thank you, yes.'

As I led her out on to the floor, I found my thoughts straying to the Netherfield ball, but I quickly controlled them and made myself think of Miss Farnham.

'Have you been in town long?' I asked her.

'No, not very long,' she said.

At least, I believe that is what she said. She has a habit of whispering which makes it difficult to hear her.

'Are you enjoying your stay?'

'Yes, I thank you.'

She relapsed into silence.

'Have you been doing anything of interest?' I asked.

'No, not really,' she said.

'You have been to the theatre, perhaps?'

'Yes.'

She said nothing more.

'What play did you see?' I coaxed her.

'I cannot recall.'

'You have been to one of the museums, perhaps?' I asked, thinking the change of subject might stimulate her.

'I do not know. Is the museum the large building with the columns outside? If so, I have been there. I did not like it. It was very cold and draughty.'

'Perhaps you prefer reading books to visiting museums?' I asked her.

'Not especially,' she whispered. 'Books are very difficult, are they not? They have so many words in them.'

'It is one of their undeniable failings.'

Elizabeth would have smiled at this, but there was no humour in Miss Farnham's voice when she whispered: 'That is exactly what I think.'

We lapsed into silence, but realizing that my thoughts were beginning to turn to Elizabeth, I determined to persevere.

'Perhaps you like to sketch?' I asked her.

'Not especially,' she said.

'Is there anything you like to do?' I asked, hearing a note of exasperation in my voice.

She looked up at me with more animation.

'Oh, yes, indeed there is. I like playing with my kittens. I have three of them, Spot, Patch and Stripe. Spot has a black spot, but otherwise he is entirely white. Patch has a white patch on his back, and Stripe – '

'Allow me to guess. He has a stripe?'

'Why, have you seen him?' she asked in amazement.

'No.'

'You must have done, else how could you know?' she said, round-eyed. 'I think my aunt must have showed him to you when I was out.'

She continued to talk of her kittens until the dance was over.

I did not let my lack of success with my first partner shake my resolve to enjoy myself, and I danced every dance. I came home pleased that I had not thought of Elizabeth above two or three times all evening.

Does she think of me ever? Does she, perhaps, think of my letter? I am satisfied that she believed me when I spoke of Wickham, for she has not asked my cousin about it, but does she understand why I spoke to her as I did when I offered her my hand? She must. She cannot be unaware of her low position in life, and on reflection she has undoubtedly decided that it was not ungentleman-like of me to speak to her in such a manner. She must have realized I was right to do so.

And what of her feelings on the way I dealt with her sister's affections? She sees now, I hope, that I acted for the best. She cannot fail to understand, or to acknowledge that what I did was right.

As for George Wickham, she knows him now for the scoundrel he is. But does she still have feelings for him? Does she still prefer his company to mine? Is she laughing with him at this moment, in her aunt's house? Does she think it better to speak to a man who has all the appearance of gentility, than one who has true worth?

If she should marry him…

I will not think of it. If I do, I will go mad.

May

Wednesday 7th May

I met Bingley at Lady Jessop's ball this evening. He has been in the north, visiting his family, and he has now returned to town.

'Darcy! I did not expect to find you here.'

'Nor I you.'

'How did you enjoy your stay with your aunt?'

'It was well enough,' I replied. 'Did you enjoy yourself in the north?'

'Yes,' he said, but there was a lack of spirit in his voice.

Have I done wrong in separating him from Miss Bennet? I wonder. He has found no new flirt since her, and though he danced all evening, he never asked any young lady to dance more than once.

My own evening was no more enjoyable. I was claimed by Mrs Pargeter almost as soon as I arrived.

'Darcy! Where have you been hiding yourself? You must come out to the country to see us. See the stud. Margaret will show it to you. Margaret!' she called.

Margaret joined us. I remembered Caroline Bingley's comment of the year before, that Miss Pargeter spent so much time with horses that she had come to resemble one.

'Should be thinking of putting yourself out to stud before long, Darcy,' said Mrs Pargeter. 'Margaret has clean lines. Excellent pedigree. Good breeding-stock.'

Margaret looked at me with interest.

'Any madness in the family?' she asked me.

'None that I am aware of.'

'Any sickness?'

'My cousin has a weak chest,' I replied.

'So she has. Anne de Bourgh. Forgotten that,' said her mother. 'Better keep looking, Margaret.'

It seemed superfluous after that to ask Margaret to dance. I partnered several other young ladies who were amusing enough, but like Bingley, I did not ask anyone twice.

Thursday 15th May

Bingley dined with Georgiana and me this evening. I have abandoned all thoughts of encouraging a match between them. She grows more lovely every day, but I am persuaded their temperaments would not suit. There are other impediments to the match, too. Bingley was distracted for most of the evening. Can it be that he still has not forgotten Miss Bennet?

What did I say to Elizabeth, regarding her sister? I cannot remember. I struggle to recall the words. Was I arrogant? Rude? Ungentleman-like? No, surely not that. And yet to claim that her sister was not a fit wife for Bingley…I am beginning to think I was wrong. There is nothing against her. She has a goodness of character and sweetness of disposition that match his own. But her relatives…no, it would not have done. Yet I was prepared to overlook them in my own case. I had admitted as much to Elizabeth. Yes, and she had roundly abused me for it.

I roused myself from my thoughts.

'Georgiana and I are holding a picnic next month, Bingley,' I said.

'That sounds very pleasant.'

'Will you still be in town?'

'Yes.'

'Then you must come.'

'Yes, Mr Bingley, that would be very pleasant,' said my sister shyly.

'I would be delighted. Caroline and Louisa will be in town then, too, and Mr Hurst.'

I tried to hide my lack of enthusiasm, and said: 'You must bring them with you.'

June

Saturday 7th June

We had good weather for our picnic. We went into the country, and ate beneath the spreading branches of an ancient oak.

Georgiana was very shy to begin with, but she welcomed her guests with civility and with growing ease. After lunch, I was pleased to see Caroline go over and talk to Georgiana, my sister being at that moment alone. I went over to them and congratulated Georgiana on her success.

'I am glad I have pleased you,' she said.

'I was telling Georgiana how well she looks,' said Caroline. 'You, too, look well, Mr Darcy. The warmer weather agrees with you.'

For some reason her compliments irk me. I said only: 'It agrees with us all.'

'Georgiana has been telling me that you visited Rosings at Easter. Miss Eliza Bennet was one of the party, I hear.'

'Yes, she was.'

'And how were her fine eyes?' asked Caroline.

'They were as bright as always.'

She smiled, but the reply did not seem to please her.

'I understood there was some little unpleasantness towards the end of her stay.'

She can have heard nothing from Georgiana, but I wondered if Colonel Fitzwilliam had said anything indiscreet. I did not satisfy her curiosity.

'No. None at all.'

After a moment she began again.

'I passed through Longbourn recently.'

I said nothing, but my interest was caught.

'That is why I thought there had been some little unpleasantness,' she said.

Ah. So it was not my cousin. I thought it would not have been.

'I partook of lunch at the inn, and the servants were gossiping, as servants will. Mr Collins had written to Mr and Mrs Bennet. He had told them of his surprise at seeing you at Rosings, and his letter said something about Miss Eliza Bennet being taken ill.'

'He cannot have been surprised at my visit. I often visit Rosings. As for Miss Elizabeth Bennet's illness, I can recall nothing more than a headache,' I said. 'Was the doctor called?'

Her smile dropped a little.

'No, I think not.'

'It cannot have been of any great matter then,' I observed.

She tried again.

'I hear that George Wickham is engaged...'

I felt myself grow pale at the sound of the name, and paler still at the knowledge that he was engaged. He could not be engaged to Elizabeth. Surely, after all I had told her, she would not accept his hand in marriage? Not after she had refused mine. Unless she had not believed me.

'...to an heiress,' went on Caroline.

I felt my colour begin to return. If he was engaged to an heiress, then my fear that he was engaged to Elizabeth was unfounded. I felt relief flow through me. But my relief was short-lived.

'But her family removed her from his vicinity,' said Caroline. 'I wonder why?'

She waited for me to speak. She knows only that Wickham behaved badly towards me, and was waiting for me to tell her more, but I did not do so. I felt sorry for my sister, who was stirring uncomfortably at my side. To be reminded of Wickham was most unfortunate.

'Miss Howard has no one to talk to,' I said to Georgiana. 'I believe you should go and ask her how she does.'

Georgiana retreated gratefully.

'Such a beautiful girl,' said Caroline, watching her go. 'And so elegant. She is the same age as Miss Lydia Bennet, and yet how different the two girls are. Lydia is to go to Brighton, I hear,' Caroline added drolly. 'She is determined to chase the officers, and if they are sent to France she will probably take the first ship.'

I wished she would not talk of the Bennets, but I could not stop her without it seeming particular. I did not like to hear her abusing Miss Lydia Bennet, no matter how justified her censure. To abuse someone else never sounds well.

As I thought it, I felt myself grow uneasy. I had abused Lydia in just such a way, and to her sister. It was small wonder that Elizabeth had not liked to hear it. I had congratulated myself at the time for my honesty, but I began to agree with my cousin, that some things, no matter how truthful, are better left unsaid.

'Her father no doubt feels the sea air will do the family good,' I remarked.

But Caroline was not to be quelled.

'Her father does not take her. He does not like to take any trouble where his family are concerned.'

'He has let her go to Brighton in the care of her mother?' I asked, before I could stop myself.

'Lydia does not go with her mother. She goes alone, in the company of Colonel and Mrs Forster.'

I could not believe that even Mr Bennet would be so negligent as to let a girl of Lydia's temperament go to a watering-place without her family. She would surely disgrace them, and thereby disgrace Elizabeth. My poor Elizabeth! How I felt for her, and how I railed against the injustice of the situation. Her name would be tarnished by a sister over whom she had no control.

And yet, unjust though it was, had I not tarnished her with the faults of her family, and had I not told her that she was beneath my notice because her sisters behaved badly?

I find it difficult to believe that I was so ungenerous, but I know that such was the case.

What was it she said to me? That I was ungentleman-like? How well the remark was deserved. If I had been going to tell her that I never wished to see her again, then there might have been an excuse for letting her see in what low esteem I held her, but to tell her she was not my equal, to say that I would be lowering myself to con-nect myself to her, and then to have the audacity to ask for her hand! And to ask for it in such a way, as though I had every expectation of being accepted! I cannot believe that I, who have always prided myself on my fair-ness and good judgement, could have behaved so badly.

To divert Caroline from any further discussion of the Bennets, I asked her about her brother. She told me of his affairs in the north, and said how pleased they were to be invited to Pemberley again for the summer.

I watched Bingley as we spoke of general matters, interested to see if he singled out any young lady for his attentions. Again, he did not. He spoke to every young lady there, he laughed and was gay, and yet there was something in his manner that was reserved, as though he held some small part of himself back.

'Does your brother have a flirt in the north?' I asked Caroline.

'No. No one has taken his fancy.'

'You do not think he still has feelings for Miss Bennet?'

'None in the world,' she answered decidedly.

But I think she is wrong. I mean to watch him to make sure, but once I am convinced, I mean to speak to him and tell him that I was wrong about Jane being indifferent to him. I must mend the damage I have done.

Monday 23rd June

I presented Georgiana with a new parasol this morning, and I was pleased to see how much pleasure it gave her.

The colour was particularly becoming to her complexion.

As I thought this, I could not help my thoughts going to Elizabeth. Her complexion was always healthy. She liked the outdoors, and was always walking, which brightened her eyes and made her face glow.

Where is she now? Is she at Longbourn? Does she think of me? Does she despise me, or has she forgiven me?

Wednesday 25th June

I am now convinced that Bingley is still in love with Jane Bennet. I have watched him for more than six weeks, and I know that the time is fast approaching when I must tell him what I have done. To take it upon myself to tell him whom he should and should not marry was an act of arrogance, and to employ the art of deceit to carry my way was impertinence of the worst kind.

'You look pensive, Darcy,' said Colonel Fitzwilliam, coming up beside me. 'Has Bingley done something to worry you?'

'No. It is I who have done something to worry him.'

'Oh?'

'I think I spoke to you once of a friend I had saved from a disastrous marriage. I am beginning to think I was wrong to interfere.'

'It seemed to me as though you had done him a service.'

'And so I thought, at the time, but he has lost his interest in young ladies since then.'

'The young man was Bingley, was he not?'

I admitted it.

'He is young. He will find someone else.'

'I am not so sure. At the time I thought I was acting through kindness, but I see it differently now. It was interference.'

'Then you are in harmony with Miss Bennet!'

'Miss Bennet?' I asked.

'Yes. Miss Elizabeth Bennet. She was of the opinion it was interference as well. Oh, never fear,' he said, as he saw my expression. 'I gave her no particulars, only that you had saved Bingley from a disastrous match. I did not mention the lady's name, indeed I did not know it. You need not be afraid that she might have known the family.'

I said nothing. Indeed, I was too horrified to speak. So Elizabeth had heard of my meddling, and she had heard of it in a congratulatory fashion, with my cousin, in all innocence, telling her how useful I had been.

It is small wonder she had been so angry with me at the parsonage. I only wonder now that she was not even angrier. I begin to see clearly why she refused me. And to see that, through my own pride, arrogance and folly, I have lost the woman I love.

July

Friday 4th July

I am unsure how to act. If I tell Bingley that Miss Bennet is partial to him, then I may do more harm than good. It is now more than two months since I spoke to Elizabeth on the subject, and it is possible that in that time, Jane has found another young man to love. I have decided that I will not tell him of Miss Bennet's affections, but I will encourage him to return to Netherfield after his visit to Pemberley. If she has any feelings for him, he will soon discover it.

When Elizabeth berated me for her sister's unhappiness I thought it a lesser charge than her berating me for Wickham's misfortunes, but I begin to think it was not so. I now know something of what Jane suffered, having felt the pain of rejection myself. If I have caused her to feel the emptiness I have felt for the last two months then I am truly sorry.

Monday 7th July

'How quiet we are now that Mr Bingley and his sisters have gone to visit their cousin,' said Mrs Annesley as we sat together after dinner this evening.

'We will be seeing them again before long,' said Georgiana, as she sat by the window with her needlework. 'They are coming to Pemberley with us.'

'I am looking forward to seeing Pemberley,' said Mrs Annesley. 'I understand it is a very fine estate.'

By this gentle sentence she persuaded my sister to tell her about it, and I thought how lucky I had been to find her. She has helped Georgiana to grow in confidence, and between us we will steer my sister towards a safe and happy womanhood.

Tuesday 8th July

I returned to Pemberley today, as I wanted to give Mrs Reynolds news of my impending visit, and to let her know how many guests I will be bringing. I could have written, but our conversation last night filled me with a longing to see it again.

As I turned in at the lodge and rode through the park I could not help thinking: Here I could have brought Elizabeth. I rode through the wood, following the trail upwards until I reached the top. I reined in my horse and let my eyes rest on Pemberley House, at the far side of the valley. My gaze ran over the house, its mellow stone glowing in the sunlight; on the stream in front of it; and on the wooded ridge behind.

Of all this Elizabeth could have been the mistress. But she had refused my hand. She had not allowed any considerations of position or wealth to sway her, and I honoured her for it. I did not know another woman who would have acted in such a way.

I felt again all the misery and pain of having lost her.

I rode on, descending the hill and crossing the bridge before riding to the door. As I dismounted, and stood before the house, I realized how much I would have valued her as my wife; how the liveliness of her spirits would have softened my own, and her lack of improper pride tempered mine.

I went in. I found the house well cared for, and Mrs Reynolds was pleased to know that I will be visiting with a party of friends in August.

'It will be good to see Miss Georgiana again, sir.'

'She is looking forward to being here. She misses Pemberley.'

If Elizabeth had accepted my hand, Georgiana would be living here again, not on her own, but with her family. She and Elizabeth would have been sisters…but I must not torture myself.

I went round the home farm with Johnson, and saw the repairs he had commissioned. He is an asset to the estate, and I am glad to have him.

When I returned to the house, Mrs Reynolds had drawn up a plan of the rooms, allotting to Bingley and his sisters their usual chambers. They will be staying with me on my return. She had also drawn up a selection of menus. I gave them my approval, and spent the evening in discussing with her some changes I would like to see in the east wing, before retiring to bed.

Friday 18th July

I returned to town, and mean to finish my business before spending the rest of the summer at Pemberley.

Saturday 19th July

I was surprised to see Bingley today, when I was riding in the park.

'I thought you were visiting your cousin,' I said to him.

'I was, but I have come back a week early. You are right about me, you see, I have no constancy.'

I was glad of the opening this offered me.

'I thought, in one matter, perhaps you had,' I ventured.

'Oh?'

He said no more, but I could see where his thoughts were tending.

'Did I tell you I visited Rosings at Easter?' I asked. 'I went to stay with my aunt, Lady Catherine de Bourgh.'

'Yes, I believe I heard something of it,' said Bingley without interest. 'I hope Lady Catherine is well?'

'Yes, thank you. She was in good health and spirits. She had visitors staying with her, a party from Longbourn.'

He changed colour at this.

'Longbourn? I did not know that. What were they doing in Kent?' he asked, as we turned into the park.

'They were visiting the rectory. Perhaps you remember Mr Collins, a heavy young man who was a rector in my aunt's parish?'

'No, I cannot think I do.'

'He was staying at Longbourn before Christmas. He attended the ball at Netherfield, with the Bennets.'

'Ah, now I remember. There was a rumour he was to marry Elizabeth Bennet.'

'It was nothing but a rumour.' Thank God, I thought. 'He did find a wife, however, and married Charlotte Lucas.'

'The charming daughter of Sir William?' asked Bingley, turning towards me.

'Yes.'

'A good match,' he said, pleased. 'I know she wanted her own establishment. I am happy for her. Was she in good spirits when you saw her?'

'Yes. She had reason to be so. Her family were paying her a visit. Her father and sister were staying with her. Sir William stayed only a week, but her sister Maria stayed with her longer.' I paused. 'She had another visitor, Miss Elizabeth Bennet.'

He started, but said only: 'Yes, I believe they were friends.' After a moment he said: 'Was she well?'

'She was.'

'I liked Miss Elizabeth Bennet very much. She was as lively a girl as one could ever wish to meet. And her parents, were they well?'

'Yes, I believe so.'

'And her…sisters?' he asked, studiously ignoring my gaze.

'They were well, although Miss Bennet I believe was not in spirits.'

'No?' he asked, torn between hope and concern.

'No,' I said firmly.

'She missed her sister, perhaps. She was very fond of her, and would not want to be parted from her.'

'She had been in low spirits before her sister left.'

'She missed Caroline, then. They saw a great deal of each other when we were all at Netherfield, and were friends.'

'Perhaps. But it is not usual for a young lady to fall into low spirits because her friend has gone.'

'No.'

He hesitated, then said: 'What do you think, Darcy? Should I give up Netherfield?'

'Is that what you wish to do?'

'I am undecided. It is a fine house, and a fine country, and the company was good – though, perhaps, not what you are used to,' he said with a trace of anxiety.

'Perhaps not, but there were several people who made the neighbourhood very pleasant.'

'Indeed. Sir William had been presented at St James's.'

'I was not thinking of Sir William.'

Though I was meant to be helping my friend, I could not prevent an image of Elizabeth rising before my eyes.

'I might perhaps go there for a few weeks towards the end of the summer. What do you say to that idea?' he asked.

'I think it an excellent one.'

'Then I think I will go after my visit to Pemberley.'

I said no more. I do not wish to give him too much hope, lest Jane should have put her hurt aside and become attached to one of the neighbouring young men. But if he returns to the neighbourhood, then a very little time will show them if they are meant to be together, and this time, I will not be so impertinent as to interfere.

August

Sunday 3rd August

Bingley and his sisters joined Georgiana and me soon after breakfast and we set out for Pemberley. To begin with, Caroline talked of her visit to her cousin, but then her conversation turned to flattery.

'What a fine coach you have, Mr Darcy,' she said, as it rattled through the streets. 'Charles has nothing like it. I keep telling him he should buy something in this style.'

'My dear Caroline, if I bought everything you wanted me to buy I would be bankrupt by the end of the year!' said Bingley.

'Nonsense. Every gentleman should have his coach, should he not, Mr Darcy?' she asked.

'It is certainly useful,' I admitted.

'Darcy! I relied on you to take my part! I was sure you would think it an extravagance.'

'If you mean to travel a great deal, then it is cheaper than hiring a coach.'

'There you are,' said Caroline, directing a smile at me. 'Mr Darcy agrees with me. How companionable it is when two people have but one mind. You should have squabs in just this colour, Charles,' she said, looking at the seats.

'I shall make sure they are in a completely different colour,' he returned, 'otherwise I will not know which is my coach and which is Darcy's.'

'How comfortable it is,' said Caroline. 'Is it not, Georgiana?' she asked, appealing to my sister.

'Yes, it is,' said Georgiana.

'And how well sprung. Charles, you must make sure your coach uses just these springs.'

'If I do, Darcy's coach will be sadly uncomfortable without them.'

'And you must have a writing desk built into the coach.'

'I dislike writing letters when I am still, and I have no intention of doing it whilst being jolted over every rut and pothole.'

'But your fellow travellers might like to write. What do you say, Georgiana? Would it not be useful?'

'Yes,' my sister ventured.

'There you are, Charles. Georgiana thinks it would be useful, and not only for writing, I am sure. It would also be useful for sketching. How is your sketching progressing?' she asked Georgiana.

'Well, I thank you.'

'My sister gave me a sketch of Hyde Park only last week,' I said.

'And was it prettily done?' Caroline asked.

'It was very well done indeed,' I said with a warm smile.

'I remember my own schooldays. How I loved to sketch! You must let me see the picture, Georgiana.'

'I left it in London,' my sister said.

'No matter. I will see it the next time we meet.'

We travelled in easy stages and stopped for the night at the Black Bull. It is a respectable hostelry. The food is good and the rooms comfortable. I have told my man to

wake me early. I have some letters to write before we
travel on.

Tuesday 5th August

I cannot believe it. I have seen Elizabeth. I scarce know
what I am writing. It was so strange.

We were returning to Pemberley, Bingley, his sisters,
Mr Hurst, Georgiana and I, when we stopped for lunch
at an inn. The day was hot and the ladies were tired. They
did not wish to travel further, and indeed I had told my
housekeeper we would not arrive until tomorrow. But I
was restless. I decided to go ahead, meaning to see Johnson and put some of the estate business out of the way
before my guests arrived.

I rode on to Pemberley. It was a beautiful afternoon,
and I enjoyed the ride. I was just leaving the stables and
walking round to the front of the house when I stopped
short. I wondered if I was hallucinating. The day was hot,
and I wondered if I had caught the sun. For there in front
of me was a figure I knew well. It was Elizabeth.

She was walking across the lawn to the river, in the
company of two people whom I did not know. At that
moment she turned to look back. She saw me. I stood
rooted to the spot. We were within twenty yards of each
other. There was no question of avoiding her, even had I
wished it. Our eyes met and I saw her blush. I felt my
own countenance grow hot.

At last I recovered myself. I advanced towards the
party. She had instinctively turned away, but stopping on

my approach, she received my compliments with great embarrassment. I felt for her, and would have made it easier for her if I could.

As I spoke to her I could not help wondering what she was doing there. To be at Pemberley! It seemed so strange, and yet at the same time so right.

'I hope you are well?' I asked.

'Yes, thank you,' she said, flushing, and unable to meet my gaze.

'And your family?'

As soon as I said it I saw her flush more deeply, and I felt an answering flush cross my face. I had no right to ask after her family, having abused them so roundly to her face, but she answered me civilly enough.

'They are well, thank you.'

'How long ago did you quit Longbourn?'

'Almost a month.'

'You have been travelling?'

'Yes.'

'You are enjoying it, I hope?'

'Yes.'

I repeated myself thrice more, asking her if she had enjoyed herself, until I felt it was better if I remain silent, since I could think of nothing sensible to say. After a few moments I recollected myself and took my leave.

To find Elizabeth, here, at Pemberley! And to find her willing to talk to me. She had been embarrassed, but she had not turned away. She had answered every question with more civility than I deserved.

What was she thinking? I wondered. Was she pleased to have met me? Mortified? Indifferent? No, not that last. She had blushed when I approached. She had been angry, perhaps, but not indifferent.

The thought gave me hope.

I went into the house, but instead of making for the steward's room I found myself going into the drawing-room.

She had not been at ease, that much was clear, and I had done nothing to help her. I had been so overcome with surprise, and a range of other emotions I dare not put a name to, that I had been incoherent.

A gentleman would have set her at ease. A gentleman would have made her feel at home. A gentleman would have asked to be introduced to her companions. How far below this mark I had fallen! I resolved to mend matters at once.

Going out into the grounds, I enquired of one of the gardeners which way the visitors had gone, and set off after them.

I saw them down by the river. I approached. Never had a walk seemed so long. Would she be pleased to see me? I hoped, at least, she would not be displeased.

I came upon her. She began speaking at once, with something more of ease than previously.

'Mr Darcy. You have a delightful estate here. The house is charming, and the grounds are very pleasant.'

She seemed about to go on, then coloured. I believe we both thought the same: the house could now be hers, if she had accepted my hand.

To help her over her distress, I said: 'Will you do me the honour of introducing me to your friends?'

She looked surprised, then smiled. There was a trace of mischief in it, and as soon as I saw it, I realized how much I had missed her.

'Mr Darcy, may I introduce my aunt and uncle, Mr and Mrs Gardiner,' she said.

I understood the cause of her mischievous smile at once. These were the very relatives I had railed against, and yet I had been wrong to despise them. They were not the low connections I had been fearing. Indeed, before she had introduced them I had taken them to be people of fashion.

'We were just returning to the house,' said Mr Gardiner. 'The walk has tired my wife.'

'Allow me to walk back with you.'

We fell into step.

'You have a fine estate here, Mr Darcy.'

'Thank you. I believe it to be one of the finest in England – but then I am partial!'

Mr and Mrs Gardiner laughed.

'Your man has been showing me the trout in the river,' said Mr Gardiner.

'Do you enjoy fishing?'

'Yes, when I have the opportunity.'

'Then you must fish here as often as you choose.'

'That is very kind of you, but I have not brought my tackle.'

'There is plenty here. You must use it when you come.' I stopped. 'That is a good stretch of the river,' I said, pointing out one of the best stretches for trout.

I saw Elizabeth and her aunt exchange glances, and I could not help but notice Elizabeth's look of astonishment. Did she think me incapable of being polite? Perhaps. I had given little evidence of it in Hertfordshire.

I could not help looking at her, though I talked to her uncle. Her face, her eyes, her mouth, all held me. I thought she looked well, and though she seemed embarrassed, I saw no hostility in her expression.

After a little time, Mrs Gardiner took her husband's arm, and I was left to walk by Elizabeth.

'I did not know you would be here,' she began at once. 'My aunt had a fancy to see Pemberley. She lived in the neighbourhood when she was a girl. But we were told you would not return until tomorrow.'

So she had discovered that, and had only come on the understanding she would not see me. My spirits sank, but rose again as I realized that fate had played into my hands. If I had not decided to tend to my estate business, I would be with Georgiana at the inn, instead of here with Elizabeth.

'That was my intention, but a matter to be settled with my steward brought me here a few hours before my companions. They will join me early tomorrow, and among them are some who will claim an acquaintance with you – Mr Bingley and his sisters.'

I could not help but think of all that had passed
between us on the subject of Bingley, and I guessed her
thoughts tended in the same direction. I wondered
whether I should say something; give her some indica-
tion of my change of sentiment; but I did not know how
to begin.

Instead, I said: 'Will you allow me, or do I ask too
much, to introduce my sister to your acquaintance during your stay at Lambton?'

'I would like that very much.'

There was a warmth in her voice, and in the smile that
accompanied it, that greatly relieved my fears.

We walked on in silence, but more easily than before.
The air was not so tense, and there was, if not ease
between us, at least no more embarrassment.

We reached the carriage. Her aunt and uncle were
some way behind.

'Will you come into the house? Would you like some
refreshment?'

'No, thank you,' she said. 'I must wait for my aunt and
uncle.'

I was disappointed, but I did not press her.

I tried to think of something to say. I wanted to tell
her how wrong I had been. She, too, looked as though
she wished to speak, but what she wanted to say I did not
know.

At last she began, but it was only to say: 'Derbyshire is
a beautiful county.'

'Have you seen much of it?'

'Yes. We have been to Matlock and Dove Dale.'

'They are well worth seeing.'

My conversation was inane. Hers was little better. There was so much that lay unspoken between us, but now was not the time. Perhaps, in a few days, when we came to know each other better again…

Her aunt and uncle drew closer. I invited them in for refreshment, but they declined. I handed the ladies into the carriage and it drove away. I watched it for as long as I could without my regard seeming particular, and then walked slowly into the house.

I had not said any of the things I wanted to say, but the knowledge that I would be seeing Elizabeth again sustained me.

My spirits felt lighter than they had done for a very long time.

Wednesday 6th August

I was out of bed very early. I could not sleep. I looked for Georgiana and at last she arrived, with Bingley and his sisters. I greeted them warmly, and then telling Georgiana I wished to show her a new specimen of tree in the grounds I invited her for a walk. She went with me readily. When we were some distance from the house I said:

'Georgiana, there is someone I would like you to meet.'

She looked at me enquiringly.

'When I was in Hertfordshire last autumn, I met a young lady by the name of Elizabeth Bennet. I liked her very much.'

Georgiana looked surprised, then pleased.

'She is visiting Derbyshire, and she is staying at a nearby inn. If you are not too tired, I would like to take you to meet her this morning.'

I knew that it was sudden, but now that I had found Elizabeth again, I could not wait to introduce her to my sister.

'No, I am not too tired. I would like to meet her.'

We returned to the house. Caroline and Louisa were upstairs, and Georgiana followed them, promising to come down when she had washed the grime of travelling from her hands and face, and when she had changed her gown.

Bingley was in the library.

'There is someone I think you will like to see, staying nearby,' I said.

'Oh?' He looked up.

'Miss Elizabeth Bennet. She is travelling with her aunt and uncle. By chance, they visited the house yesterday, just as I arrived. I said I would visit her this morning. I will be taking Georgiana with me, and I thought you might like to come.'

He looked surprised, but said: 'Of course, Darcy. I would like to see her again.' He hesitated, then said: 'Might it be better if I do not ask after her sister? Or would that seem particular?'

'I think you should certainly ask after her.'

He smiled, and I was pleased with the turn events had taken.

Georgiana returned to the room. I ordered the curricle to be brought round and we drove to Lambton, with Bingley following on horseback. I hoped Elizabeth would not have gone out. I caught a glimpse of her at the window and was reassured.

I believe I was as nervous as Georgiana when we were admitted. Elizabeth seemed embarrassed, but no sooner had I introduced Georgiana than she regained her composure. Between the two of them there seemed a genuine warmth. Georgiana was shy, and spoke in no more than monosyllables at first, but Elizabeth persevered, asking her questions and gently leading her to speak. Georgiana grew easier in her manner, and before long they were sitting together.

'You must not forget you promised to fish in my river,' I said to Mr Gardiner.

He looked surprised, as though he thought I might have changed my mind, but he agreed readily enough.

I could not help my gaze drifting to Elizabeth, and I believe it would have remained there had we not been interrupted by Bingley. Fortunately his sisters had not come downstairs by the time we departed, or we should have been obliged to invite them to go with us.

Elizabeth's expression softened on seeing him. She did not hold his inconstancy against him, then. I was glad. I had been the cause of it, not he. If not for his natural modesty, he would have pursued his own course instead of listening to me.

'Your family are well, I hope?' said he.

'Yes, quite well, I thank you.'

'Your mother and father?'

'They are in good health.'

'And your sisters?'

'Yes, they are well.'

'Good.' He paused, as embarrassed as I had been the day before. 'It is a very long time since I had the pleasure of seeing you.' She opened her mouth to reply, but he went on: 'It is above eight months. We have not met since the twenty-sixth of November, when we were all dancing together at Netherfield.'

How long ago it seemed. And what dramas had unfolded since then.

'When will you be returning to Longbourn?' he asked.

'Soon. In a little less than a week.'

'You will be pleased to see your sisters again.'

Elizabeth smiled. She could not be ignorant of the cause of all this talk about her sisters.

'Yes.'

'And they to see you.'

'I'm sure they will.'

'I am thinking of returning to Netherfield myself,' he said nonchalantly.

'Oh? I had heard a rumour you meant to quit it.'

'Not at all. It is quite the pleasantest house I have ever come across.'

'And yet you have been a long time away.'

'I had business to attend to,' he said. 'But now I am my own master.'

Elizabeth's eyes met mine, and we smiled. I was sure she knew what Bingley meant when he said, Now I am my own master.

I noticed her aunt glancing from one to the other of us, but I did not disguise my admiration for her niece. Let her know it. I would like to let all the world know. I am in love with Elizabeth Bennet.

I made it my concern to be agreeable. It was not difficult. I simply pretended that I had known the Gardiners all my life. It is remarkable how simple it is to be easy with strangers once one has the knack. And the determination, I could not help admitting. I would not give myself the trouble before. Now, I made an effort to be liked.

We stayed above half an hour. It was a little over-long for a morning visit, perhaps, but I could not tear myself away. At last I noticed Mrs Gardiner glancing at the clock, and knew we must be on our way.

'I hope you will join us for dinner before you leave the neighbourhood,' I said, glancing at Georgiana so that she joined me in the invitation.

'Yes, we would like it very much if you could join us,' she said shyly.

I looked to Elizabeth, but she looked away. I was not concerned. There was a look of awkwardness, not hostility on her face, but in time I hoped we would come to know each other better, and her awkwardness would fade away.

'We would be delighted,' said Mrs Gardiner.

'Shall we say the day after tomorrow?'

'The day after tomorrow it is.'

'I will look forward to it,' said Elizabeth.

She caught my eye as she said it, and I smiled. I saw an answering smile rise to her own lips, and I was satisfied.

'I am also looking forward to it,' said Bingley to Elizabeth. 'We have a great deal to talk about. I would like to hear about all my Hertfordshire friends.'

We departed, and returned to Pemberley.

Georgiana returned to her room to remove her pelisse and bonnet. I went into the morning room with Bingley, to find Caroline and Louisa there.

'You have been out?' asked Caroline.

'Yes, visiting Miss Bennet,' said Bingley.

'Jane Bennet is here?' asked Caroline in surprise.

'I should have said, Miss Elizabeth Bennet.'

Even worse, said Caroline's expression. She quickly schooled it, however.

'Dear me, what a coincidence that she just happens to be in Derbyshire when you return, Mr Darcy.'

'Yes. It is fortunate, is it not?' I asked.

She looked as though she would like to say something satirical, but thought better of it.

'I would like to see her again. I think I will pay her a call. What do you say, Louisa? Will you come with me?'

'There is no need,' said her brother. 'She is coming here.'

'Here?' Caroline sounded horrified.

'Darcy invited her to dinner.'

'With her aunt and uncle,' I added.

'Not the attorney from Meryton?' she asked in a droll voice.

'No, the uncle who lives in Cheapside,' I replied, removing her sting.

She looked annoyed. 'And is he very vulgar?' she asked.

'He must be. My dear! Cheapside,' said Louisa with a shudder.

'He is in fact a gentleman-like man, and his wife is a lady of fashion.'

'And are we to meet these paragons?' said Caroline, with a flash in her eyes. 'How entertaining.'

I listened with complaisance as she ran on in a similar fashion. Nothing she could say could pierce my happiness. I thought only of Elizabeth. She had not repulsed me. She had not spoken to me with disgust and contempt. She had been polite, and agreeable, and there had been that in her manner which led me to hope she was not indifferent to me.

When I think how once I had taken it for granted that she would marry me! That I had not even considered the possibility that she might refuse me. And now, though I felt hope rising inside me, I cautioned myself that my feelings might not be returned.

But I will not think so far ahead. I am to see her the day after tomorrow. It is enough.

Thursday 7th August

Mr Gardiner arrived here early this morning and I took him down to the river, together with some other of my house-guests. He is knowledgeable about fishing, and I provided him with tackle so that he might try his luck at catching something. My other guests had brought their own. I was about to join them when a chance remark of Mr Gardiner's made me change my mind.

'It was very civil of your sister to pay us a visit yesterday, Mr Darcy. My wife and niece were much struck by the attention,' he said. 'They have resolved to return the call this morning.'

'That is very good of them,' I said, when I could master my surprise.

'They did not want to be backward in any attention.'

'I hope you enjoy your fishing,' I said to the gentlemen. 'If you will excuse me, I have to return to the house.'

My house-guests murmured civilities, assuming I had business to attend to, but I saw a look of comprehension on Mr Gardiner's face. So he knows. I am not surprised. I took no care to guard my feelings when I visited his niece. I am beyond feigning a lack of interest.

I returned to the house and went into the saloon. My eyes went immediately to Elizabeth. I knew instantly that she belonged there. As I watched her, I saw a future stretching out in front of me, a future in which I saw Elizabeth and myself living at Pemberley. I wanted it more than I have ever wanted anything, and I can only hope she wants the same.

'Miss Bennet, Mrs Gardiner, it is very good of you to call on my sister so soon,' I said.

'Oh, yes, very good,' said Georgiana, blushing. 'I did not expect it.'

'We could not do otherwise, after your kindness in welcoming us,' said Mrs Gardiner to Georgiana.

Georgiana blushed again, but I had eyes only for Elizabeth. Her gaze met mine. She looked away, embarrassed, and yet I thought I saw a welcome in her eyes before she turned away.

Caroline and Louisa were sitting silently, making no contribution to the conversation and leaving Georgiana to perform her duties as a hostess alone.

Mrs Annesley helped her, saying to Elizabeth: 'The grounds at Pemberley are very fine. I believe you saw them a few days ago?'

'Yes, we enjoyed walking round them very much,' said Elizabeth. 'The trees are very handsome.' She glanced out of the window at some specimens.

'They are Spanish chestnuts,' Georgiana said softly, pleased to be able to add something to the conversation.

'Have they been here long?' asked Elizabeth, turning towards her encouragingly.

'Oh, yes, they are very old.'

Georgiana looked at me for approval and I smiled at her. She has not had much experience of welcoming guests, and none at all of welcoming people whom she does not know, but she acquitted herself very well.

Caroline evidently felt she had been silent long enough.

'Pray, Miss Eliza, are not the militia removed from Meryton? They must be a great loss to your family.'

I had never heard her speak with such venom. Her satirical comments were usually uttered with some semblance of a smile, but there was nothing humorous about them today, and I realized for the first time how truly poisonous Caroline can be.

I saw Elizabeth's distress. A thousand recollections flooded my mind. My own ungenerous remarks concerning her younger sisters; her face as she flung an accusation of ruining Wickham at me; my angry retaliation; and then my letter.

I felt for her, but she had no need of my assistance in repelling the attack. After a moment's distress she replied: 'It is always sad to lose the company of intelligent and good-natured people. There are those who enter a neighbourhood with a view of mocking all they see, or an intention of forming false friendships with which to while away their time whilst giving no thought to the feelings of those who must remain. But we were fortunate with the officers. They were polite and well-bred. They gave us pleasure when they were with us, and left nothing but pleasant memories behind when they went.'

I caught Elizabeth's eye and smiled. Caroline was silenced, and my sister was relieved from the acute embarrassment she had experienced when Caroline's words had reminded her of George Wickham. I was relieved of a great burden. By her calm manner I believed Elizabeth's infatuation with Wickham to be over.

The visit came to an end, but I could not bear to let Elizabeth go.

'You must let me see you to the carriage,' I said, as Mrs Gardiner rose to take her leave.

'Thank you,' she said.

I walked with them, glad of the opportunity it afforded me to be with Elizabeth. Her aunt walked a little ahead, so that I could talk to her alone.

'I hope you have enjoyed your morning.'

'Yes, thank you, I have.'

'I hope I will see you here again.'

We had reached the carriage, I could say no more. But my feelings were in my glance. She blushed, and looked down, from confusion, I hope. There is still some little awkwardness between us, but that will pass, and then I will discover if her feelings towards me are still what they were at Easter.

I handed Mrs Gardiner into the carriage. I handed Elizabeth in after her, and the carriage pulled away.

Little had I known when I had returned to Pemberley that it would hold so much of interest for me. It would soon have a new mistress, I hoped. I looked across the sweeping lawns and pictured my sons going down to the river to fish. I looked to the house and saw my daughters returning from a walk, their petticoats covered in mud. If I could be sure it would come to pass, I would think myself lucky indeed.

I was loath to return to the saloon, but knew it must be done. I could not leave Georgiana alone with Caroline and Louisa. They had done nothing to help her during Elizabeth's visit, and had indeed added to her distress. If it was possible to invite Bingley to Pemberley without his sisters I would willingly do so.

'How very ill Miss Eliza Bennet looks this morning,' said Caroline, as soon as I entered the room. 'She is grown so brown and coarse. Louisa and I were agreeing that we should not have known her again.'

It was clear to me that Caroline's remarks were inspired by jealousy. I had wondered, on occasion, if she fancied herself the next Mrs Darcy, but dismissed the notion. Now I was sure of it. I was determined not to let her ill-natured remarks ruin my happiness, however.

'I saw nothing different about her, except that she was rather tanned, no miraculous consequence of travelling in summer.'

'For my own part,' she went on spitefully, 'I must confess that I never could see any beauty in her.'

As she went on to criticize Elizabeth's nose, chin, complexion and teeth I grew more and more annoyed, but said nothing, even when she added: 'And as for her eyes, which have sometimes been called so fine, I never could perceive anything extraordinary in them.'

She looked at me challengingly, but I remained determinedly silent.

'I remember your saying one night, after they had

been dining at Netherfield: "She is a beauty! – I should as soon call her mother a wit".'

'Yes,' I replied, unable to contain myself, 'but that was only when I first knew her, for it is many months since I have considered her as one of the handsomest women of my acquaintance.'

And so saying, I walked out of the room.

Caroline's impertinence goes beyond all bounds. If she was not Bingley's sister I would tell her to leave. To insult Elizabeth, to me! She must be far gone with jealousy indeed.

But she cannot pierce my happiness. I love Elizabeth. Now it only remains to be seen if Elizabeth loves me.

Friday 8th August

I could not sleep last night, but this time the cause was happiness. I think Elizabeth is not averse to me. In time, I think, she might come to like me. I thank the happy fate that brought her to Derbyshire, and the happier one that prompted me to ride ahead of the rest of my party, in time to meet her. In London, I tried to forget her, but it was impossible. Now, I must try to win her.

I went to the inn, therefore, this morning, hoping to sit with her. I was shown up to the parlour by the servant. As we went upstairs I wondered what expression would cross her face when I entered the room. By that, I might know much. A smile would show I was welcome. Embarrassment would give me leave to hope. A cold look would dash me completely.

The door opened. But instead of seeing Elizabeth sitting with her aunt, I saw her darting towards the door, her face pale and her manner agitated. I started, thinking some great calamity must have befallen her to produce such a look, but before I had a chance to speak she turned anguished eyes to mine and exclaimed: 'I beg your pardon, but I must leave you. I must find Mr Gardiner this moment, on business that cannot be delayed; I have not an instant to lose.'

'Good God! What is the matter?' I asked, longing to be of service to her. As soon as the words were out, I knew how unhelpful they had been. Collecting myself, I said: 'Let me, or let the servant, go after Mr Gardiner. You are not well enough; you cannot go yourself.'

'Oh, yes, the servant.' She called him back and said breathlessly: 'You must find my uncle. Fetch him at once. It is a matter of the utmost urgency. Send a boy. Tell him his niece needs him immediately. Tell my aunt. She must come, too.'

The servant promised to do so, and left the room.

I saw Elizabeth's knees tremble and I moved forward, ready to lend her my assistance, but she sat down before I could reach her, looking so miserably ill that I could not have left her, even if I had wanted to.

'Let me call your maid,' I said gently, feeling suddenly useless. I knew nothing about helping ladies in such circumstances. A sudden thought hit me. 'A glass of wine, shall I fetch you one?'

'No, I thank you,' she said. I saw her wrestle with herself and control the worst of her agitation. 'I am quite well. I am only distressed by some dreadful news which I have just received from Longbourn.'

She burst into tears. I longed to go to her and comfort her. I longed to put my arms around her and ease her pain. But I could do nothing. For the first time in my life I cursed civility, good manners and breeding. They had always seemed so important to me, but they now seemed valueless because they were keeping me from Elizabeth.

A moment longer and I believe I would have thrown convention to the wind, but she recovered herself and said: 'I have just had a letter from Jane, with such dreadful news. My youngest sister has left all her friends – has eloped – has thrown herself into the power of – of Mr Wickham. They are gone off together from Brighton. You know him too well to doubt the rest. She has no money, no connections, nothing that can tempt him – she is lost for ever.'

I could not believe what I was hearing. This was perfidy indeed. To steal a young girl away from her relatives and friends. And yet he had done it before, or at least he had tried to do it and would have succeeded if he had not been foiled in the attempt.

'When I consider that I might have prevented it! I who knew what he was,' she said.

No, I wanted to say. You are not to blame. I should have made his nature known. But the words were pouring out of her in a torrent, and I could do nothing but let her speak. At last, her flow came to an end.

'But is it certain, absolutely certain?' I asked.

News travels fast, especially bad news, but it is often distorted along the way. I could not think that Wickham would elope with Miss Lydia Bennet. She had nothing to tempt him, and he had no score to settle with the Bennets. He must know that such behaviour would make him an outcast. It was too great a price to pay for the pleasure of marrying a silly young girl with no name and no fortune. And then, indeed, how could he marry her? She was under age. He could take her to Gretna Green but the journey would cost a great deal, and I knew he would not spend half that amount unless his bride was a considerable heiress.

'They left Brighton together on Saturday night and were traced almost to London, but not beyond; they are certainly not gone to Scotland.'

I began to gain an idea of what must have happened. Wickham knew London. He knew where he could lie concealed. And when he had taken his pleasure, he could abandon Miss Lydia Bennet with impunity.

All this had followed from my insufferable pride. If I had made Wickham's character known it could not have happened, but I had disdained to do it, and in consequence I had hurt the woman I loved.

'What has been done, what has been attempted to recover her?' I asked.

I needed to know, so that I would understand how best to use my time, and how to conduct my own search. I would not rest until Elizabeth's sister was returned to her.

'My father is gone to London, and Jane has written to

beg my uncle's immediate assistance, and we shall be off, I hope, in half an hour.'

Half an hour! After all my hopes, to lose Elizabeth so soon, but of course it must be done.

'How is such a man to be worked on? How are they even to be discovered? I have not the smallest hope. It is every way horrible!'

I could say nothing, do nothing, but give her my silent sympathy and hope it strengthened her. I longed to embrace her, but her uncle would be returning at any minute, and to do so would make the situation worse.

'When my eyes were opened to his real character. Oh! Had I known what I ought, what I dared to do! But I knew not. I was afraid of doing too much. Wretched, wretched mistake!'

I knew she must be wanting me gone. It was I who had enjoined her to secrecy; I who had said she must tell no one. And this had been the result. A sister ruined, a family in turmoil....She would not look at me. I was not surprised. I managed a few incoherent words, telling her I had nothing to plead in excuse of my stay but concern.

'This unfortunate affair will, I fear, prevent my sister's having the pleasure of seeing you at Pemberley today?'

As soon as I spoken, I thought how ridiculous the words were. Of course it would prevent it. She did not seem to mind, however, for she answered me directly.

'Oh, yes. Be so kind as to apologize for us to Miss Darcy. Conceal the unhappy truth as long as it is possible.

I know it cannot be long.'

'You can rely on my secrecy. I am sorry it had come to this – I wish you a happier conclusion to events than now seems possible.'

Because if a happy conclusion is possible, I will contrive it somehow, I thought.

With that I left her to her solitude and returned to Pemberley.

'You have been abroad early,' said Caroline as I entered the saloon. 'You have been visiting Miss Eliza Bennet, perhaps?'

I saw the jealousy in her eyes, and heard it in her voice. I had never realized until that moment how deeply she wanted me. Or perhaps it would be fairer to say, how deeply she wanted Pemberley. Without it, she would have regarded me as nothing. My handwriting could have been the most even in the world and she would not have thought fit to comment on it.

'Yes, I have,' I returned.

'And how is she this morning?'

'She is very well.'

'And we will be seeing her later, I suppose? How these country people bore one with their visits.'

'No, she will not be calling.'

'Not bad news from home, I hope?' asked Caroline. 'Lydia Bennet has not run off with one of the officers?'

I started, but then controlled myself. She could not have heard about it. Elizabeth had told no one but myself. Caroline's words were the result of spite, and their accuracy was nothing more than luck.

'Or perhaps her accomplished sister – Mary, is it not? – visited Lydia in Brighton and attracted the attention of the Prince of Wales? Perhaps he has invited the whole family to stay with him, so that they can share in Mary's triumph as she entertains him at the Marine Pavilion,' she said in a droll voice.

'Her uncle has had to take her home. He has been forced to curtail his holiday, as an urgent business matter has called him back to London.'

'These city men and their urgent business,' said Caroline, conveniently forgetting, as is her habit, that her father made his fortune from trade.

'That is what comes of having an uncle in Cheapside,' said Louisa. 'I pity Miss Eliza Bennet. It must be mortifying to have to cut short a holiday on account of business.'

'It reminds me that I, too, have business to attend to, which I have neglected for too long,' I said shortly. 'You will excuse me for a few days, I am sure.'

'You are going to London?' asked Bingley.

'Yes.'

'What a good idea. I should love a few days in London,' said Caroline.

'In all this heat?' asked Louisa.

'The heat is nothing,' she said.

'Can your business not wait?' said Bingley to me. 'I have to go to London myself at the end of the month. We could go together.'

'Unfortunately it is urgent. Stay and enjoy Pemberley.

There is plenty for you to do here, and my sister will make sure you are well looked after. I will not be away very long.'

'I think I will take advantage of the opportunity to go to London with you and do some shopping,' said Caroline, standing up. 'I will call in on my dressmaker. You would not object to taking me with you in the carriage, I am sure.'

'You will not wish to leave Georgiana,' I said. 'I know how much you enjoy her company.'

Caroline was silenced. She quite doted on Georgiana, or so she was fond of saying, and she could not pursue me without revealing her friendship to be false. She might betray Miss Bennet, but she would not care to betray Georgiana, particularly since I knew a plan fermented in her brain, similar to one I had once entertained, of Georgiana becoming her sister-in-law.

I felt a moment of compunction for abandoning my sister to such ill-natured company, but reflected that she would have her music and sketching to occupy her, and would have Bingley to amuse her, as well as Mrs Annesley, so that she would not be too sorely tried. Besides, I had no choice. I must find Wickham and repair the damage he had done.

I wanted to leave straight away, but various preparations had to be made, and I resolved to leave first thing in the morning.

Saturday 9th August

I arrived in London today and I knew where to start my search: with Mrs Younge. It was fortunate that I had turned her off without giving her a chance to pack her bags, because it meant that she had had to leave an address to which they could be sent. I found it soon enough, a large house in Edward Street.

'Mr Darcy!' she said in astonishment when she opened the door. Then she became wary. 'What are you doing here? If it is to accuse me of taking the silver serving-spoons when I left Ramsgate, then it is a lie. I never touched them. I had my suspicions of Watkins – '

'My visit has nothing to do with serving-spoons,' I said, grateful that this was one domestic trouble I had been spared. 'May I come in?'

'No, you may not,' she said, drawing herself up and pulling her shawl about her shoulders. 'It's lucky I have a roof over my head after you turned me off so cruelly, without even a reference. I had nowhere to go – '

'But you seem to have done well for yourself,' I remarked. 'Tell me, Mrs Younge, how did you afford to take a house like this?'

She licked her lips. 'I was left a legacy,' she said. 'And a good thing I was, after – '

'I am looking for George Wickham,' I said, not wanting to waste any more time on listening to her lies and deciding it would be useless to try and persuade her to let me in.

She looked surprised. 'Mr Wickham?'

'Yes. George Wickham.'

She became tight-lipped. 'I haven't seen him,' she said.

It was obvious she was lying, but I knew I would get no more from her for the present.

'Tell him I am looking for him. I will call back later. Good day.'

I knew that, eventually, greed would compel her to seek me out. And with that I returned to Darcy House.

Monday 11th August

Mrs Younge came to see me this morning, as I knew she would.

'You said you were looking for Mr Wickham?' she asked, as my butler showed her in.

'I am.'

'I know where he is. I happened to meet him by chance in the park yesterday,' she said. 'I mentioned that you were in town, and he said he would be delighted if you would call on him.'

He thinks he can extract money from me, no doubt.

'Very good. What is his address?'

'Well, now, let me think. It was a funny name,' she said, holding out her hand.

I put a sovereign into it.

'If I can just remember it.'

It took me five sovereigns, but at last I found out what I wanted to know.

I went immediately to the address she had given me, and found that Wickham was expecting me.

'My dear Darcy,' he said, looking up at my entrance. 'How good of you to find time to visit me.'

I looked around his lodgings. They were small and mean, and told me his situation must be desperate. I was pleased, as I knew it would make him more compliant.

'Do sit down,' he said.

'I prefer to stand.'

'As you wish.'

He himself sat down and lolled in his chair, resting his legs over the arm.

'What brings you here?' he asked, smiling up at me.

'You know what brings me.'

'I confess I am at a loss. You have decided to give me a living, perhaps, and have come to tell me the good news?'

His insolence angered me, but I kept my temper.

'I have come to tell you what your own conscience should have told you, that you should never have abducted Miss Bennet.'

'Miss Bennet?' he asked, feigning astonishment. 'But I have not seen Miss Bennet. I have been in Brighton, and she remained at Longbourn.'

'Miss Lydia Bennet.'

'Ah, Lydia. I did not abduct Lydia. She came with me of her own free will. I was leaving Brighton as my creditors were becoming rather vocal, and Lydia suggested she came with me. I tried to put her off. To be truthful, Darcy, she bores me. She is too easy a conquest. She convinced herself I was the handsomest man in the regiment, and the thing was done. I told her I had no money but she did not care. "I am sure you will have some one day," she said. "Lord, what a lark!" I grew so tired of her pleading that it was easier to let her come with me than it was to make her stay behind. Besides, she has her uses,' he said impudently.

At that moment the door opened, and Lydia herself came in.

'Lord, what a surprise! Mr Darcy!' she said, going over to Wickham. She stood beside his chair and rested one hand on his shoulder.

'Mr Darcy has come to reprimand me for abducting you,' said Wickham, covering her hand with his own.

She laughed at me.

'My dear Wickham did not abduct me! Why should he? I was eager to see London. I told him he must take me with him. What fun it has been!'

'Have you no thought for your family?' I asked her coldly. 'They have been worried about you ever since you left the care of Colonel Forster. They have no idea where you are.'

'Lord! I forgot to write,' said Lydia. 'I have been so busy with my dear Wickham. We have had such a time! But never mind. I will write as soon as we are married. What fun it will be, to sign my name, Lydia Wickham!'

She squeezed his hand and he, the insolent dog, pulled her into his lap and kissed her, then smiled at me whilst caressing her.

'So you see, Darcy, your concern is misplaced,' he said.

Lydia's words had told me one thing: that at least she

expected to be married. I felt she would be less eager to remain with him if she knew that Wickham had no such intention. I did not think he would tell her, however – why should he lose an eager companion? – and so I felt it necessary for me to do so.

'I would like to talk to Miss Bennet alone,' I said to Wickham.

'Very well,' said he, pushing her off his lap. 'Try and talk her into going home if you will. She is a baggage. But I cannot see why her fate matters to you,' he added as he stood up.

'It matters because I could have made your character known in Meryton and did not. It would have been impossible for you to have behaved in this way if your true self were known.'

'Perhaps,' he said, 'but I do not believe that is the reason. I doubt if you would have sought me out if I had run off with Maria Lucas.'

I did not flinch. If I let him once guess that I had a personal reason for seeking him out, he would be difficult to buy off at any price.

'Stay,' said Lydia, snatching at his hand as he walked towards the door.

'Mr Darcy wishes to speak with you alone. He is afraid I am keeping you here against your will, and he wants to give you a chance to go home with him.'

'As if I would wish to go back to stuffy old Longbourn,' she said, twining her arms round his neck and kissing him on the lips.

He put his arms round her and returned her kiss, then looked at me tauntingly before leaving the room.

'Is he not handsome?' asked Lydia, as the door closed behind him. 'All the girls were wild for him in Meryton, and Miss King would have married him if her guardian had not put a stop to it. It was the same in Brighton. Any number of them would have run away with him. Miss Winchester – '

'Miss Bennet, you cannot stay here,' I interrupted her.

'It is a little shabby, to be sure, but we will have something better by and by. I would like your help though, Mr Darcy.'

'Yes?' I said, hoping she had seen sense at last.

'What do you think? I cannot decide. Does my dear Wickham look better in his red coat or his blue?'

'Miss Bennet!' I rapped out. 'You cannot stay here with Wickham. He has no intention of marrying you. I know he has said he has, but it was a lie, to make you elope with him.'

'He did not make me elope with him, it was I who made him elope with me. Brighton was growing boring,' she said with a yawn. 'Colonel Forster was so stuffy. He would not let me go to half the things I wanted to, and I had to sneak out of the camp on two occasions to attend my Wickham's parties. Denny helped me. I dressed as a man. You should have seen me. My own mother would not have recognized me.'

'Your reputation will be in ruins! He will abandon you as soon as he tires of you, and you will be left in

London without a protector, with no money and nowhere to live. Come back with me now, and I will do what I can to persuade your family to receive you.'

'Lord! I do not want to go home! I would die of boredom. I am sure we shall be married some time or another, and if not, it does not much signify,' she said.

She was immovable. She would not leave him. Since such were her feelings, I could do nothing but try and make sure a marriage took place.

Wickham came back into the room, carrying a decanter in one hand and a glass in the other. He put his arm round Lydia and she turned to kiss him immediately.

'Well, Darcy? Have you persuaded her to leave me?' he asked, when he had done.

'She is lost to all sense,' I said angrily, 'but since she will not leave you, you must marry her.'

'Come now, Darcy. You know I cannot do that. My pockets are to let. I have debts all over the country. There are unpaid bills in Meryton, and worse in Brighton. I need to many an heiress.'

'Do you hear this?' I demanded of Miss Bennet.

She only shrugged.

'It does not signify. An heiress would bring us some money, then we could have a better house,' she said.

It was only because of Elizabeth that I stayed. My inclination was to walk out and leave her sister to the life she had made for herself. But the thought of Elizabeth's pale face sustained me.

'Meet me at my club tomorrow,' I said to Wickham.

'My dear Darcy, you know I am not welcome there.'

'I will make sure you are admitted.'

He looked surprised, but said: 'Very well.'

As I left the house, the memory of his insolent smile went with me.

Thursday 14th August

I met Wickham at my club and the negotiations began.

'You must marry her,' I said to him shortly.

'If I do that, I give up for ever the chance of making my fortune through marriage.'

'You have ruined her,' I said. 'Does that mean nothing to you?'

He crossed one ankle over the other and lay back in the chair. 'She ruined herself,' he said.

A waiter passed, and he ordered a whisky. I did not react, knowing he did it only to annoy me.

'How much do you owe?' I asked, going straight to the heart of the matter.

'Several hundred pounds.'

'Whether that is true or not, I do not know but I shall. If you give your bills to my agent, he will pay them for you. In return, you will marry Lydia.'

'Come now, as you are so anxious to see her wed, she is worth a lot more than that. Is it Miss Bennet who has caught your fancy, or is it the lovely Elizabeth?'

'I am doing this for my own conscience,' I said.

He laughed in my face.

'No man goes to such lengths to ease his own

conscience. Let me guess. It is the beautiful Jane Bennet. Sweet-natured, beautiful Jane. She would make a splendid addition to Pemberley. I congratulate you, Darcy.'

'I have no intention of marrying Miss Bennet.'

'Then it is Elizabeth.'

I said nothing, but he must have guessed it from my face.

'Ah! So it is! Her liveliness appeals to you. I would not have thought it. You are so pompous, Darcy, but they say that opposites attract.'

He had the upper hand, and he was enjoying using it.

'Have a care,' I warned him. 'I will do much to save Lydia Bennet from disgrace, but if you go too far, instead of having your debts paid and something more besides, you will find yourself pursued by every creditor in Brighton, and maybe the army, for I will give them all your address.'

'I can go to Bath, or Lyme, or the Lake District,' he said. 'I do not have to live here.' But I could tell he had no stomach for further flight.

'Do so,' I said, calling his bluff. I stood up and turned towards the door.

'Wait,' he said.

I paused.

'I will marry her – '

'Good,' I said, sitting down again.

'– for thirty thousand pounds.'

'What?' I cried.

'It is the sum I should have had from Georgiana.'

I mastered my temper with difficulty. 'I will give you nothing of the kind.'

'Very well, then, twenty thousand.'

I stood up and left the club.

He will come to me soon enough. He has nowhere else to go.

I do not relish seeing him, but the knowledge that it will case Elizabeth's fears recompenses me for any time or trouble I might take, and I hope that, before very long, I will see her happy again.

Friday 15th August

Wickham called on me this afternoon, as I knew he would. His situation is desperate, and he cannot afford to throw away assistance. Only the thought of Elizabeth's happiness sustained me throughout the ordeal, which was as unpleasant as our last encounter. If not for her, I would have abandoned the matter. We settled at last on a thousand pounds to pay his debts and a further thousand.

'And a commission,' he said.

'I cannot believe you will be welcome in the army.'

'You have some influence there. Come, Darcy, I must have something to live on. How else am I to support a wife?'

At last I agreed, on condition he join a regiment in the far north. I do not want to see him when Elizabeth and I are married. If Elizabeth and I are married. I made the mistake once before of thinking that she was wanting me to propose to her, but I was wrong. I will not make the same mistake again.

Having settled everything with Wickham, I decided to call on Mr Gardiner to let him know what had been decided. I soon found his house, but when I asked to see him I learnt from the servants that Mr Bennet was with him. I hesitated. In the first flush of discovery, I feared Mr Bennet might do something rash. On further enquiry I found that Mr Bennet will be returning home tomorrow. I therefore judged it wiser to wait, thinking it would be easier to talk to Mr Gardiner than Mr Bennet. Mr Gardiner is of necessity less closely involved, and therefore he is likely to be more rational.

Saturday 16th August

I called on Mr Gardiner and this time found him alone. He was surprised to see me, but welcomed me cordially.

'Mr Darcy. I did not know you intended to visit town so soon. How is your sister? Well, I hope?'

'Very well.'

'We were delighted to meet her in Derbyshire. She is a beautiful girl.'

'Thank you. You are very kind. It is not about my sister I have come to talk to you, however, but about your niece.'

I saw him change colour.

'Will you not sit down?'

'Thank you. I called on her shortly after her sister's letter was delivered,' I said, 'and learnt the unhappy truth. I felt responsible for the situation, for I knew of Wickham's character and yet I kept silent. He had done something similar before, but I had not mentioned it because

I had wanted to protect the young lady's reputation. If I had made his perfidy known, then no woman would have been able to love him, and Miss Lydia Bennet would have been safe.'

His expression said that nothing would have kept a girl as wild as Lydia safe.

Aloud he said: 'It is really not your fault.'

'Nevertheless, I took it upon myself to track him down. I knew his acquaintances, and knew how to find out where he might be. I have seen him, and persuaded him that a marriage must take place.'

He looked more and more surprised as I unfolded the details. He refused to let me undertake any of the financial arrangements, but as I argued it with him back and forth, a thoughtful expression began to cover his face. He suspected the nature of my feelings for Elizabeth, I am sure of it, but said nothing. How could he? He said at last that we had talked long enough, and invited me to call on him again tomorrow. I think he wishes to consult his wife as to how far I should be allowed to help.

I left him and retired to my club. Everything will soon be settled, I am confident of it. As soon as Elizabeth hears of it she will be relieved of care, and it is that thought that sustains me. She will be able to laugh again, and tease me, and she will forget all about her sister.

Sunday 17th August

I called upon Mr Gardiner again, and this time Mrs Gardiner was with him. They welcomed me warmly, and after exchanging pleasantries, I said again that I expected to settle Wickham's debts. That they agreed to, but they would not agree to me settling anything else. There are some arrangements still to be made, however, and I mean to work on Mr Gardiner again tomorrow, until he agrees to let me settle the whole.

Monday 18th August

All has finally been settled. I have at last managed to have my own way. Mr Gardiner had an express sent off to Longbourn, and it gave me great satisfaction to know that it will relieve Elizabeth from distress. Mr and Mrs Gardiner are to offer Lydia their protection until the marriage can be arranged. I do not envy them. She has shown no remorse for what she has done, and seems to think it a great joke. She is one of the most worthless girls of my acquaintance.

Tuesday 19th August

I returned to Pemberley, and I was pleased to find that my guests had noticed nothing strange about my absence. If they knew that I had been arranging a marriage, instead of attending to business, how astonished they would be!

Saturday 30th August

I travelled to London, and tomorrow I have the unpleasant task of making sure Wickham attends his own wedding.

September

Monday 1st September

Today Lydia was married, and her reputation saved.

The morning started badly. I called on Wickham in his lodgings at half past ten as arranged and found him only half-dressed.

'What is this?' I asked. 'You have to be at the church in half an hour.'

He poured himself a drink and threw it off.

'It will only take us ten minutes to get to the church. There is plenty of time.'

'If you are beyond the hour you will not be able to marry today,' I said.

'Do you know, Darcy, if you had given me the living I wanted when I applied for it, all this unpleasantness could have been avoided.'

I made no reply.

'It would have suited me better to marry other people rather than being married myself. I am beginning to think I do not want to be married at all,' he said.

'Then you must face your debtors.'

'Ah. I would like that even less.'

He put his glass down and picked up his coat. He shrugged himself into it and tied his cravat, then we went out to the waiting carriage.

'This is like our boyhoods,' he said to me, as we climbed in. 'The two of us together. I always thought you would stand up with me at my wedding. Lately I began to doubt it, but here we are you see, friends again.'

'You are no friend of mine,' I said.

He smiled tauntingly. 'Unless I miss my guess we will soon be closer than friends. We will be brothers.' He lolled back on the squabs. 'How happy it would have made our fathers, to know we will be so close to each other. We were almost brothers last year...' He paused, and I required all my self-control not to respond. 'But alas, fate had other ideas. Or, at least, you did. How is Georgiana?'

'Better for being away from you.'

'A pity. I did not think she would forget me so soon. I rather thought she was in love with me. I am looking forward to seeing her again, when Lydia and I visit Pemberley.'

'That is something you will never do,' I said with finality.

The journey to St Clement's was a short one. The church had been chosen because it was in the same parish as Wickham's lodgings, and the rector was willing to perform the ceremony. He knew nothing of what had taken place in order to bring the marriage about, only that a young couple wished to wed. He greeted us with smiles as we entered the church and we waited for Lydia to arrive.

'Perhaps she has changed her mind,' said Wickham. 'You could not hold that against me. You would still have to pay my debts.'

'She will be here. Her aunt and uncle will see to it.'

At that moment Lydia entered the church. She glanced towards the altar then broke out in effusive spirits when she saw that Wickham had already arrived.

Her aunt and uncle bade her remember where she was, and walked with her to the front of the church.

'I will be glad when this is all over,' said Mr Gardiner to me in an undertone.

'I agree,' said his wife. 'I tried to make her understand the worry she has caused her parents, the disgrace she has brought on her family and the gratitude she owes to those who have rescued her from ruin, but to no avail. She paid no attention to me and instead talked constantly of Wickham, with every now and then a complaint that we never set foot outside the house.'

The ceremony began, and the marriage which had taken so long to bring about was quickly accomplished.

'I hope you will thank Mr Darcy for all he has done,' said Mrs Gardiner when it was over.

'Mrs Wickham. How well it sounds!' said Lydia, ignoring her aunt and gazing at the ring on her finger.

A number of curious people had entered the church, and Lydia showed them all her ring, telling them that they must congratulate her and be the first to call her by her new name.

'How envious my sisters will be,' she said, as we left the church. 'Not one of them is married, though they are all older than me. I should be ashamed to be more than twenty and still not married. Jane is fast becoming an old maid. She will have to give up her place to me at the table, for I am a married woman now. What fun it will be! "Jane," I will say, "I take your place now, and you must go lower, because I am a married woman." '

Mr and Mrs Gardiner exchanged glances.

'They will all be so jealous of me and my handsome husband. I was so worried this morning, when we were coming to the church. I had a horror of him wearing black, but my happiness was complete when I saw he had chosen his blue coat.'

I felt a surge of satisfaction as I realized that Lydia will be just as silly as her mother, and I took enjoyment in the knowledge that Wickham will, after all, be punished for his iniquities, because he will have to live with her for the rest of his life.

Tuesday 2nd September

I dined with the Gardiners this evening. We were all relieved that everything had passed off well. The last few weeks have been a strain, but everything turned out for the best.

They are a most pleasing couple. Mr Gardiner is intelligent, and Mrs Gardiner has a great deal of common sense. They are cultured and well-bred, and I spent a very pleasant evening in their company – so pleasant that I forgot I was in Gracechurch Street. I have spent many a worse evening at a better address.

To think I once dismissed them without even knowing them, and rejected Elizabeth because her relations did not fit my notion of what they should be! Had I turned such a critical eye on my own relatives I might have realized that she was not alone in having undesirable connections. Lady Catherine, for all her elegance, disgraced herself by suggesting that Elizabeth – her guest! – should practise the piano in the housekeeper's room, something I am persuaded Mrs Gardiner would never do. And Bingley's relations are hardly any better. Caroline Bingley might be a woman of breeding and fashion, but she is also a woman who is eaten up by jealousy and spite.

Wednesday 3rd September

I returned to Pemberley to find that Caroline and Louisa were full of plans to visit Scarborough.

'Do come with us, Mr Darcy,' said Caroline. 'Scarborough is so invigorating at this time of year.'

'I have too much to do on my estate,' I said.

'But it would be so good for Georgiana. I do believe she has not seen the sea since last summer, when she stayed in Ramsgate. She must be pining for it.' She turned to Georgiana. 'Would you not like to see it again?'

Georgiana blushed, and said she had no desire to do so. Caroline turned to me.

'You would return to Pemberley refreshed, and manage twice as much work as if you had never gone,' she said.

'My intentions are fixed. But you must go,' I said as she opened her mouth to change her mind. 'The sea air will do you good.'

'Sea air,' said Mr Hurst, then retreated into his stupor.

Thursday 4th September

Caroline, Louisa and Mr Hurst departed for Scarborough. They tried to persuade Bingley to go with them, but he said he had no wish to be blown about and would remain at Pemberley. Caroline encouraged the idea. She still believes he will marry Georgiana, and wants him to see her more often, though it is obvious to an impartial eye that he never will.

Monday 8th September

'I think I will go to Netherfield again,' said Bingley nonchalantly as we rode out this morning.

'A good idea. If you mean to keep the house, you should use it from time to time.'

'That is exactly what I think. Will you come with me? I should like to repay your hospitality.'

My spirits rose. If I went to Netherfield, then I would have an opportunity of seeing Elizabeth again.

'When do you intend to go?' I asked.

'In about a week. I thought I would send the servants tomorrow, to ready the house.'

'Yes, I will come.'

He looked pleased.

'It is almost a year to the day that I took it. I little thought then…'

His voice trailed away, and it was not difficult to guess what direction his thoughts had taken. I said no more, but let him lose himself in day-dreams. Perhaps they will become reality before very long. And my dreams…what of them?

Wednesday 17th September

We arrived at Netherfield this afternoon. Bingley declared his intention of riding into Meryton as soon as we arrived, and it was only the onset of rain that made him put his visit off.

Thursday 18th September

Sir William Lucas called this morning, to welcome us back to the neighbourhood.

'Mr Bingley,' he said with a low bow, 'you do us too much honour in returning to our humble neighbourhood. We thought we had not joys enough to hold you and yet here you are, fresh from your triumphs in town, to honour our humble village with your presence. Mr Darcy,' he said, with a low bow to me. 'It seems but a moment since we were all taking tea with Lady Catherine in the delightful dining-parlour at Rosings Park. You enjoyed your stay, I trust?'

Enjoyed it? That was hardly the way I would have described my feelings during those turbulent few weeks, but he took my silence to mean that I had.

'Have you visited your estimable aunt since that time?' he asked.

'No,' I said shortly.

'I hope to visit my daughter again before very long,' he said.

He embarked on a rambling speech, extolling the virtues of his daughter's position. How long he would have gone on if Mr Long had not called I do not know!

When our guests had left, Bingley said: 'It was after Sir William called last year that Mr Bennet called on us. Do you suppose he will do so again?'

I thought of Mr Bennet's indolent habits and hesitated.

'Perhaps I could call on the Bennets even without this civility,' suggested Bingley.

'Wait and see whether he calls tomorrow,' was my advice.

Saturday 20th September

Mr Bennet did not call again yesterday, and this morning, Bingley made up his mind to visit Longbourn.

'Come with me, Darcy,' he said.

Telling myself I would go with him so that I could see whether Miss Bennet had any regard for him, I agreed, but my real reason was to see Elizabeth. I was as eager to see her as Bingley was to see her sister, and I was just as apprehensive about it.

We set out. Bingley was silent, and I too was lost in my thoughts, wondering how I should be received. If Elizabeth resented me for being the cause of Lydia's ruin I could hardly blame her, more particularly because she did not know that I had helped to set matters to rights.

I had been particularly concerned that she should not know. I did not want her gratitude. If she had developed any tender feelings for me I wanted to know they sprang from love, and nothing else.

We arrived. The servant showed us in. I immediately saw Elizabeth drop her gaze, embarrassed, and busy herself with her needlework. What did it mean? I wished I knew. Did it mean she was alive to the awkwardness of the situation, or did it mean that she could not bear to look at me?

'Why, Mr Bingley!' cried Mrs Bennet, jumping up with a smile. 'How delightful to see you at Longbourn again. We have missed you. You quit us in such a hurry last year you did not have time to say goodbye! I hope you will not be thinking of leaving us again so quickly?'

'No, I hope not,' said Bingley, looking at Miss Bennet.

I observed her smile, and drop her gaze. She, at least, I could understand, and it was clear that Bingley's hopes would not be disappointed.

'And Mr Darcy,' said Mrs Bennet in an ill-humoured voice, turning to me.

I took no notice of her humour, and I found it difficult to believe that only a few months ago I had thought it a reason for not proposing to Elizabeth. What did it matter if her mother was silly and vulgar? I did not want to marry Mrs Bennet.

I could not take a seat next to Elizabeth, her younger sisters being by, but I asked her how her aunt and uncle did. She replied sensibly, but then turned her attention back to her work.

Outwardly I was calm. Inwardly, I was otherwise, but I could do nothing. I was not close enough to Elizabeth to continue the conversation without it seeming particular, and what could I say to her, under her mother's eye, that I wanted to say?

To distract my thoughts, I looked at Miss Bennet and wondered how I could not have seen her partiality for Bingley last year. Her feelings for him were there in every gesture, and every look and every smile. Had I blinded myself, wanting Bingley to marry Georgiana? I wondered. I had not thought so at the time, but I realized now that I had.

I glanced again at Elizabeth, wishing I could read her mind.

After a time, she said: 'Miss Darcy is well, I hope?'

'Yes, thank you,' I said, glad to hear the sound of her voice.

There was chance for nothing more. Her mother began talking of Lydia's wedding. Elizabeth would not look up. Did she know that I had been involved? But no, I am sure she did not. I had sworn the Gardiners to secrecy, and I knew they would not betray me. Her confusion came from the subject, knowing what she does about my relations with Wickham.

'It is a delightful thing, to be sure, to have a daughter well married,' said Mrs Bennet, a speech that would have revolted me a few months before, but which now left no impression. I care nothing for Mrs Bennet. Let her be the silliest woman in Christendom if she chooses. It will not prevent me marrying Elizabeth, if she will have me.

Mrs Bennet continued to talk of Wickham, saying he had gone into the regulars, and adding: 'Thank Heaven!

He has some friends, though perhaps not so many as he deserves.'

Elizabeth's face was a fiery red, and her eyes sparkled with mortification. How I wanted to help her! But how I thought the colour became her.

She did, at last, raise her head and speak.

'Do you mean to stay in the country, Mr Bingley?' she asked.

I wished I was Bingley at that moment, so that she had spoken to me. Why did she favour my friend? Why would she not look at me? Did she not wish to? I was in misery.

At last the visit drew to an end. I would have stayed all day if I could, but it was impossible.

'You will come to dine with us on Tuesday, I hope, Mr Bingley?' said Mrs Bennet as we rose to leave. She turned cold eyes to me, adding unwelcomingly: 'And Mr Darcy.'

What did I care for her manner? I was to see Elizabeth again.

The next meeting will surely tell me whether she has any feelings for me, whether she can forgive me the grievous wrongs I have done her family and whether she can love me.

I will be in torment until I know.

Sunday 21st September

'I thought Miss Bennet looked well last night,' said Bingley to me this morning.

'She did.'

'I thought she looked very well,' he said a few minutes later.

'Yes, she did.'

'And in spirits. She has enjoyed the summer, I suppose,' he said wistfully.

'It is to be hoped so. You would not wish her to be unhappy?'

'No, of course not,' he replied hastily.

'I thought she did not look quite so blooming when we went in,' I said to him.

'No?' he asked hopefully.

'No. But she appeared to blossom when she saw you.'

Bingley smiled. 'Mrs Bennet is a wonderful woman. Truly charming. And so polite. I did not expect her to ask me to dinner so soon. It is a courtesy I do not deserve.'

Anyone who can think Mrs Bennet is a wonderful woman is in the grip of more than an infatuation. He is in love! I am glad for Bingley, and I only hope my own fortune can be as good.

Tuesday 23rd September

Bingley was ready to leave for Longbourn half an hour too early.

'We cannot go so soon,' I said, though I was just as eager to set out.

'We might be delayed on the way,' he said.

'Not on such a short journey,' I replied.

'Jennings will not want to drive the horses too fast.'

'We will reach Longbourn too soon, even if they walk all the way.'

'There might be a branch in the road.'

'We can drive round it.'

'Or the carriage might lose a wheel.'

'We cannot go for half an hour,' I said, settling myself down with a book.

I wished I felt as complacent as I seemed. I was as anxious to go as Bingley, and yet I was reluctant to go as well. He had the happiness of knowing his feelings were returned. I had no such assurance. To see Elizabeth again! I hardly dared think about it. If she smiled, what joy! If she avoided my gaze, what misery.

Bingley walked over to the window.

'You should do as I do, and choose a book,' I said.

He walked over to me and took it from my hands, then turned it round before handing it back to me.

'You will do better if it is the right way up,' he said.

He looked at me curiously, but I did not enlighten him as to the cause of my distraction. Instead, I kept my eyes on the page, but they saw nothing. At last the appointed time came, and we set out for Longbourn. We were both of us silent. We arrived. We went in. Mrs Bennet greeted Bingley with an excess of civility, and gave me a cold bow. We repaired to the dining-room. Miss Bennet happened to look up as we entered and Bingley took his place next to her. Happy Bingley! I had no such fortune. I was almost as far from Elizabeth as it was possible to be. Even worse, I was seated next to her mother.

Mrs Bennet had gone to a great deal of trouble with the dinner, and it was not difficult to see why. Her constant glances towards her eldest daughter and Bingley showed what direction her thoughts were taking. The soup was good, and it was followed by partridges and venison.

'I hope you find the partridges well done?' Mrs Bennet asked me.

'Remarkably so,' I replied, making an effort to be agreeable.

'And the venison. Did you ever see a fatter haunch?'

'No.'

'You will take some gravy, I hope?' she pressed me.

I had little appetite, and I declined her offer.

'I suppose you are above a simple gravy,' she said. 'You will be used to a variety of sauces in London.'

'I am,' I replied.

'You have dined with the Prince of Wales, I suppose?'

'I have had that honour.'

'Some people think that sort of gluttony genteel, but I confess I have always thought it vulgar. We do not have twenty sauces with every dish. We are not so wasteful in the country.'

She turned her attention back to Bingley, and I endeavoured to eat my meal. I watched Elizabeth, hungry for a glance in a way that I was not hungry for the food, but she did not look at me.

The ladies withdrew. The gentlemen sat over the port. I took no interest in the conversation. The iniquities of

the French did not interest me. The Prince of Wales's follies could not hold my attention. I glanced at the clock,
and then at the other gentlemen. Would they never stop
talking?

We rejoined the ladies and I went towards Elizabeth,
but there was no space near her. The dinner party was a
large one, and as she poured out the coffee I could not
get close. I tried nonetheless, but a young lady who will
be for ever blighted in my eyes moved close to her and
engaged her in conversation.

Did Elizabeth look vexed? I thought she did, and the
thought gave me hope. I walked away, but as soon as I
had finished my coffee, which burned my mouth, so
quickly did I drink it, I took the cup over to her for
refilling.

'Is your sister still at Pemberley?' she asked.

She seemed cool, aloof.

'Yes, she will remain there till Christmas,' I said.

She asked after Georgiana's friends, but said no more.
I did not know whether to speak or whether to be silent.
I wanted to speak, but I had so much to say I scarcely
knew where to begin, and on reflection I realized that
none of it could be said in a crowded drawing-room.

My silence drew notice from one of the ladies and I
was obliged to walk away, cursing myself for not having
made more of my opportunity.

The tea-things were removed and the card-tables
placed. This was my opportunity! But Mrs Bennet
demanded my presence at the whist-table and I could

not refuse without giving offence. I nearly gave it. I nearly said: 'I would much rather talk to your daughter.' What would she have said? Would she have told me that she had no intention of inflicting such a disagreeable man on Elizabeth, or would she have been stunned, and fallen blissfully silent? I was tempted to try, but I could not embarrass Elizabeth.

I could not keep my mind on the game. I lost repeatedly. I looked for an opportunity to speak to Elizabeth before I left, but I could not find one, and I returned to Netherfield in sombre mood.

Bingley, by contrast, was brimming with happiness. I have decided that, tomorrow, I must tell him that Miss Bennet was in town, and that I kept it from him. He will not be pleased, but the deception has gone on for long enough.

Wednesday 24th September

'Is Miss Bennet not the most beautiful girl you have ever seen?' Bingley asked me this evening as we played billiards.

'She is.'

'I think there might be hope,' he said.

'I am sure there is.' I hesitated, but I had to speak. 'Bingley, there is something I have to tell you.'

'Oh?'

He looked at me in all innocence, and I felt guilty for the part I had played in deceiving him.

'I have done you a great disservice. Last spring, Miss Bennet was in town.'

'But I did not see her!' he said in surprise.

'No. I know. I should have told you, but I thought you had forgotten her. No, let me be honest, I hoped you had forgotten her, or would forget her, if you did not see her again.'

'Darcy!' He was hurt.

'I am sorry. I had no right to meddle in your affairs. It was impertinent of me.'

'So she followed me to London?' he said, forgetting my deceit in the happiness of thinking that she had followed him.

'She went to stay with her aunt and uncle, but she tried to see you. That is, she wrote to Caroline.'

'Caroline! She knew of it, too?'

'Yes. I am ashamed to say that Caroline cut Miss Bennet, and that I encouraged her.'

'Darcy!'

He was vexed.

'I behaved very badly, and I beg your pardon.'

'If she agrees to be my wife, you will have it. But perhaps in the future you will consider that I can manage my own affairs.'

'I will, and better than I manage mine.'

He looked at me enquiringly.

I said no more. I cannot speak of my love for Elizabeth until I know it is returned. Unless I know it is returned.

Thursday 25th September

I have been obliged to return to town. How long I stay for will depend on circumstances.

Tuesday 30th September

I had a letter from Bingley this morning, evidently written in haste. It was blotted and so badly written as to be almost illegible. But at last I made it out.

> *My dear Darcy,*
> *Congratulate me! Jane and I are to be married!*
> *She is the sweetest, most adorable angel! I cannot believe I have been lucky enough to win her. Her mother is in raptures. Her father is pleased. Elizabeth is delighted. I have time for no more. Caroline bids me send you her greetings. She is already planning her dress as the maid of honour, and looks forward to seeing you at the wedding.*
> *Charles Bingley*
>
> *PS I forgot to ask. You will stand up with me?*
> *C.B.*

I wrote to him, sending him my heartiest congratulations and telling him that of course I will stand up with him. I was tempted to return to Netherfield and give him my best wishes personally, but Georgiana is unwell and I intend to remain in town until she is better.

As I sit with her, I cannot help thinking of Elizabeth. The two of them would be friends if Elizabeth consents to be my wife. It is in every way such a longed-for conclusion of everything that has happened, and yet I am apprehensive. I have seen no sign in Elizabeth's words or manner to make me think my feelings are returned. And yet I saw nothing to make me think she is irrevocably set against me. I am almost afraid to return to Longbourn. Whilst I am with Georgiana I still have hope, but once I return to Longbourn it may be dashed for ever.

October

Thursday 2nd October

Colonel Fitzwilliam called to see how Georgiana was getting on. She is much recovered, and I will be able to return to Netherfield in a few days' time.

'You have been to Netherfield, I understand?' he said.

We were eating in the dining-room. Georgiana, still listless from her illness, took dinner in her room.

'Yes.' I told him of Bingley's engagement.

'And do you mind?'

'No. I am very happy for him. I am happy for them both.'

'Did Miss Elizabeth Bennet speak to you about your letter? Has she accepted that you did not ruin Wickham?' he asked hesitantly.

'She has said nothing, but I think she has accepted it.'

'And has it softened her feelings towards you?'

I did not know how to reply.

'These affairs are painful whilst they last, but they should not be allowed to last for ever,' he said. 'It is time you looked to the future again, Darcy. You should marry. It would be good for Georgiana to have a woman in the house.' He took a mouthful of turbot, then said: 'Anne has been expecting your proposal for several years.'

'Anne?' I asked in surprise.

'Come now, Darcy, you know Lady Catherine has regarded your marriage as a settled thing since you were in your cradles. I was surprised you offered your hand to Elizabeth, but as it was none of my business I held my peace. Now that she has rejected you, however, I think you should formalize your engagement to Anne.'

'I have no intention of marrying Anne,' I said.

'But Lady Catherine expects it. She and your mother betrothed you and Anne in your cradles.'

'She is not serious in that? I have heard her say it many times, but I took it for an idle fancy, such as: "When you were a baby, my sister and I decided you would go into the army", or "When you were a child, I decided you would go into politics".'

'I do assure you, she means it.'

'And Anne?' I asked.

'Yes, she too expects it. It is why she has never married.'

'I had thought it was because she was so young…'

'She is eight and twenty, as you are. Have you forgotten that you were in your cradles together, and that all three of us played together when we were children?'

I had forgotten. She used to trail after my cousin and me. No, not trail after us. She could run almost as fast as I could. My cousin, being five years older, could outstrip us both.

'Do you remember how she beat us to the top of the oak tree?' he asked. 'She was not meant to climb it. She tore her frock, and was confined to the nursery on bread and milk for a week.'

'I remember. I also remember how you took her a cold beef sandwich and slice of pie, wrapped up in a handkerchief. I thought you would surely fall as you climbed across the roof to her window. Did you ever get caught for stealing from the kitchen?'

'No. Mrs Heaney blamed it on the dog.'

'Poor Caesar! I had forgotten about Anne's exploits. She was much more lively as a child, when her health was good,' I remarked.

'And when she had Sir Lewis to defend her. He found out about Lady Catherine's orders that she be confined to the nursery, and he went there himself to give her half a sovereign.'

'Did he indeed?' I said with a smile.

I could imagine it. Sir Lewis had always been very fond of Anne, and she in turn had been very fond of her father. It had been a sad blow to her when he had died.

'I have often wondered...' began my cousin.

'Yes?'

'Have you noticed that her cough is always worse when her mother is by?'

'No.'

'And not only her cough, but her shyness. She is much more spirited when she is with me.'

'She is never spirited with me,' I said in surprise.

'But then, she is in awe of you.'

'Of me?'

'You are quite a figure, Darcy, particularly when you are out of sorts. Let the weather be bad, and your boredom turns you into an ogre.'

I was about to tell him he was talking nonsense when I recalled Bingley saying something similar.

'I am sorry for it. But Anne need suffer no further. I will visit Rosings and tell her that a marriage between us is out of the question.'

'There is no need. Lady Catherine is in London, and Anne is with her. I saw them both this evening, before I came here. Lady Catherine means to call on you before she returns to Rosings.'

We finished our meal, and after sitting with me for an hour Colonel Fitzwilliam left. He is remaining in London for the next two weeks, and has promised to call on Georgiana every day to make sure she is well and happy.

Saturday 4th October

Lady Catherine called this morning, bringing Anne with her. I was about to enquire after their health, when my aunt began without preamble.

'You must put an end to this nonsense at once, Darcy,' she said, as soon as she had seated herself.

I did not know what she was talking about, but before I could say anything, she went on:

'I heard from Mr Collins that you were about to propose to Miss Elizabeth Bennet. Sit down, Anne.'

Anne promptly sat down.

'Knowing such a report to be a grotesque falsehood, I visited Longbourn in order to have Miss Elizabeth Bennet deny it. The audacity of the girl! The perverseness! Though what else can one expect with such a mother and an uncle in Cheapside? She refused to give the lie to the report, though I knew it must be false. I have never met such an impudent girl in my life. She trifled with me in the most vulgar way. When I told her that she must contradict the report, she replied only that I had declared it to be impossible, so it needed no contradiction. Of course, it is impossible. You are too proud a man to be drawn in, whatever arts she employed. To ally yourself with such a family! And through them, to ally yourself with George Wickham, the son of your father's steward. He, to call you brother! It is not to be thought of. To put an end to her schemes, I told her you were engaged to Anne, and do you know what she said to me?'

'No,' I said, not knowing what to make of Elizabeth's speech, but hoping – for the first time having reason to hope – that she was not firmly set against me.

'That if it was so, you could not possibly make an offer to her! She is lost to every feeling of propriety. Honour, decorum and modesty all forbid such a match! And yet she would not tell me the rumour was false. She thought nothing of the disgrace she would bring to a proud name, or the pollution she would inflict on the shades of Pemberley. Pemberley! When I think of such an ignorant girl at Pemberley! But of course it is impossible. You and Anne are formed for each other. You are descended from the same noble line. Your fortunes are splendid. And yet this upstart, without family, connections or fortune, would not give me an assurance that she would never marry you.'

My hopes soared. She had not decided against me! If she had, she would have told my aunt. Then there was still a chance for me.

'Well?' Lady Catherine demanded.

'Mama – ' began Anne timidly.

'Be silent, Anne,' commanded my aunt. 'Well, Darcy?' she demanded.

'Well?' I asked.

'Will you assure me that you will never ask this woman to be your wife?'

'No, Aunt, I will not.'

She glared at me.

'Then you are betrothed?'

'No, Aunt, we are not.'

'Ah. I thought not. You could not be so lost to what is right and proper, and to all common sense.'

'But if she will have me, I mean to make her my wife.'

Her silence was awful, and was followed by a torrent of words.

'You need not think you will be welcome at Rosings, if you marry that upstart. You will not bring such shame and degradation on my own house, even if you are absurd enough to bring it on your own. Your sainted mother would be appalled to discover what woman is to succeed her at Pemberley.'

'My mother would be glad I had chosen so well.'

'You have a fever. It is the only explanation,' she said. 'If you marry that girl you will be cut off from family and friends. They will not visit you, nor invite you to visit them in turn. You will be ostracized, cast out. I will give you a week to come to your senses. If I do not hear from you in that time, saying that you have been wholly mistaken in this preposterous plan, and if you do not beg my forgiveness for sullying my ears with this objectionable nonsense, then I will be aunt to you no more.'

I made her a cold bow and she swept out of the room. Anne hung back.

'I am sorry,' I said to her. 'I never knew you took our marriage as a settled thing until my cousin told me of it, or I would have made sure you knew that I did not regard myself as betrothed to you.'

'There is no need to be sorry. I did not want to marry you,' she said.

She smiled, and I was taken aback. There was no timidity in her smile, and as she walked up to me she looked confident and assured.

'Am I then so terrible?' I asked.

'No, not that. As a friend and a cousin I like you very well – as long as the weather is fine, and you are not forced to remain indoors – but I do not love you, and the thought of marrying you made me miserable. I am glad you are to marry Elizabeth. She is in love with you. She will tease you out of your stiffness, and we will all be friends.'

'She is in love with me? I wish I could be so sure.'

'One woman in love recognizes another,' she said.

She smiled again and then followed Lady Catherine out of the room.

Monday 6th October

I am once again at Netherfield. I arrived here with more

hope than I have ever felt, but still I dare not take Elizabeth's love as a settled thing. Bingley and I left Netherfield early and soon arrived at Longbourn. Miss Bennet was full of blushes and had never looked more becoming. Elizabeth was harder to understand. She, too, blushed. I wish I knew the cause!

Bingley suggested a walk.

'I will fetch my bonnet,' said Kitty. 'I have been longing to see Maria. We can walk to the Lucas's.'

Mrs Bennet frowned at her, but Kitty did not notice.

'I am not a great walker, I am afraid,' said Mrs Bennet, turning to Bingley with a smile. 'You must excuse me. But Jane loves to walk. Jane, my dear, fetch your spencer. That man, I suppose, will go, too,' she said, looking at me as though I was a disagreeable insect.

Elizabeth blushed. I ignored the remark as best I could, and thought that only my love for Elizabeth could induce me to set foot in that house ever again.

Bingley looked helpless.

'Lizzy, run and fetch your spencer, too. You must keep Mr Darcy company. I am sure he will not be interested in anything Jane has to say.'

'I am too busy to walk,' said Mary, lifting her head from a book. 'I have often observed that those who are the best walkers are those who lack the intellectual capacity to instruct themselves in the serious matters of life.'

'Oh, Mary!' said Mrs Bennet impatiently.

Mary returned to her book.

Elizabeth and her sister returned, having put on their

outdoor clothes, and we set out. Bingley and his beloved
soon fell behind. Kitty, I knew, would soon leave us to go
to visit her friend. Would Elizabeth go too? I hoped not.
If she remained with me, then I would be able to talk to
her. And talk to her I must.

We reached the turning to the Lucas's.

'You can go on by yourself,' said Elizabeth. 'I have
nothing to say to Maria.'

Kitty ran off down the path, leaving Elizabeth and me
alone.

I turned towards her.

Elizabeth, I was about to say, when she stopped me by
speaking herself.

'Mr Darcy, I am a very selfish creature; and, for the
sake of giving relief to my own feelings, care not how
much I may be wounding yours.'

I felt myself grow cold. All my hopes now seemed like
vanity. She was going to wound my feelings. I had been
wrong to read so much into her refusal to deny the
report of our engagement. It had meant nothing, except
that she would not deign to deny an idle report for the
benefit of my aunt.

She was obviously finding it difficult to continue.

She is going to tell me never to come to Longbourn
again, I thought. She cannot bear the sight of me. I have
given her a disgust of me that is too great to be overcome. I have not used my opportunities. I have visited
Longbourn with Bingley and said nothing, because I had
too much to say. Yet none of it could have been said in

front of others. And now it is too late. But I will not let
it be too late. I will speak to her, whether she wants me
to or not.

But then she went on, even as those thoughts were
going through my mind.

'I can no longer help thanking you – '

Thanking me? Not blaming me, but thanking me? I
scarcely knew what to think.

'– for your unexampled kindness to my poor sister.'

Unexampled kindness? Then she does not hate me!
The thought made my spirits rise, though cautiously, for
I did not know what she had heard of the business, or
what else she was going to say.

'Ever since I have known it, I have been most anxious
to acknowledge to you how gratefully I feel it. Were it
known to the rest of my family, I should not have merely
my own gratitude to express.'

Gratitude. I did not want her gratitude. Liking, yes.
Loving, yes. But not gratitude.

'I am sorry,' I said, 'exceedingly sorry, that you have
ever been informed of what may, in a mistaken light,
have given you uneasiness. I did not think Mrs Gardiner
was so little to be trusted.'

'You must not blame my aunt,' she said. 'It was Lydia
who told me of it, and then I asked my aunt for greater
detail. Let me thank you again and again,' went on
Elizabeth, 'in the name of all my family, for that generous compassion which induced you to take so much
trouble, and bear so many mortifications, for the sake

of discovering them.'

Generous compassion. She thought well of me, but in what way? I was in an agony of suspense.

'If you will thank me, let it be for yourself alone,' I said. My voice was low and impassioned. I could not hold my feelings in. 'Your family owe me nothing. Much as I respect them, I believe I thought only of you.'

I stopped breathing. I had spoken. I had let out my feelings. I had offered them to her, and could only wait to see if she would fling them back in my face. But she said nothing. Why did she not speak? Was she shocked? Horrified? Pleased? Then hope rose in my breast. Perhaps she was kept silent by pleasure? I had to know.

'You are too generous to trifle with me,' I burst out. 'If your feelings are still what they were last April, tell me so at once. My affections and wishes are unchanged. But one word from you will silence me on this subject for ever.'

It seemed to be an age before she spoke.

'My feelings are so different...' she began.

I started to breathe again.

'...that I am humbled to think you can still love me...'

I began to smile.

'...now I receive your assurances with gratitude and...and pleasure...'

'I have loved you for so long,' I said, as she slipped her hand through my arm and I covered it with my own. To claim her was a joy. 'I thought it was hopeless. I tried to forget you, but to no avail. When I saw you again at Pemberley I was overcome with surprise, but quickly blessed my good fortune. I had a chance to show you that I was not as mean-spirited as you thought me. I had a chance to show you that I could be a gentleman. When you did not spurn me, when you accepted my invitation, I dared to hope, but your sister's troubles took you away from me and I saw you no more. I could not let matters rest. I had to help your sister, in the knowledge that by doing so I was helping you. Then, when she was safely married, I had to see you. I was as nervous as Bingley when we arrived at Longbourn. It was clear that your sister was a woman in love, but I could tell nothing from your face or manner. Did you love me? Did you like me? Could you even tolerate me? I thought yes, then I thought no. You said so little – '

'Which was not in my nature,' she said with an arch smile.

'No,' I said, returning the smile. 'It was not. I did not know whether it was because you were displeased to see me or merely embarrassed.'

'I was embarrassed,' she said. 'I did not know why you had come. I was afraid of showing too much. I did not want to expose myself to ridicule. I could not believe that a man of your pride would offer his hand when it had already been rejected.'

'His hand, no, but his heart, yes. You are the only woman I have ever wanted to marry, and by accepting my hand you have put me forever in your debt.'

'I will remind you of it, when you are cross with me,'

she said teasingly.

'I could never be cross with you.'

'You think not, but when I pollute the shades of Pemberley, it is possible that you might!'

I laughed. 'Ah yes, my aunt expressed herself forcefully to both of us.'

'She told me I would never live at Pemberley,' said Elizabeth.

'I ought to dislike her for it, but I am too much in charity with her. It is her visit that brought me to you.'

'She came to see you?'

'She did. In London. She was in high dudgeon. She told me that she had been to see you, and that she had demanded that you contradict the rumour of our impending marriage. Your refusal to fall in with her wishes put her sadly out of countenance but it taught me to hope.'

I spoke of my letter. 'Did it,' I said, 'did it soon make you think better of me? Did you, on reading it, give any credit to its contents?'

'It made me think so much better of you, and so immediately, that I felt heartily ashamed of myself. I read it through again, and then again, and as I did so, every one of my prejudices was removed.'

'I knew that what I wrote must give you pain, but it was necessary. I hope you have destroyed the letter.'

'The letter shall certainly be burnt, if you believe it essential to the preservation of my regard; but, though we have both reason to think my opinions not entirely unalterable, they are not, I hope, quite so easily changed as that implies.'

'When I wrote that letter, I believed myself perfectly calm and cool, but I am since convinced that it was written in a dreadful bitterness of spirit.'

'The letter, perhaps, began in bitterness, but it did not end so. The adieu is charity itself. But think no more of the letter. The feelings of the person who wrote, and the person who received it, are now so widely different from what they were then, that every unpleasant circumstance attending it ought to be forgotten. You must learn some of my philosophy. Think only of the past as its remembrance gives you pleasure.'

I could not do it. I could not let the past go without telling her of my parents, good people in themselves who yet encouraged me to think well of myself and meanly of others. I told her how I was an only son, indeed an only child for much of my life, and how I had come to value none beyond my own family circle. 'By you, I was properly humbled. I came to you without a doubt of my reception. You showed me how insufficient were all my pretensions to please a woman worthy of being pleased.'

We talked of Georgiana and of Lydia, and of the day at the inn when Jane's letter had arrived. Talk of Jane naturally led to her engagement.

'I must ask whether you were surprised?' asked Elizabeth.

'Not at all. When I went away, I felt that it would soon happen.'

'That is to say, you had given your permission. I

guessed as much,' she teased me.

By this time we had reached the house. It was not until we went indoors that I realized how long we had been away.

'My dear Lizzy, where can you have been walking to?' asked her sister, as we sat down at the table.

Elizabeth coloured, but said: 'We wandered about, not paying attention to where we were going, and became lost.'

'I am sure I am sorry for it,' said Mrs Bennet, in a whisper loud enough for me to hear. 'It must have been very trying for you, having to talk to that disagreeable man.'

Elizabeth was mortified, but I caught her eye and smiled. Her mother may be the most dreadful woman it has been my misfortune to meet, but I would tolerate a dozen such mothers for the sake of Elizabeth.

I could not speak to her as I wished to during the evening. Jane and Bingley sat close together, talking of the future, but until I had asked Mr Bennet for Elizabeth's hand, she and I could not indulge in such discussions.

It was time for Bingley and me to return to Netherfield. I was able to relieve my feelings a little in the carriage going home.

'I have already wished you happy,' I said. 'Now you must do the same for me.'

Bingley looked surprised.

'I am to marry Elizabeth.'

'Elizabeth?'

'Yes. I proposed during our walk. She has agreed to marry me.'

'This is capital news! Almost as good as my own. She is just the wife for you. She is the only person I have ever met who can stand up to you. I shall never forget the way she teased you when she stayed with us at Netherfield, when Jane was ill. You were bored and in one of your stately moods. Caroline was admiring everything you said and did. I remember thinking it would be a tragedy if you married her, knowing she would confirm you in your conceit. She would convince you that you were above everyone else in every way. Not that you needed a great deal of convincing!'

I laughed.

'Was I really so arrogant?'

'You were,' said Bingley. 'You know you were! But Elizabeth will make sure you never become so again. When do you mean to marry?'

'As soon as possible. Elizabeth will need time to buy wedding clothes, and if she wishes me to make any alterations to Pemberley before she arrives then I will need time to attend to it. Otherwise, I would like to marry at once.'

'Changes to Pemberley? It must be love,' Bingley said. 'I am sure I hope you will be very happy.'

'We have been talking about that, Elizabeth and I. We have decided that you and Jane will be happy, but that we will be happier.'

'Oh no, on that we will never agree.'

The carriage rolled to a halt.

'Will you tell Caroline, or shall I?' asked Bingley, as we went in. Then he went on immediately: 'It might be better to let me tell her, or she might say something she regrets on first hearing the news.'

'As you wish.'

On entering the house, I retired to the library, to think of Elizabeth, and of the future.

Tuesday 7th October

I met Caroline at breakfast, and I was pleased to see how well she comported herself.

'I understand I am to wish you happy,' she remarked.

'Yes. I am to be married.'

'I am delighted,' she said. 'It is time you took a wife. Who would have thought, when we came to Netherfield last year, that both you and Charles would find true love.'

I ignored her droll tone.

'Perhaps one day you might be as fortunate.'

'I do not think I will ever marry,' she declared. 'I have no desire to let a man master me. When is the wedding to be?'

'Soon.'

'Then I must see my dressmaker. Two weddings in so short a space of time will require careful planning.'

'Oh, yes,' said Louisa. 'We must have something new.'

Soon after breakfast, Bingley and I set out again for Longbourn.

'Caroline was very well-behaved,' I said to him. 'I thought she took the news well.'

'She was not so very well-behaved when I told her,' said Bingley, 'but I reminded her that if she was not civil about it she would find herself excluded from Pemberley.'

We arrived. Mrs Bennet was all smiles as she greeted Bingley, and all grimaces as she made me a curtsy. How will she react when she knows I am to be her son-in-law?

Bingley looked at Elizabeth warmly, so that I am sure she guessed I had told him, then he said: 'Mrs Bennet, have you no more lanes hereabouts in which Lizzy may lose her way again today?'

Mrs Bennet was all too ready to fall in with his suggestion, eager to allow him a little privacy with Jane. She suggested we walk to Oakham Mount. Bingley, in lively humour, said he was sure it would be too much for Kitty, and Kitty agreed she would rather stay at home. It is a change to have Bingley ordering my life for me! But I could not complain, since a few minutes later I found myself out of doors and free to talk to Elizabeth.

'I must ask your father for his consent to the marriage,' I said, as we wandered towards the mount.

'And if he does not give it?' she asked with an arch smile.

'Then I will have to carry you off without it,' I said. 'Do you think he will withhold it?' I asked her more seriously.

'No. I am not afraid of what he might say. At least, not once he comes to know you, though to begin with he might be surprised. When Mr Collins's letter came...'

She broke off.

I looked at her enquiringly.

'Mr Collins wrote to him, telling him that I must not marry you, as it would anger Lady Catherine!'

'And what did your father reply?'

'He is too busy savouring the joke to write back.'

'I can see I will have a difficult time with him. Will he think I am joking when I ask for your hand?'

'I don't believe he will dare,' she said.

She spoke lightly, but I could tell she was troubled.

'I will take pains to know him,' I said. 'He and I will come to understand each other better, and I will make sure he does not ever regret giving his consent.'

We walked on.

'And then there is my mother,' she said.

'Will I stop being that man, do you think?' I asked her with a smile.

'Don't,' she said with a shudder. 'If you knew how many times I have blushed for her, or wished her to be silent. I think I will tell her when she is alone,' she went on. 'Then she will have a chance to overcome the first shock, and perhaps it will make her more rational when she speaks to you.'

'Exactly Bingley's feelings, when deciding it would be better if he told Caroline!'

'I wonder if she will continue to find your handwriting so even once you are married?'

'I fear not. She will probably think it uncommonly untidy.'

We reached the top of the mount.

'Well, and what do you think of the view?' Elizabeth asked me.

I turned to look at her.

'I like it very much,' I said.

She looked so beautiful that I gave in to the urge to kiss her. She was surprised at first, but then responded warmly, and I knew our marriage would be a happy one in every way.

We walked on together, talking of the future. I am eager to show Elizabeth Pemberley, not as a visitor, but as its future mistress.

'You will not mind my aunt and uncle visiting?' she asked.

'Of course not. I liked them.'

'And my sisters?'

'Jane and Bingley will be with us often. Your younger sisters are welcome to come whenever they, or you, choose. But I will not have Wickham there.'

We rejoined Jane and Bingley and returned to Long-bourn.

Throughout the evening, Elizabeth was not at ease. I longed to put her out of her misery, but could not speak to Mr Bennet until after dinner. As soon as I saw him withdraw to the library, I followed him.

'Mr Darcy,' he said in surprise, as I closed the library door behind me.

'I would like to speak to you,' I said.

'I am at your disposal. You have heard, I suppose, of the rumour that you are to marry Elizabeth and want it stopped, but I advise you to enjoy it for its absurdity, instead of fretting over what is a harmless piece of non-sense.'

'I don't find it in the least bit absurd,' I said to him. 'I find it highly desirable. I have followed you in order to ask you for Elizabeth's hand in marriage.'

His mouth fell open.

'Ask me for Elizabeth's hand in marriage?' he repeated at last.

'Yes.'

'But there must be some mistake.'

'There is no mistake.'

'But I thought…that is, Mr Collins is such a fool! He is forever regaling me with some new and preposterous story, and I was sure he must have made a mistake. You, who have never looked at Elizabeth in your life! And yet now you tell me you want to marry her.'

'I do. I love her, and as for not singling her out for attention, I have done little else. You have not been there, however, so I cannot blame you for being surprised. When she was a guest at Netherfield, I had the pleasure of her company for almost a week, and I spent much of my time with her. I saw her again in Kent, when she was visiting Mrs Collins, and we came to know each other well. I met her more recently in Derbyshire, and each time I have met her, I have loved her more. My feelings are not of a short duration. They are longstanding, and will not change.'

'But she has always hated you!' he said. 'For any man to persist against such obvious aversion is madness.'

At this I smiled.

'I can assure you I am quite sane. Her aversion has been overcome long ago. I have already asked her to marry me, and she has said yes.'

'Said yes!' exclaimed Mr Bennet in faint tones.

'And as the two of us are in agreement, we need only your permission to set a date.'

'And if I do not give it?'

'Then I am afraid I will have to marry her without it.'

He looked at me as though deciding if I was serious. Then, collecting his wits, he said: 'If it is as you say, and Elizabeth really wishes to marry you, then you may have my consent and my blessing. But I want to hear it from her own lips. Send her to me.'

I left him and went to Elizabeth. She saw from my face that he had given his consent.

'He wants to speak to you.'

She nodded, and left the room.

Mrs Bennet, who had been talking to Jane and Bingley, looked up at this.

'Where has Lizzy gone?' she asked Jane.

'I do not know,' Jane replied, though from her face I could tell she had guessed.

'She has made an excuse to leave the room, being tired of talking to that disagreeable gentleman, I suppose,' said Mrs Bennet, not taking the trouble to lower her voice. 'I do not blame her. Now, Jane, you must have a new dress for your wedding. What colour do you think it should be? I was married in blue,' she said, 'in quite the most beautiful dress, not like the fashions nowadays. It had a wide skirt, and a pointed bodice. We must make sure you have something equally fine. Satin, I think, or Bruges lace.'

Jane cast me an apologetic look at the start of this speech, and then attended to her mother, but I scarcely heard Mrs Bennet's effusions. I was wondering what was happening in the library. Elizabeth seemed to be gone for a very long time. What was her father saying to her? Was it really taking her so long to convince him of her feelings for me?

'I have often observed, that the finery of the wedding-gown has no bearing on the happiness of the marriage,' said Mary, looking up from her book. 'Such things are all vanity, set to entrap the incautious female and lead her down the path of temptation.'

'Oh, hush Mary, be quiet, no one asked you,' said Mrs Bennet, annoyed. 'When you find a husband, you may prose on the nature of wedding gowns as much as you like.'

Mary was silenced.

'When I marry, I will have a satin underskirt and a gauze overskirt,' said Kitty, 'and I will not run off with my husband and live with him in London first.'

'Kitty, be quiet,' said Mrs Bennet. She turned to Bingley with a smile. 'What will you wear, Mr Bingley? A blue coat or a black one? Wickham was married in his blue coat. My dear Wickham!' she said with a sigh. 'Such a handsome man. But not nearly as handsome as you.'

I caught Bingley's eye. It was probable that, if Wickham had had five thousand a year, he would have been allowed to be as handsome as Bingley.

'I will wear whatever Jane wishes,' he said.

Where was Elizabeth? I felt my impatience growing. At last she returned to the room and smiled. All was well.

The evening passed quietly. I received a cold nod from Mrs Bennet when I left, and I wondered what her reception of me would be on the morrow. I saw lines of strain around Elizabeth's mouth, and I knew she was not looking forward to her interview with her mother.

'By this time tomorrow it will be done,' I said.

She nodded, then Bingley and I departed.

'Her father gave his consent?' asked Bingley, as we returned to Netherfield.

'He did.'

'Jane and I have already set a date for our wedding. We were wondering what you and Elizabeth would think of a double wedding?'

I was much struck by the idea.

'I like it. If Elizabeth is agreeable, then that is what we will do.'

Wednesday 8th October

Bingley and I were at Longbourn early this morning.

'Mr Bingley,' said Mrs Bennet, fidgeting as she welcomed him. She turned to me, and I felt Elizabeth grow tense. But her mother merely looked at me in awe and said: 'Mr Darcy.'

There was no coldness in her tone. Indeed she seemed stunned. I made her a bow and went to sit beside Elizabeth.

The morning passed off well. Mrs Bennet took the younger girls upstairs with her on some pretext, and Elizabeth and I were free to talk. When luncheon was served, Mrs Bennet sat on one side of me, and Elizabeth on the other.

'Some hollandaise sauce, Mr Darcy?' said Mrs Bennet. 'I believe you like sauces.'

I cast my eyes over the table, and saw no less than six sauce-boats. I was about to refuse the hollandaise sauce when I caught sight of Elizabeth's mortified expression and I determined to repay Mrs Bennet's new civility with a civility of my own.

'Thank you.'

I took some hollandaise sauce.

'And béarnaise? I had it made specially.'

I hesitated, but then put a spot of béarnaise sauce next to the hollandaise sauce.

'And some port-wine sauce?' she said. 'I hope you will take a little. Cook made it specially.'

I took some port-wine sauce and looked at my plate in dismay. I caught Elizabeth's eye and saw her laughing. I took some béchamel sauce, mustard sauce and a cream sauce as well, and then set about eating my strange meal.

'You are enjoying your luncheon?' asked Mrs Bennet solicitously.

'Yes, thank you.'

'It is not what you are used to, I suppose.'

I could honestly say that it was not.

'You have two or three French cooks, I suppose?'

'No, I have only the one cook, and she is English.'

'She is your cook at Pemberley?'

'Yes, she is.'

'Pemberley,' said Mrs Bennet. 'How grand it sounds. I am glad Lizzy refused Mr Collins, for a parsonage is nothing to Pemberley. I expect the chimney piece will be even bigger than the one at Rosings. How much did it cost, Mr Darcy?'

'I am not sure.'

'Very likely a thousand pounds or more.'

'It must be difficult to maintain,' said Mr Bennet. 'Even at Longbourn, it is difficult to keep up with all the repairs.'

We fell into a discussion about our estates, and I found Mr Bennet to be a sensible man. He might be negligent where his family are concerned, but his duties in other areas are carried out responsibly.

I have to forgive him the former negligence as it produced Elizabeth. Her liveliness and vitality would have been crushed under an ordinary upbringing.

I have decided that Georgiana must have a spell without a governess or a companion, so that she might develop her own spirit. I am sure that Elizabeth will agree.

Friday 10th October

Elizabeth began to ask me how I had fallen in love with her.

'How could you begin?' she asked. 'I can comprehend your going on charmingly, when you had once
made a beginning; but what could set you off in the
first place?'

I thought. What was it that had started me falling in
love with her? Was it when she had looked at me satirically at the assembly? Or when she had walked through
the mud to see Jane? Or when she had neglected to flatter me, not telling me how well I wrote? Or when she
had refused to try and attract my attention?

'I cannot fix on the hour, or the spot, or the look, or
the words, which laid the foundation. It is too long ago.
I was in the middle before I knew I had begun.'

She teased me, saying I had resisted her beauty, and
therefore I must have fallen in love with her impertinence.

'To be sure, you know no actual good of me – but
nobody thinks of that when they fall in love.'

'Was there no good in your affectionate behaviour to
Jane, while she was ill at Netherfield?'

'Dearest Jane! Who could have done less for her? But
make a virtue of it by all means. My good qualities are
under your protection, and you are to exaggerate them as
much as possible.'

'You do not easily take offence. It cannot have been
easy for you to be at Netherfield – you were not made
very welcome – and yet you were amused rather than
otherwise by our rudeness.'

'I like to laugh,' she admitted.

'And you are loyal to your friends. You berated me

over my treatment of Wickham – '

'Do not speak of him!' she begged me. 'I can hardly bear to think about it.'

'But I can. He is a loathsome individual, but you did not know that at the time, and you defended him. There are not many women who would defend a poor friend against a rich and eligible bachelor.'

'However undeserving the "friend" might be,' she said ruefully.

'And you were not afraid to change your mind when you learnt the truth. You did not cling to your prejudices, regarding either Wickham or myself. You admitted the justice of what I said.'

'Yes, I acknowledged that a man who does not give a living to a wastrel is not a brute. That is a sign of great goodness, indeed!'

'You did everything in your power to help Lydia, even though you knew her to be thoughtless and wild,' I pointed out.

'She is my sister. I could hardly abandon her to a rogue,' she replied.

'But I am allowed to exaggerate your good points,' I reminded her. 'You said so yourself.'

She laughed.

'Poor Lydia. I thought she had ruined my chance of happiness with you for ever. I could not imagine you would want to be connected to a family in which one of the girls had eloped, especially not as she had eloped with your greatest enemy.'

'I never thought of that. You had taught me by then that such things do not matter.'

'I had taught you more than I realized, then. When you came to Longbourn, after Lydia's marriage – '

'Yes?'

'You said so little. I thought you did not care about me.'

'Because you were grave and silent, and gave me no encouragement.'

'I was embarrassed,' she said.

'And so was I.'

'Tell me, why did you come to Netherfield? Was it merely so that you could ride to Longbourn and be embarrassed? Or had you intended any more serious consequence?'

'My real purpose was to see you, and to judge, if I could, whether I might ever hope to make you love me. My avowed one, or what I avowed to myself, was to see whether your sister were still partial to Bingley, and if she were, to make the confession to him which I have since made.'

'Shall you ever have courage to announce to Lady Catherine, what is to befall her?'

'I am more likely to want time than courage, Elizabeth. But it ought to be done, and if you will give me a sheet of paper, it shall be done directly.'

Whilst I composed my letter to Lady Catherine, Elizabeth composed a letter to her aunt and uncle in Gracechurch Street. Hers was easier to write than mine, because it would give pleasure, whereas mine would give distress. But it had to be done.

> *Lady Catherine,*
> *I am sure you will want to wish me happy. I have asked Miss Elizabeth Bennet to marry me, and she has done me the great honour of saying yes.*
> > *Your nephew,*
> > *Fitzwilliam Darcy*

'And now I will write a far pleasanter letter,' I said. I took another sheet of paper and wrote to Georgiana.

> *My dear sister,*
> *I know you will be delighted to hear that Elizabeth and I are to marry. I will tell you everything when I see you next.*
> > *Your loving brother,*
> > *Fitzwilliam*

It was short, but I had time for no more. I read it through, sanded it and addressed the envelope.

'Shall you mind having another sister?' I asked Elizabeth.

'Not at all. I am looking forward to it. She will live with us at Pemberley?'

'If you have no objection?'

'None at all.'

'She can learn a great deal from you.'

'And I from her. She will be able to tell me all about the Pemberley traditions.'

'You must alter anything you do not like.'

'No, I will not alter anything. My aunt and I are already agreed, Pemberley is perfect just as it is.'

Tuesday 14th October

Elizabeth is delighted with Georgiana's letter, which arrived this morning. It was well written, and in four pages expressed Georgiana's delight at the prospect of having a sister.

Less welcome was Lady Catherine's letter.

> *Fitzwilliam,*
>
> *I do not call you nephew, for you are no longer a nephew of mine. I am shocked and astonished that you could stoop to offer your hand to a person of such low breeding. It is a stain on the honour and credit of the name of Darcy. She will bring you nothing but degradation and embarrassment, and she will reduce your house to a place of impertinence and vulgarity. Your children will be wild and undisciplined. Your daughters will run off with stable hands and your sons will become attorneys. You will never be received by any of your acquaintance. You will be disgraced in the eyes of the world, and will become a figure of contempt. You will*

*bitterly regret this day. You will remember that I
warned you of the consequences of such a disastrous act, but by then it will be too late. I will
not end this letter by wishing you happiness, for
no happiness can follow such a blighted union.*
                          Lady Catherine de Bourgh

Wednesday 15th October

I dined with Elizabeth this evening, and I was surprised
to find a large party there, consisting of Mrs Philips, Sir
William Lucas and Mr and Mrs Collins. The unexpected
appearance of the Collinses was soon explained. Lady
Catherine has been rendered so exceedingly angry by
our engagement that they thought it wiser to leave Kent
for a time and retreat to Lucas Lodge.

Elizabeth and Charlotte had much to discuss, and
whilst the two of them talked before dinner, I was left to
the tender mercies of Mr Collins.

'I was delighted to learn that you had offered your
hand to my fair cousin, and that she, in her gracious and
womanly wisdom, had accepted you,' he said, beaming. 'I
now understand why she could not accept the proposal I
so injudiciously made to her last autumn, when I knew
nothing of the present felicitous happenings. I thought at
the time that it was strange that such an amiable young
woman would refuse the wholly unexceptionable hand of
an estimable young man, particularly one who possessed
so fine a living, and who, if I may say so, had the advantages of his calling to offer her as well as the advantages of

his person. The refusal seemed inexplicable to me at the time, but I fully comprehend it now. My fair cousin had lost her heart to one who, if I may say so, is, by virtue of his standing, more worthy even than a clergyman, for he has the clergyman's fate in his hands.'

I saw Elizabeth looking satirically at me, but I bore his conversation with composure. I might even, in time, grow to be amused by it.

'Admirably expressed,' said Sir William Lucas, as he joined us. He bowed to me, and then to Mr Collins, and then to me again. 'Only such worth could resign us to the fact that you will be carrying away the brightest jewel of our county when you carry Elizabeth to Derbyshire,' he continued with another bow. 'I hope we will all of us meet very frequently, either at Longbourn or at St James's.'

Fortunately we then went in to dinner, but though I was relieved from the company of Mr Collins and Sir William, I found myself seated next to Mrs Philips. She seemed too much in awe of me to say very much, but when she did speak, it was all of it very vulgar.

'So, Mr Darcy, it is true you have ten thousand a year?' she asked.

I looked at her quellingly.

'I am sure it must be, for I have heard it talked of everywhere. And is Pemberley bigger than Rosings?'

When I did not reply, she asked the question again.

'It is,' I said.

'And how much was the chimney-piece? Mr Collins was telling me that the chimney-piece at Rosings cost eight hundred pounds. I expect the chimney-piece at Pemberley must have cost over a thousand pounds. My sister and I were talking of it only the other day. "Depend on it," I said, "it will have been well over a thousand pounds". "Very likely it cost more than twelve hundred pounds", she returned. It is a good thing Lizzy did not marry Mr Collins, after all, though my sister was annoyed enough at the time, but what is Mr Collins to Mr Darcy? Even Lady Lucas agrees that he is nothing whatsoever. Ten thousand a year. The dresses, the carriages she will have.'

I bore her remarks as best I could, and I look forward to the day when I will have Elizabeth with me at Pemberley, free of all her relations.

Tuesday 28th October

I did not know that I could feel so nervous, but this morning I felt almost as nervous as the day on which I asked Elizabeth to marry me. Bingley and I went to the church together. I believe he was even more anxious than I was when we went in and took our places at the front.

The guests began to arrive. Mr Collins was the first. His wife was not with him, for she was to be Elizabeth's attendant. Mrs Philips followed closely after. The Lucases arrived, then a number of Elizabeth's acquaintances. Of my own relatives there was only Colonel Fitzwilliam and my sister, Georgiana. Lady Catherine and Anne did not attend. I did not expect it, and I was relieved that aunt had decided to stay away, but I would have liked to have seen Anne, and I suspect she would have liked to see me married safely to Elizabeth.

The church filled. The guests took their seats. Bingley and I exchanged glances. We looked to the door. We looked back again. I glanced at my watch. Bingley glanced at his. He smiled nervously. I smiled reassuringly. He nodded. I clasped my hands. And then we heard a sigh and, looking round, I beheld Elizabeth. She was walking up the aisle on her father's arm, with Jane on his other arm. But I had no eyes for Jane. I had eyes only for Elizabeth. She looked radiant. I felt my nervousness leave me as she joined me, taking her place next to me as Jane took her place next to Bingley.

The service was simple but it touched me deeply. As Elizabeth and I exchanged vows I thought there could not have been a happier man in all England.

We left the church, and as I looked down at Elizabeth I knew she was now Mrs Darcy.

'Mrs Darcy!' said her mother, echoing my thoughts. 'How well it sounds. And Mrs Bingley! Oh! If I can but see my other two daughters so well married I will have nothing left to wish for.'

We returned to Longbourn for the wedding-breakfast, and then Elizabeth and I set off for a tour of the Lake District. Jane and Bingley went with us. We stopped for the night at a small inn and I am making the most of the opportunity to write my diary, for there will not be time later. I am looking forward to this evening. After dinner, our true marriage will begin.

November

Tuesday 11th November

Today we returned to Pemberley, after our honeymoon by the lakes. Elizabeth looked well and happy. I watched her as the carriage rolled up the drive, seeing in her face her delight at her new home.

The carriage pulled up outside the door. We went in. Mrs Reynolds had assembled the staff, and they welcomed us. Mrs Reynolds, I know, is delighted to see a mistress at Pemberley again.

We went up to our rooms. I went into her suite with Elizabeth. It was the only set of rooms she wanted altered, and it had been decorated just as she wished.

'Do you like it?' I asked.

She looked round her appreciatively. 'It is perfect.'

I went over to her and kissed her.

'Do you like it?' she asked, looking round at the room again.

'It does not matter if I like it or not.'

'I think it does,' she teased me. 'After all, you will be a frequent visitor.'

I smiled and kissed her again.

It was some hours later when we went downstairs.

'Are you sure you do not want any of the other rooms redecorated?' I asked her, as we entered the dining-parlour.

'No, I like them just the way they are. They remind me of my first visit to Pemberley.' She walked over to the window and looked out. 'It is a beautiful prospect.'

I agreed. The wooded hill was lovely, and the river sparkled as it wound its way through the valley. I love every tree and every blade of grass, and it warms me to know that she loves it, too.

'What did you think when you first saw it?' I asked her.

She smiled mischievously. 'That I might have been the mistress of all this, if I had accepted you!'

'And did you regret it?'

'For a minute – until I remembered that I would not have been allowed to welcome my aunt and uncle here.'

'I cannot believe I was ever so proud. If not for your aunt and uncle, we might never have met again. We will welcome them any time you wish to do so.'

I put my arms round her.

'We must have them to stay soon. I have promised my aunt she can ride round the park in a phaeton and a pair of ponies.' She turned in the circle of my arms and stroked my cheek. 'But we will not invite them just yet.'

Tuesday 18th November

We have been at Pemberley for a week, and Elizabeth and Georgiana are getting on together as well as I could have hoped. Georgiana is starting to lose some of her shyness through her nearness to Elizabeth, and although she is not as playful as Elizabeth, she has ventured to tease me on one or two occasions.

I finally feel I can be a brother to Georgiana again, and not a father and mother. She is growing up now, and with Elizabeth to guide me, I no longer worry that I do not understand young ladies. If I am ever in doubt, I have only to ask Elizabeth.

Life is a great deal easier for Georgiana, too, because she has a confidante as well as a sister in Elizabeth.

Thursday 20th November

Elizabeth received a letter from Lydia this morning, asking for help with some bills. I came upon her by chance as she was reading it in her bedroom. She looked up guiltily as I walked in.

'Secrets?' I asked.

She looked rueful.

'It is from Lydia. She is so extravagant that she has exceeded her income again. She writes to me that it must be nice to be so rich, and she asks for my help.'

'You will not give it to her?' I saw her face. 'You will.'

'She is my sister, after all,' she said.

'Let her ask Jane.'

'She has already asked Jane,' said Elizabeth, her playfulness returning. 'I feel she means to ask us each in turn.'

'You should say no. Then she will learn to manage.'

'Not Lydia! She will run up bills until the shopkeepers demand payment, and then she and Wickham will change lodgings and start all over again. Think of it this way, I am not helping Lydia, I am helping the shopkeepers she is cheating.'

With this she knew I would agree.

'I never cease to wonder how it is that you and Jane turned out so well, when your other sisters turned out so ill,' I said, going over to her and kissing her on the cheek.

'Kitty is not so bad,' said Elizabeth. 'I was thinking of having her to stay with us. After our Christmas party next month, I am going to invite her to stay on. Some superior company will do much to influence her for the better.'

'If you must, you must. I would rather have you to myself.'

'She will not be indoors all the time. She will go for long walks with Georgiana,' said Elizabeth.

'Or long carriage rides,' I said, kissing her on the lips.

'Or picnics,' said Elizabeth, kissing me in return.

'My love, I had better lock the door.'

December

Friday 5th December

Elizabeth has ordered a phaeton and pair for Christmas. Her aunt and uncle will be joining us, and they will be here in just over a fortnight. Elizabeth has persuaded me that I must invite my aunt, too. It is time to put an end to the hostilities, she says, and she is right. I cannot be on bad terms with Lady Catherine for ever.

Jane and Bingley are coming to stay, and they are bringing with them Caroline and Louisa. Mr and Mrs Bennet will also be coming with Mary and Kitty, and Lydia will be one of their party. I have reluctantly agreed to welcome her, but on condition that Wickham does not come with her. I will not have him at Pemberley, now or ever. Elizabeth understands. She has no wish to see him, and we both know it would be mortifying for Georgiana.

The two people we will not see are Mr and Mrs Collins. Charlotte is in an interesting condition and cannot travel. Elizabeth has reminded me to look for a living for Mr Collins, something better than the one he has at present.

'A larger house for Charlotte,' said Elizabeth, 'and one with plenty to keep Mr Collins occupied. If there is something for him to do outside the house, perhaps some alms-houses to run, so much the better. And make sure the house has two pleasant rooms, so that Charlotte can have one as well as her husband.'

'Very well, but I will not have them within an hour's drive of Pemberley. I like Charlotte well enough, but not even your friendship with her can reconcile me to her husband.'

In this, Elizabeth and I are as one.

Saturday 13th December

Our guests will all be arriving on Monday. One more has been added to their number. Colonel Fitzwilliam will be coming with Lady Catherine and Anne.

Monday 15th December

At last, they are here. Bingley and Jane were the first to arrive, bringing with them Caroline and Louisa.

'Mrs Darcy,' said Caroline, with an excess of civility. 'How pleased I am to see you again.' She smiled as though she and Elizabeth had always been the best of friends, then turned to me. 'Mr Darcy, how well you look,' she said. 'And Georgiana. How you have grown! It must be this Derbyshire air. It is so invigorating.'

Louisa was less vocal but greeted us pleasantly. Mr Hurst merely grunted before retiring to the billiard room. Caroline and Louisa went upstairs, led there by Georgiana, and Elizabeth and I were free to talk to Jane and Bingley.

'So Lydia is coming?' asked Bingley, as we all sat down in the drawing-room.

'Yes, she is, though not her husband,' said Elizabeth. 'You do not think it wrong of me not to invite him?' she asked Jane.

'Dear Lizzy, of course not. It is not as though he and

Lydia have nowhere else to go. They have been to stay with us twice already. It is cheaper for them to stay with us than to live on their own. They gave up one set of lodgings before coming to us, so that they would not have to pay any rent, and then they took another set when they returned.'

'How very distressing,' said Elizabeth.

'Not to Lydia. She is the same as ever, exuberant and high spirited. She thrives on the change.'

'The next time they come, I think I will have the servants say we are not at home!' said Bingley.

'We are too convenient at Netherfield, that is the trouble,' said Jane. 'They visit Longbourn, and then they come to us when they have outstayed their welcome there. And it is not only Lydia who visits us. It seems that every day my mother finds some reason to call. We are thinking of taking a house elsewhere.'

'Poor Jane! You must come and live in Derbyshire,' said Elizabeth.

'There are some very fine properties hereabouts,' I said.

'I think we might,' said Bingley.

A coach drawing up outside alerted us to the fact that Lady Catherine had arrived. She descended with all state and entered the house. A few minutes later she swept into the drawing-room without waiting to be announced.

She looked round with a jaundiced eye.

'The furniture has not been replaced, I see,' she said, without greeting either myself or Elizabeth. 'I thought you would have put my sister's furniture in the attic and replaced it with something of inferior workmanship.'

'Your ladyship cannot think I would wish to spoil my own home,' said Elizabeth.

'Your home. Hah!' said my aunt.

Elizabeth cast me a satirical glance, but making a determined effort she welcomed Lady Catherine, Anne and Colonel Fitzwilliam.

'We meet again,' he said.

'We do.'

'And in happy circumstances. Darcy is a lucky man,' he told her.

'Darcy is no such thing,' said my aunt. 'He should have married Anne.'

Anne cast her eyes to the floor.

'You had a good journey, I hope?' Elizabeth asked her.

Anne raised her eyes a little but did not reply. I was struck by the difference in her demeanour from the last time I had seen her, and I thought of what my cousin had said, that she had much more spirit away from her mother.

'Anne's health is precarious. She never travels well,' said my aunt.

'But the journey was good,' said Colonel Fitzwilliam. 'Lady Catherine's coach is comfortable, and the roads were not too bad.'

'Let me show you to your rooms,' said Elizabeth.

'That is the housekeeper's job,' said Lady Catherine disdainfully.

'Then I will ask Mrs Reynolds to show you the way,' said Elizabeth. She turned to Anne. 'Allow me to show you to your room,' she said. 'It is the room you always have. I asked Mrs Reynolds which one was yours.'

Anne cast a worried glance at her mother, but allowed Elizabeth to lead her upstairs. Jane went with them, whilst my aunt had to wait for Mrs Reynolds.

Colonel Fitzwilliam laughed. 'Elizabeth is afraid of no one,' he said, when Mrs Reynolds had taken Lady Catherine upstairs.

'Of course not,' said Bingley. 'She married Darcy! Though I think he is not quite so awful as he used to be. Marriage suits him.'

'It suits both of you. Perhaps I ought finally to take the step myself,' said the Colonel.

Elizabeth rejoined us, and soon the other ladies found their way to the drawing-room. My aunt and Anne already knew Caroline and Louisa, and once the four of them had exchanged greetings, my aunt began to speak, only to break off as she heard another carriage arrive.

'Who is this?' she asked, glancing out of the window.

'My aunt and uncle!' cried Elizabeth, jumping up.

'The uncle who is an attorney, or the uncle who lives in Cheapside?' asked Lady Catherine contemptuously.

Elizabeth did not reply, but went forward to greet her guests as soon as they entered the room.

'Elizabeth! How well you look,' said Mrs Gardiner.

She was dressed fashionably, and had an air of style about her.

'Positively blooming,' added Mr Gardiner.

I saw that Elizabeth was pleased by the look of surprise on Caroline's face. We exchanged glances, and our thoughts went back to the first time I had met the Gardiners, when I, too, had been pleasantly surprised.

There followed the usual conversation about the roads, and then talk of the Gardiner's carriage led on to Elizabeth saying: 'I have the phaeton and pair all ready for you, just as you requested. As soon as you feel like travelling again, we will take it round the park.'

'A phaeton and pair? What is this? An equipage for an outing? I must have my share of the pleasure. I like a ride round the park of all things. I would have learned to drive if Sir Lewis had taught me, and I would have excelled at it,' said Lady Catherine. 'Sir Lewis told me so himself. You must let me know when you mean to go. I will come with you, and so will Anne.'

'But there are only two seats,' Elizabeth pointed out.

'Then Anne and I will take the carriage.'

'I am persuaded your ladyship will not like the expedition,' said Elizabeth. 'We will not only be going down by the river, we will also be going through the woods.'

'What does that signify?' demanded Lady Catherine. 'The woods are my greatest pleasure. When my sister was alive, we drove there often.'

'But, as your ladyship informed me at our last meeting, my presence has polluted them,' said Elizabeth archly.

My aunt could think of no reply. I have never known her to be lost for words, and it was a welcome experience.

She was not to be bested, however, and after a minute she overcame her astonishment and said: 'Your mother and sisters are coming, I understand?'

'Yes, they are.'

'All of them?'

'Yes, all of them.'

'What, even the one who ran off with the son of Darcy's steward?'

'Yes. Even Lydia,' said Elizabeth gravely, but with a smile in her eye.

'I hear your mother received her at Longbourn, after her scandalous behaviour. It cannot be true, of course. The report must be false. No mother could endorse such infamy on the part of her daughter. She would immediately cast her off and leave her to suffer the consequences of her behaviour.'

In her estimation of Mrs Bennet's character she was entirely wrong. Mrs Bennet arrived soon after her brother and his wife, and not only did she endorse Lydia's behaviour, she gloried in it.

'Lady Catherine, how good it is to see you again,' she said as she made her curtsy. 'It seems like only yesterday you were visiting us at Longbourn, bringing us word of Charlotte on your way through the village. If you had told me then what I know now, I should not have believed you. My Lizzy, to marry Mr Darcy! Of course, it is not to be wondered at. She has always been a very good sort of girl, quite her father's favourite, and though Jane has more beauty, Lizzy has more wit, though of course I should not call her Lizzy any more, I should call her Mrs Darcy. Mrs Darcy! How well it sounds. And to think, she is the mistress of Pemberley! I knew she could not be so lively for nothing. Pemberley is a very fine house. I had no idea it would be quite so fine. Lucas Lodge is nothing to it, and it is even better than the great house at Stoke. As for Purvis Lodge, it has the most dreadful attics, but Lizzy – Mrs Darcy – assures me that the attics at Pemberley are quite the best she has ever seen.'

'I am sure she will give you a tour of them, if you ask her nicely,' said Mr Bennet dryly, as he stepped forward and kissed Elizabeth. 'How are you, Lizzy? You look well.'

'I am well, Papa.'

'Darcy is treating you well?'

'Yes, he is.'

'Good. Then I do not have to challenge him to a duel.'

'I hope you will go fishing with me instead, sir,' I said.

'I will be glad to do so.'

'And you, too, are included in the invitation, of course,' I said to Mr Gardiner.

'It will give me great pleasure.'

'What do you think of my bonnet, Lizzy?' asked Lydia, coming forward. 'Is it not delightful? I got it yesterday.'

'I thought you needed to economize,' said Elizabeth.

'I did,' said Lydia. 'There were three bonnets I liked in the shop, and I bought only the one.'

'From all I have read, the practising of economy does not come naturally to females,' said Mary. 'They must study it diligently if they are not to let their expenditure exceed their income.'

'Well said, Mary. Very well put,' said Mrs Bennet. She turned to Colonel Fitzwilliam. 'Such an accomplished girl. She reads I do not know how many books. She will make some lucky soldier an excellent wife.'

For the first time in my life, I saw my cousin non-plussed. He was not required to reply, however, for whilst Lydia went over to the mirror and began to admire her-self, Mrs Bennet resumed her conversation.

'When you drove away from us after your visit to Longbourn, Lady Catherine, I had no more idea of our being related than I had of the cat going to see the queen, but now we are family.'

'Indeed we are not,' said my aunt indignantly.

'But yes! Your nephew is married to my daughter. That makes us cousins of a sort. My cousin, Lady Catherine! How envious Lady Lucas was when I told her, for she is not a real lady of course, she was only made a lady when Sir William was given a knighthood, on account of an address he made to the king. She was plain Mrs Lucas before that, and her husband was in trade in Meryton. He gave it up when he was made Sir William, but birth shows.'

'It does indeed,' remarked Lady Catherine pointedly. 'And this is the girl who ran off with the steward's son?' she demanded, turning to Kitty.

'No, I am not,' said Kitty, blushing.

'This is my second youngest, Kitty,' said Mrs Bennet. 'Such a good girl! Such manners! And in the way to becoming a beauty. She will turn heads before she is much older, mark my words. Not that she has not already done so. Captain Denny was very taken with her, and there were one or two other officers who singled Kitty out, though she is so young, but – '

'It cannot be you,' said Lady Catherine, cutting across Mrs Bennet and turning to Lydia. 'You are a child.'

Lydia did not turn round but, having removed her bonnet, fluffed her curls in front of the mirror.

'La! What nonsense you do speak!' she declared. 'I have been married these four months. My dear Wickham and I were married in September. I am quite the matron.' She turned round and faced Lady Catherine. 'I am so pleased to meet you,' she said, extending her hand as though she was a duchess and my aunt a farmer's wife. 'My dear Wickham's told me all about you.'

'Has he indeed,' said Lady Catherine awfully, ignoring her hand.

Lydia dropped it, unabashed, and turned to Colonel Fitzwilliam, going towards him with hand outstretched.

'La! An officer. It does my heart good to see a red coat. It reminds me of my dear Wickham.'

'I always liked a man in a red coat,' said Mrs Bennet to Lady Catherine. 'Lydia takes after me.'

'Unfortunately for those of us who like rational conversation,' said Mr Bennet. 'Darcy, do you have a billiard room here?'

'I do, sir. Allow me to show it to you. Gentlemen?'

And so saying, I rescued them from the ladies.

'My wife is a constant source of amusement to me,' said Mr Bennet as we left the room, 'and Lydia even more so. I had great hopes of Mary, but she has become less silly now that she goes out more, and doesn't suffer in comparison with her sisters, though her outburst today gives me hope that her silliness has not entirely disappeared. Kitty, too, looks set to disappoint me. She has become so rational a creature now that she spends two days out of every three at Netherfield that I fear she will grow up to be a sensible young lady after all.'

I am still not easy with Mr Bennet's way of speaking of his daughters, but as his levity helped to shape Elizabeth's playful character, I suppose I cannot complain.

Tuesday 16th December

Elizabeth took her aunt through the grounds in the phaeton and pair today as promised, and the two of them returned with bright eyes and a healthy glow on their cheeks.

'And do you like Pemberley as much as the last time you visited?' I asked her.

'Far better,' she replied. 'Then, it was simply a fine house. Now it is Elizabeth's home.'

'It must be an enjoyable way of seeing the grounds,' said Anne.

There was a trace of wistfulness in her voice. Elizabeth heard it, and said, 'You must take a drive with me this afternoon.'

I blessed her for it. Anne has little pleasure in her life, I believe.

They set out after lunch, and though their trip was shorter than the previous one, they returned in lively mood.

'I think I have misjudged Anne,' said Elizabeth later. 'I, who used to pride myself on my ability to judge people on first impressions, seem to have done nothing but mistake people this year. I made a grievous mistake with you, and I believe I have made a mistake with Anne, too. I took her to be sickly and cross, and I thought – '

She stopped abruptly.

'Yes, what did you think?' I asked.

'I thought that the pair of you deserved each other,' she said mischievously.

'It is a pity I did not know this sooner, or I could have obliged you by marrying her,' I teased her.

I never knew what it was to tease or be teased before I met Elizabeth, but I am learning.

'She is not nearly as sickly or cross as I supposed. In fact, the farther we went from the house, the more lively she became.'

'She used to be very much more lively when we were children, until the winter when she had a bad cold, and a cough settled on her chest. My aunt took her away from the seminary and said she was not well enough to go back.'

'Ah. So she was alone at Rosings with Lady Catherine from then on?'

'She had her companion.'

'It would be a brave companion who would stand up to Lady Catherine.'

I agreed.

'What did you talk of to Anne?'

'To begin with, we talked of the park. She has fond memories of it from childhood visits, and she pointed out the spot at which she lost her doll, and the spot at which Colonel Fitzwilliam found it – though he was not a colonel then. But he seems to have been a nice boy. It could not have been pleasant for him to have had a little girl trailing after him, yet he seems to have shown her a great deal of kindness.'

'He was always fond of Anne.'

'And then we talked of books. She has read a great deal, and we enjoyed a lively debate. I think she is better away from her mother. I will ask my Aunt Gardiner to take her out in the phaeton tomorrow. Between the two of us, we should be able to separate her from Lady Catherine for most of her stay.'

Thursday 18th December

The house party is proving to be surprisingly enjoyable. Mrs Bennet is content with walking the length and breadth of Pemberley, memorizing its finery so that she can confound her neighbours with accounts of its splendours on her return to Longbourn. Lydia spends her time flirting with the gardeners. It is useless to try and stop her, and at least it keeps her out of doors. Mr Bennet sits in the library most of the time, venturing out only for our fishing trips. Lady Catherine has taken to instructing Kitty and Mary on the correct behaviour for young ladies, and Kitty is so in awe of my aunt that she sits and listens to her with flattering attention for hours together. Mary, too, sits and listens, interposing her own profound thoughts from her reading. Caroline and Louisa occupy themselves with fashion journals, whilst Mr Hurst sleeps for most of the time.

Anne has made the most of this chance to escape her mother's notice, and has taken to walking in the grounds, where she is often joined by Colonel Fitzwilliam. Her cough seems to trouble her far less than formerly, and she says it is the exercise which is doing her good.

When the others are occupied, it is with Jane and Bingley, Georgiana and Mr and Mrs Gardiner, that Elizabeth and I are able to spend most of our time.

Saturday 20th December

Elizabeth and I rode out with Jane and Bingley this morning to see a property some ten miles from Pemberley. It is a fine house, with good views. We looked around, and Jane and Bingley were much taken with it.

'If we find nothing better, I think we will buy it,' said Bingley.

'I do believe you are learning caution,' I said to Bingley. 'A year ago you would have taken it straight away.'

'Impossible for me to do so now,' he said, shaking his head. 'If I have learnt anything from you, Darcy, it is that I must not take a house without first enquiring about the chimneys!'

'I reprimanded Bingley for not asking any sensible questions when he took Netherfield,' I explained, when Elizabeth looked mystified.

'It is a good thing he did not ask too much,' said Elizabeth, 'or else we might never have met.'

We rode back to the house, where we found Mrs Bennet deep in conversation with Mrs Reynolds, ascertaining how much the curtains had cost, and what were the exact dimensions of the ballroom.

Anne was in the drawing-room with Mrs Gardiner, and their laughter reached us as we entered the room. Anne is looking much better than formerly. There is an animation about her that was wholly missing when she was confined with Lady Catherine, and, I own, when she thought she would have to marry me.

'Did you like the house?' asked Mrs Gardiner.

'Yes, very much,' said Jane. 'It is a little smaller than Netherfield, but it is still a good-size house.'

'Smaller than Netherfield?' asked Mrs Bennet, coming into the room. 'That will never do.'

'But it is an easy distance from Pemberley,' said Jane.

'To be sure, that is in its favour. Then I might visit you both at once. I can stay with Lizzy first and then, dear Jane, I can stay with you. It is a long journey into Derbyshire to visit one daughter, but an easy distance to visit two. I dare say I shall be here all the time.'

'I thought the park was rather small,' said Bingley, with a glance at Jane.

'And the attics were poor,' she said.

'Oh, if the attics are poor I should not contemplate it,' said Mrs Bennet. 'You had much better stay at Nether-field.'

Monday 22nd December

It was a wet day today. After dinner, Lady Catherine retired early. Kitty and Lydia were engaged in trimming bonnets, and Mrs Bennet was telling Kitty that when she was married she must make sure she had a house as fine as Pemberley. Mr Gardiner and Mr Bennet were playing chess, whilst Mrs Gardiner was looking through a book of engravings.

'Would anyone care for a game of billiards?' asked Colonel Fitzwilliam.

'Darcy will play with you, and I will watch,' said Elizabeth. 'Anne, will you join us?'

Anne agreed, and the four of us went to the billiard room. We had hardly entered it, however, when Elizabeth excused herself on account of a headache, and asked me to help her back to the drawing-room.

As the door of the billiard room closed behind us, her headache seemed to disappear.

'I think Fitzwilliam and Anne will do better without us,' she said.

I looked at her in surprise.

'He needs only a little encouragement to realize that he is in love with her.'

'Fitzwilliam and Anne?'

'I think they would suit well. Her eyes follow him

whenever he is in the room, and she can scarcely talk about another subject without somehow mentioning him. For his part, he has always been fond of her, and it would be a suitable match as well as a love match. He needs to marry an heiress, and Anne is to inherit Rosings and a considerable fortune besides.'

I was even more surprised.

'How do you know he needs to marry an heiress?'

'He told me so.'

'When did he do that?'

'At Rosings, when we were all there together last Easter. I suspect it was to put me on my guard, and warn me that I must not expect an offer from him.'

'What arrogant men we are! Both of us thinking you wanted an offer from us!'

'Perhaps I did want one from the Colonel,' she teased me.

'My love, I warn you that I am a jealous husband. I will ban my cousin from Pemberley unless you tell me this minute that you did not want an offer from him,' I returned.

'Very well, I did not. But Anne, I think, does.'

'It might not be a bad thing,' I said. 'In fact, the more I think of it, the more I am pleased with it.'

'Lady Catherine, too, will be pleased.'

'So you are encouraging it to please Lady Catherine?' I asked her innocently.

'Mr Darcy, you are becoming as impertinent as your wife!' she teased me.

'But I am not so sure Lady Catherine will approve,' I said thoughtfully.

'She cannot complain about his birth.'

'Perhaps not, but he is a younger son, and impoverished,' I reminded her.

'But Anne's fortune is big enough for two.'

'My cousin has no house.'

'He will live at Rosings,' she said.

'Sending Lady Catherine to the dower house.'

'Whereas, if you had married Anne, she would have been the mistress of Pemberley, and Lady Catherine would have continued to be the mistress of Rosings.'

We both of us imagined how Lady Catherine would react when she learnt that she would have to move to the dower house.

'Do you think Anne will find the courage to stand up to her mother?' I asked.

'It will be interesting to see.'

Thursday 25th December

Little did I think, when I celebrated Christmas with Georgiana in London last year, that the next time I celebrated it I would be married. Pemberley is looking very festive. Greenery is twined round the banisters, whilst holly, thick with red berries, adorns the pictures and mistletoe hangs from the chandeliers.

We awoke to a smell of baking, and after breakfast we attended church. The weather was so fine that Elizabeth, Jane, Bingley and I decided to walk to the church whilst the rest of our guests were conveyed there by carriage.

'This reminds me of the walks we took when Jane and I were newly engaged,' said Bingley, as we crunched the frost beneath our feet, 'although then it was not so cold.'

'You and Jane were in the happy position of being acknowledged lovers. You could spend your time talking to each other and ignoring everyone else, whilst Elizabeth and I could not even sit together.'

'But you managed to become lost in the country lanes whenever we were out of doors,' said Bingley with a smile.

'The lanes were very useful,' said Elizabeth.

'And our mother helped you a great deal, by insisting you occupied that man,' said Jane.

'I have never been so mortified in my life,' said Elizabeth, but she was laughing as she said it.

We came to the church and went in. Our guests were already assembled, and no sooner did we enter than the service began. It was lively and interesting, full of the good cheer of the occasion. Lady Catherine complained about the hymns, the sermon, the candles and the prayer books, but I am persuaded that everyone else was uplifted by the service.

We had a splendid dinner, and afterwards we played at charades. Caroline chose Colonel Fitzwilliam as her partner, but Elizabeth thwarted her efforts to claim his attention later in the evening by inviting him to open the dancing with Anne. They made a lively couple, and disproved Lady Catherine's dire warnings that Anne would suffer a coughing fit.

Kitty danced with Mr Hurst, and even Mary was persuaded to take to the floor, though she protested that dancing was not a rational activity and declared that she would much rather read a book.

When all our guests had retired, we went upstairs.

'Tired?' I asked.

For answer, she lifted her hand above her head, and I saw she was holding a sprig of mistletoe.

Monday 29th December

Our party broke up this morning. Lady Catherine and Anne were the first to leave, accompanied by Colonel Fitzwilliam. Elizabeth had hoped to hear of an engagement, but although Fitzwilliam and Anne have spent a great deal of time in each other's company, nothing has been said.

The Bennets went next. Last to leave were Jane and Bingley.

'You must come and visit us at Netherfield,' said Jane.

'And bring Georgiana,' said Bingley.

We have promised to go and see them before too long.

At last we had the house to ourselves.

'It is very pleasant to have guests,' I said, as the last carriage departed. 'But it is even better to see them go.'

We returned to the drawing-room. Georgiana and Elizabeth were soon reliving the visit, discussing the people we had seen. Georgiana ventured a humorous remark about Lady Catherine and then looked at me to see if I had been offended. On seeing my face, her own relaxed. She has lost much of her shyness, and is on the way to becoming an open and confident young woman. For this, as for so many things, I have to thank Elizabeth.

March

Wednesday 4th March

Mr and Mrs Collins arrived this morning, and are to stay for a week. They thought it best to leave Kent as Lady Catherine is in a rage. She has just learnt that Anne is to marry Colonel Fitzwilliam.

'Her ladyship was not unhappy with the idea at first, although she graciously confided in me that she would rather have had a man of fortune as a son-in-law. But the estimable Colonel has an old and revered name, and she magnanimously thought it fitting that he should ally himself with her own, most esteemed, branch of the family. She was condescending enough to give her consent, and to say that Anne would make the most elegant bride of the year. I was able to please her ladyship by saying that Miss de Bourgh would grace any church in which she should choose to wed.'

'But her ladyship changed her mind when Anne made it clear she intended to live at Rosings, and that she intended her mother to move to the dower house,' put in Charlotte.

'Lady Catherine most amiably declared it to be impossible. She honoured me with the most obliging confidence, saying that she would not move out of her home to suit the convenience of a thoughtless chit, and she went on to graciously inform me that Anne was a headstrong girl who had no proper gratitude.'

'Anne pointed out that, if she were a man, her mother would have had to leave the house on her marriage, to which her ladyship replied that Anne was not a man, and that therefore she would remain. I expected Anne to give way,' said Charlotte, 'but she did nothing of the kind. Love has made her strong.'

'The atmosphere has unfortunately not been of the most harmonious. Of all things, I dislike an air of dissension. It offends a man of my calling in a way I can scarcely describe. I tried to offer an olive branch, saying that the dower house was a very fine building, with elegant apartments and sumptuous gardens, but Lady Catherine turned on me such a look of disapprobation that my courage faltered, and I was compelled to add: "But not as fine as Rosings." I think that pleased her ladyship.'

'But not her daughter,' I said.

Mr Collins's face fell.

'No. I fear it is impossible to remain on good terms with both of them, and so we felt it better to come away.'

'And there was another reason for our visit. I wanted you to see Elinor,' said Charlotte.

The nurse brought Elinor forward. I have never seen any attraction in babies, but Elizabeth was delighted with the little girl, and took her from the nurse. As she cradled the infant in her arms, she looked at me in a way that made my heart stand still, and suddenly babies became the most interesting thing in the world to me.

I thought last year was the happiest of my life, but I think this one is going to be even better.

About the Author

Amanda Grange is a bestselling author of historical fiction in the U.K. She specializes in creative interpretations of classic novels and historic events, including Jane Austen's novels and the *Titanic* shipwreck. Her novels include *Lord Deverill's Secret, Mr. Knightley's Diary* and *Titanic Affair.* She lives in England.